I0614086

Hidden Obsession

by

Susan Vaughan

Obsession, Book Two

This is a work of fiction. Names, characters, places, and incidents are either the product of the author's imagination or are used fictitiously, and any resemblance to actual persons living or dead, business establishments, events, or locales, is entirely coincidental.

Hidden Obsession

Cover Art by *Kim Mendoza*

The Wild Rose Press, Inc.
PO Box 708
Adams Basin, NY 14410-0708
Visit us at www.thewildrosepress.com

Publishing History
First Edition, 2023
Trade Paperback ISBN 978-1-5092-4888-9
Digital ISBN 978-1-5092-4889-6

Obsession, Book Two
Previously Published 2019
Published in the United States of America

Comet picked up the toy lobster at Sheri's feet and deposited it on the toe of Justin's boot. She sat at attention, tail swishing on the carpet.

A rich laugh from Sheri shot a dart of heat into him. He shifted in his seat.

"You fickle little beast." She wagged a finger at the dog. "I was your new best friend for all of ten minutes. Until he arrived."

"Comet's a fine judge of character." As he bent to scratch beneath the dog's chin, he eyed the soft-sided briefcase by Sheri's chair. "You here on business?"

The corners of her mouth tightened. "Deb and I are old friends."

"Can't come up with why, but your name's familiar."

"Harte is a common name. A Maine family dating back to the 1800's."

"But not Sheridan Harte. You from around here?"

"Originally, but not for a long time. I live near Portland. Detective, should I show you my ID so you can check me for priors?"

"Just making conversation."

She huffed. "Seems more like police interrogation than simple conversation."

"My mother says the same thing." So did too many other women. A hazard of the profession. And he wasn't just making conversation. Something about this woman intrigued him.

Dedication

To all the dogs I've known and loved whose charm and sweetness led to Comet's personality—to Freya and Sarah and Sasha, all rescues and unidentifiable mixes. I've added to Comet the traits missing in those sweet girls—playing with toys and fetching a ball or stick. Hidden Obsession is my only book to include a dog. I hope readers enjoy Comet as much as I did writing her.

Chapter One

SHERIDAN HARTE ORDERED her fingers to relax on the steering wheel, but her cramped digits wouldn't obey. Dragon Harbor, Maine, looked much the same as she'd left it twenty years ago. The fishing-net draped Wheelhouse Bar and Grill, white clapboard and cedar-shingled houses, lobster gear stacked in dooryards, and men clustered around a pickup at Buddy's Garage and Bait Shop. Fog veiled the Pepsi sign on the general store and blotted out the harbor's rock formation that gave the town its name.

Past the post office and the general store, changes to the village surprised her enough that she slowed to twenty-five, a nod to the speed limit no one here ever obeyed. Shops and businesses, some familiar and others new, filled the business block between the Baptist and Episcopal churches. A long building, once a garage, housed two shops and a restaurant. Its sandwich board announced, "Italian cuisine and seafood!"

In spite of her misgivings about returning, Sheri grinned. No restaurant on the coast could survive without local seafood on the menu. The place must be doing well to expect diners this early in spring. Maine's ocean peninsulas and towns ranged between quiet and dormant in the cold months, but came to life when summer residents and tourists arrived.

According to the calendar and the melting banks of

dirty snow lining the roadside, that wouldn't be for a few more months.

On her way out of the village proper, the *Welcome - Come Again* sign jeered at her.

Sheri Harte welcome? The daughter of George Harte? Not likely.

The road veered right, away from the water. Here and there between antique Capes and staid white Colonials, private lanes led to oceanfront properties. A few houses and a stand of trees past the Saltview Grange, she steeled herself.

The Tardiff farmhouse slumped amid bare, overgrown lilacs and brown witch-grass. The porch railing had fallen across one sagging step. Fog wraiths trailed around the peeling clapboards and through broken windowpanes. Off to the side, the garage was caving in, holes in its roof open to the weather. Its doors long gone, the gaping doorway seemed to accuse her.

She pressed a hand to her belly and fought back tears. The urge to turn around clawed at her—as if leaving meant she could forget any of what had happened. But she couldn't afford to pass up a client, and the advance had gone to pay bills. She would spend here the minimum amount of time her work required.

Willing away seventeen-year-old images, she visualized the rest of the route. The drive would take about the five minutes until her ten o'clock appointment. Another half mile, and then a left sent her onto the narrow road of Echo Cliff Point, where she and her friends used to ride bikes. They'd try to hit the tide right so they could hear the breakers boom in the cavern below. They threatened to push each other off the cliff. Mist smelling of salt and seaweed closed in around the

SUV, forcing her to squint as she negotiated the curve.

Houses faced the cliff and islands beyond that strung like beads out toward the Gulf of Maine. In clear weather a gorgeous view, but today it resembled dirty cotton wadding. Depressing. Past a couple of cottages and ranch-style houses, she swung into the Littlefield driveway and pulled to a stop behind her friend's minivan.

The Painted Lady's slate blue façade, its turret and porches accented with moss green and gold, splashed the only color on this gray point of land. The gazebo reminded her of the one her dad had built. She closed her eyes, calling up mind-snapshots of carefree summers selling lemonade and playing Barbies. Qualms eased, she focused on the reason for coming.

When she opened her eyes, a hooded figure was running toward her from the house. She'd know that sure stride anywhere.

The driver's door opened wide, and Debra Delano, née Littlefield, spread her arms wider. "Sheri! Hon, come out here this minute! I need a hug. Big time!"

Instead of the laughing gaze and sunny smile Sheri expected, she saw red-rimmed eyes and a wobbly mouth. Wearing an oversize orange slicker that dwarfed her, Deb was a forlorn doll. They'd had lunch in the Old Port only two weeks ago and phoned and texted often. So what could've happened recently?

Sheri slid out and bent into an embrace fragrant with the light scent of rose-and-jasmine cologne but rife with the same desperation as her words. Crushed against the boobs she'd envied when hers maxed out at 34B, she conjured a thousand disasters. But questions could wait as she delivered the requested hug. She squeezed in an extra measure of comfort.

After a moment Sheri straightened, gripping her friend's frigid hands. "What's the matter? Something with your grandmother? Len? The boys?"

Deb shook her head, her ponytail flinging drops onto her slicker. "Family's good. No, it's... this morning... he—" She pulled loose and flapped a hand toward where the road disappeared around the bend.

Lights flashed holes in the fog pudding. Red and blue lights. Sheri's pulse hitched. "An accident?"

"I wish. Well, maybe." Deb wrapped her arms around her midriff. A tear slid down her cheek. "Let's get out of this shit."

What was going on? *Crap* was the harshest expletive uttered by the former potty mouth since she gave birth to Len Junior eight years ago. Now *shit*? Sheri flipped up her raincoat hood and hooked her leather carryall from the backseat. She tucked inside the matching clutch.

"Not in the house. Not yet. Better if I tell you before I take you in to meet Miriam."

Looping the tote onto her shoulder, Sheri followed her to the gazebo.

The screened structure offered no more warmth than the outside. A bench encircled the gazebo's interior. Sheri stepped around small puddles and urged Deb away from them to sit beside her. She kept an arm curved around her friend's shoulders while she composed herself.

Even draped in outsized foul-weather gear and eyes devoid of mascara, Deb carried herself with style. She always had, even in high school. As opposed to her own lanky build, blah fashion choices, and blah hair, at the moment limp in the humidity despite her efforts earlier with the curling iron. People bandy about the term BFF but in their case, Best Friends Forever was an accurate description, despite being opposites in almost every way.

The friendship had begun the first day of kindergarten. Sheri hung back on the playground, observing and detached, waiting, until a laughing Deb pulled her and two other girls to the chalked hopscotch grid. Even years later when Sheri moved away, they'd kept in touch, sharing their lives and a love of romance and mystery novels.

Deb was one of the reasons she'd returned to Maine. "It's been a long time since I saw you this upset. You haven't even quizzed me."

"Leave it to you to make me feel better." Deb's lips curved in a soggy smile as she pushed back her hood. Her nose scrunched up while she thought. "Okay, the minivan. What's different?"

One reason for Sheri's success in writing was her eidetic memory. Her detailed and vivid memory of visual images guided her when her notes and recordings had gaps. It sometimes caused awkwardness in relationships. And provided entertainment to her friends. Deb's quiz was a long-running joke.

A picture of the vehicle coalesced in Sheri's mind. "New license plate. The animal welfare one." She reeled off the number-letter combo. "Ding in the bumper. Right side."

The grin widened. "One day I'll catch you. Dent's not my fault. Some idiot in the supermarket lot. Now it's my turn. Who are you carrying this week?" She gestured to Sheri's carryall.

"Not a who, a what. Coach, both the tote and the

clutch inside." She didn't admit it to any but her closest friends, but she had a handbag addiction.

Deb grinned and then blew her nose, lower lip quivering as the circumstance — whatever it was hit her again. She waved a hand around her head as if she could dispel emotions swirling around her like the fog. "Sorry I'm such a mess. Adam Spear was killed this morning. I saw it… them… *him*."

Killed? She'd implied it wasn't an accident. Did that mean a hit-and-run?

Shaken, Sheri reached for her hand. "Was he related to Steve Spear?" She remembered him as a large boy, two years ahead of them. Sullen. Often in the principal's office or detention.

"Steve's father." She dragged in a breath and dabbed at her eyes with a ragged tissue. "I already told Chief Galt everything but he said the state detective would want to talk to me. Maybe if I tell you, I can make some sense of the jumble in my head and repeating it won't be so bad later." Her breath hitched, and she squeezed her eyes shut as if to block out a sight too terrible to recall.

Sheri kept up with local news via the weekly online newspaper, but violent deaths on this bucolic peninsula were rare and usually domestic violence or drug related or— No, not going there. She shook away the image that rose in her mind. Bile stung her throat at the idea that the father of someone she knew might've been murdered.

A choking sound from her friend pulled her back. Poor Deb had witnessed… something. Sheri swallowed her horror.

"Breathe. I'm here." She linked her fingers with her friend's cold ones.

"Are you girls going to stay out there all *morning*? I

want to meet my *ghost*," called a hearty female voice that rivaled the harbor foghorn. Had to be Sheri's client, Miriam Littlefield.

"Your grandmother?" Sheri would leave calling her by her first name to Deb. Family prerogative. Her nana, if she were still alive, would slap her for such a transgression.

"We might as well go in." Deb pushed to her feet. She extracted a clean tissue from her pocket and blew her nose. "You'll hear the rest later when I tell the detective."

****

DETECTIVE JUSTIN WYLDE zipped his rain slicker and tugged his ball cap lower on his forehead. Mist darkened the granite rocks where he stood. Just once why couldn't he get called out during warm, sunny weather?

The state Evidence Response Team had finished marking and photographing. The forensic techs clustered around their house-size van as everybody waited. The body couldn't be moved until one of the medical examiners arrived.

Justin flipped open his pocket notebook and reviewed his notes on the deceased — Adam Spear, age fifty-six, five foot eight, one sixty, partner in a Bayport law practice, married, one adult son.

According to the Dragon Harbor police chief, as soon as the first responders determined Spear was dead, they covered the body with a tarp.

"No telling what evidence the EMTs trampled climbing down to the victim," Justin said.

"No footprints on this damn granite, Wylde. And my people know their business." Chief Norman Galt of the

DHPD worked his mouth and his mustache, deepening the fissures and canyons lining his cheeks. His dark gaze was unreadable. He hitched up his duty belt.

Galt topped Justin's six feet by more than four inches. At fifty plus, he still carried most of his bulk as muscle. Justin had worked with him before. Thought him a good cop. But the investigation had barely begun and the chief was stonewalling. Not being the Gentle Giant, as he was known in Maine law enforcement. *"My people."* Like the state detectives were invading enemy forces.

Justin swallowed his impatience. "And they didn't move the body?"

"Not a hair. Soon as they determined he was past helping, they covered him like you see. To preserve evidence." Galt aimed him a pointed look that underscored his earlier insistence on the first responders' professionalism. "Then they climbed back up and called the department."

Justin cast a glance at his partner nearby. Bess Peters was nodding to a tech and scribbling notes. He left her to it. He was primary on this case but they worked as a team. Bess was good people and a good detective. But sometimes he preferred to work alone, do things his way.

"What about the path?"

"People tramp back and forth on the path all the time. Shell bits, gravel, sand." Galt lifted his chief's cap by the shiny brim, dumped the accumulated water onto the ground, and settled it again on his salt-and-pepper hair. "Impossible to count shoe prints, let alone ID them. I'll provide a couple of my officers if you want to give it a go."

There, a bone. "Thanks. Might take you up on the

offer." He doubted the effort would prove effective. He peered through the fog at the Looky Lous on the nearby front lawn. Young woman holding an infant, gray-haired woman, bald man, another guy with a camera. A press pass hung on a cord around his neck.

"Local Bayport weekly," Galt said, following Justin's gaze.

"Any neighbors see anything?"

The chief's scowl gave him the answer. "Say they didn't. Came outside when they heard the sirens. I have their names, names and addresses of everyone on Echo Cliff Point. Close to two dozen houses. A couple empty now, summer people, no obvious break-in. My officers locked down the entire Point and searched everywhere they could. Two black jackets were bagged. I have 'em for you in my unit."

"Appreciate that, Chief." No wonder Galt was respected around the state. Surprising he hadn't been picked up by one of the larger burgs.

"Like I said, Debra Delano's the only witness. Told her you'd be stopping by her grandmother's later." He waved a hand, indicating the house lay back the way Justin had come.

"I'll need to talk to the EMTs too."

"Figured you would. I gave their cards to Bess."

Bess? Justin had heard stories about the chief being a player but fought the urge to press him about Bess. She could hold her own and wouldn't thank him for going all protective. Nope, she'd call him a chauvinist pain in the ass. Again. Besides, she was seeing some hotshot attorney.

"Bess?"

"She asked me earlier. Full disclosure. One of the

EMTs is my daughter. Divorced her son-of-a-bitch husband and moved back home." A wide grin softened Galt's features. "Jury's out on whether having my grandson around full time will kill me or rejuvenate me."

Chiming sounded from the chief's belt. He stepped away with his phone.

Just as well. Justin wouldn't have known what to say in reaction. Being single, his main contact with kids was with his nephews or on the job. He'd tried coaching Little League, but too many calls yanked him from practices and games. From dates too. Damned problematic having even casual dates, and let alone a relationship, which wasn't in the cards anyway.

He surveyed the crime scene. Evenly spaced stone blocks separated the paved road from the path. Nothing between the path and the rocky drop beyond. Hardly a safety barrier, more a warning of the steep descent to the icy waves.

Evidence tags on the scrapes and smears of blood marked the path of the victim's tumble. Painful way to die. Still covered by a tarp, the body lay about sixty feet down on the pink granite. Justin expected the medical examiner would make a joke about that.

He bent to tighten the laces on his hunting boots. Wouldn't surprise him if kids swam off the rocks in the summer. Today only seals and fish would dare those breakers. He began the descent, sticking to the switchback trail marked by tiny green flags.

The cliff was less a precipice and more a steeply terraced series of boulders, ledges, and loose rock, cut here and there by crevices. No ice, thank God. The granite's rough texture, although wet, made for sure footing.

He squatted beside Adam Spear and folded back the plastic. Remained silent for a moment, offering respect before mentally cataloguing the scene.

If he was lucky, the gray windbreaker might yield trace evidence. Blood and water plastered Spear's thin, light-brown hair to his pink skull. More blood and dirt daubed his soaked blue sweats and the jacket's reflective strips. Both garments bore jagged tears. Hands bagged. Good. His remaining sneaker was a Nike. Expensive. New, from the looks of the sole. The techs had the other in an evidence bag. The legs and arms sprawled in unnatural angles.

The sight made Justin's knee ache in sympathy. Or else it was the dampness leaching into his old baseball injury. Shaking off the ache, he dug his phone from an inner pocket and snapped several pictures from different angles. The crime-scene techs would've taken plenty, but he liked to have his own.

The medical examiner would be able to tell how and when the breaks occurred. Pre or post-mortem. But someone had bent and twisted Spear's limbs into a crude swastika. Someone deliberately positioned him.

Did that say something about the victim?

Or the killer?

Chapter Two

SHERI'S NANA USED to say you can identify the house of a true Mainer by noting whether the front door is accessible. In the case of this house, three planters— empty this early in spring — barricaded the steps to the front porch. She smiled as she followed Deb along the flagstone path and across the drive to a side door.

She looked forward to meeting her new client. When Deb had contacted her a month ago about ghostwriting her grandmother's memoirs, she mentioned the woman had led an interesting life. Before Sheri considered a contract with a new client, she conducted initial research so she had an idea of personality, background, and anything that raised red flags. She liked to be prepared, and this woman's vibes were go, go, go. A colorful and full life. Travel, living abroad. Accomplishment and philanthropy. Three marriages. Children, grandchildren, and great-grandchildren. After the last husband died, she returned to Maine and her first husband's name.

The door led into a mudroom, where they hung their coats on Shaker-style pegs.

"Miriam, where are you?" Deb kicked off her boots and stepped into ballet flats.

Drips from Sheri's raincoat had found their way into her clogs. If only she'd worn boots and wool socks. She kicked off the clogs and slipped on her pumps.

She turned toward clicking and scrabbling on the

hardwood floor. A black-and-tan whirlwind burst in, ears and tail flying. The small dog raced first to Deb, then to her before dashing in frantic circles. The flourish of welcome apparently completed, the animal plopped down on its haunches, flashing a big doggy-smile.

Sheri grinned at her friend. "Comet, I presume."

"How ever did you guess?" Deb leaned over to scratch floppy ears. "She's a rescue dog."

"From the local shelter where you volunteer?" Once a week, Sheri recalled.

"Yes. She's about three we think, a sheltie-spaniel mix. And Miriam seemed so alone rattling around in this big house."

"You felt she needed a furry companion."

"You could use a pet too."

"Cliché! Single woman, over thirty, owns a cat." Comet turned her eager, bright gaze on her, so she obliged with a chin scratch.

"And over thirty isn't anywhere near middle age," Deb huffed. Since they were born the same year, that assessment didn't count. Her lips curved in a sly grin. "Okay, no cat. Could be a dog, a smallish one like Comet."

"Same cliché. And no, I won't accompany you to the shelter while I'm here." She left unsaid that she wouldn't spend nights in Dragon Harbor. As Deb knew, she adored dogs and could be suckered in by pleading eyes and wagging tails. She traveled frequently and worked incessantly. No time for a pet. She pulled her hand away from Comet's silky coat and straightened.

"Comet, come," called the stentorian voice again, "and bring along the laggards." A hint of the British Isles rang in the final word.

Susan Vaughan

For a personal project like a memoir, Sheri typically spent the first month interviewing the client and examining journals, photos, and mementos. To accommodate Miriam Littlefield's advanced age, they'd work together about four hours four days a week. Sheri would make the round trip each day, an hour each way.

Deb reassured her that the dog didn't bite, but she said nothing about Mrs. Littlefield's teeth or claws. Nor did Sheri's internet research. Judging from the noblesse oblige in the woman's tone, she couldn't count on her following Comet's example.

From the hall, Sheri glimpsed the kitchen. Her mouth watered at the aroma of brewing French roast. Hot coffee would warm her up.

"She's in the library," Deb said.

Too sweet. An antique New England house complete with library. They followed the little dog down the hall and through an open arched doorway.

Floor-to-ceiling shelves were stuffed with books and family mementoes. An actual home library, not a family room that used to be a library. Petite and as erect as a ballerina, one hand decorously on a baby grand piano, neither did Miriam Littlefield disappoint.

Hair a spiky froth of silver, she swept across the oriental carpet, secure on heels two inches or higher the same peacock blue of her slim pants and cashmere sweater.

Comet dashed to her mistress, who bent to scratch her ears. "There's my good girl." The dog wriggled from tail to head before racing off again.

Violet eyes a shade lighter than her granddaughter's sparkled with welcome. She grasped Sheri's hands and air-kissed both cheeks. "My *dear* Sheridan, I'm *terribly*

14

glad to meet you at long last. For *years*, my Debra has talked about you. I can't *wait* to have you all to myself."

"Mrs. Littlefield, I'm happy to be working with you. I hope Deb hasn't divulged all our childhood secrets."

She appeared at least a decade younger than her eighty years. Obvious from whom Deb had inherited her curvy figure and sense of style. The older woman's laugh, like her voice, was low and rich. "Only a few. But you *must* call me Miriam. Mrs. Littlefield was my mother-in-law."

She slipped an arm through Sheri's and drew her toward seating grouped before the fireplace. The warmth of gas flames flickering behind the screen began to dispel the chill. Miriam lowered herself onto the sofa with care, using the arm for support, the first indication of her advanced age. Deb and Sheri took the matching upholstered club chairs opposite.

Comet reappeared, carrying a fleece lobster that leaked stuffing from one of its red claws. She deposited the toy at Sheri's feet and sat, tongue lolling from one side of her mouth.

"Does she want me to throw it?"

Miriam laughed, a contagious peal. "She's bestowing one of her *treasures* on you. A great *honor*, declaring you her new best friend."

When Comet lay down and presented her belly for scratching, Sheri was happy to oblige.

"Deb told me about the tragedy on the cliff path," she said, to get that out of the way.

"Tragedy," Miriam scoffed. "No such thing. I'm ready to uncork the *Cristal.*"

"Please stop," Deb said. "Sheri will get the wrong impression."

She huffed. "*Not* wrong. He cheated my son-in-law out of thousands of dollars. That damn money grubber *finally* got what he deserved."

What's that about? But before Sheri could formulate a tactful question, buzzing erupted from the hallway.

"That must be the detective." Deb hurried out.

Sheri settled back, hoping to be unobtrusive. She wanted to support Deb, who was still shaken. Spear's death sickened her, but she couldn't silence the questions in her head. She was a writer. Curiosity was in her DNA. She wanted to know more about what Miriam had blurted and more about what happened on the cliff.

****

JUSTIN RUBBED HIS chilled hands together as he accompanied Debra Delano into a book-lined room. The little dog bounded in circles around him before curling up near the fire. In a while Justin would boil but for now his fleece anorak's warmth felt damned good.

Deb, as she'd asked him to call her, made the introductions. Miriam Littlefield, an elderly woman who bore a marked resemblance to her granddaughter. Sheridan Harte, about his age, maybe a little younger. Tall, long and lean, a runner maybe. Black turtleneck and long belted green sweater. Unreadable brown eyes. Blond hair, a darker shade like the honey Gram used to spoon on his toast. Curls escaped a clasp at her nape. She appeared damned buttoned up. Except for a wide mouth with full lips, not artificially so, just enough to keep his gaze riveted to them.

He shook off his reaction as she rose from her chair.

"I'm Sheri." She held out a hand. If he wasn't mistaken about her expression, she'd caught him staring and was sizing him up.

"Apologies for the icy fingers."

"None necessary."

He registered her firm grip and savored the cool softness before she stepped back.

Mrs. Littlefield patted the cushion beside her. "Detective, you *must* sit by me. And *do* call me Miriam. I expected Chief Galt to investigate but my granddaughter says otherwise."

"Yes, ma'am. For most of the state of Maine, the law designates the Major Crimes Unit—that's state detectives like me—to investigate cases of suspicious deaths."

As he lowered himself onto the cushy seat, he caught amusement pulling at Sheridan Harte's lips. Shit, he'd forgotten what tie he was wearing. He kept his expression solemn, as if a tie festooned with a smirking Wile E. Coyote was the usual professional MCU attire, which in his case it was. Too obvious if he zipped up now.

He nodded toward the fireplace. "I'm grateful for the fire. Da— Doggone raw out in the fog."

"Typical of Adam Spear. Inconsiderate even in getting himself *killed*," Mrs. Littlefield said.

Across from him, a choking sound came from Deb Delano.

"Ma'am?"

"I have nothing *good* to say about the man," Mrs. Littlefield—*Miriam*—continued. "He was an arrogant son of a bitch. And a crook. Whoever killed him deserves a *medal*."

Her granddaughter popped up as if propelled by an ejector seat. "Miriam! The coffee must be ready. Come show me what cups you want to use for your guests." She hooked her grandmother's arm, hauled her to her feet, and whisked her into the hall.

Justin turned to observe Sheridan Harte. *Sheri*. The full name was somehow familiar. Composed, alert curiosity in her brown gaze as she scrutinized him right back.

"You have the same opinion of the deceased, Sheri?" he asked.

"I didn't know the man." She crossed long legs clad in tailored black pants.

"Did you see what happened on the cliff?"

"Deb's the one who witnessed… something." Her gaze shifted to the fire's glow. "I arrived at the house about twenty minutes before you did. Did someone really kill Spear?"

"The death's suspicious, but as yet there's no determination of homicide."

As she returned her attention to him, her gaze sharpened. "Meaning you don't know or you won't say?"

"Can't. Have to wait for the medical examiner. Once cause of death has been determined, the MCU will put out a statement."

Comet picked up the toy lobster at Sheri's feet and deposited it on the toe of his boot. She sat at attention, tail swishing on the carpet.

A rich laugh from Sheri shot a dart of heat into him. He shifted in his seat.

"You fickle little beast." She wagged a finger at the dog. "I was your new best friend for all of ten minutes. Until *he* arrived."

"Comet's a fine judge of character." As he bent to scratch beneath the dog's chin, he eyed the soft-sided briefcase by Sheri's chair. "You here on business?"

The corners of her mouth tightened. "Deb and I are old friends."

"Can't come up with why, but your name's familiar."

"Harte is a common name. A Maine family dating back to the 1800's."

"But not *Sheridan* Harte. You from around here?"

"Originally, but not for a long time. I live near Portland. Detective, should I show you my ID so you can check me for priors?"

"Just making conversation."

She huffed. "Seems more like police interrogation than simple conversation."

"My mother says the same thing." So did too many other women. A hazard of the profession. And it wasn't just *making conversation*. Something about this woman intrigued him.

His reply earned him a warm smile that curled inside his chest. "And the neckwear's supposed to make a felon relax and confess all his crimes?"

"Wile E. usually helps in interviews with kids. Had a case early this morning at Maine Medical Center. Four-year-old with broken arm, twist fracture, so the doc suspected abuse. Other X-rays showed previous injuries, but the boy wouldn't say anything to the doc."

"But your cartoon tie helped coax him to talk to you?" Her gaze turned solemn.

"Something did. He cried, said his mom's boyfriend threatened to do worse if he told." God, he hated to see a kid in pain. Emotional pain was worse than the physical. His knees objected to the tight grip of his hands, and he flexed his fingers.

"MCU handles abuse cases?"

"Sometimes. More to the situation than I can discuss. Shouldn't have said that much." Neighbor had found Toby outside in pajamas. Called the cops, who discovered the mom in her bed, strangled.

She started to reach toward him, but laid her hand on her lap, curled in a fist. "I should say it's forgotten, but I won't forget that poor child."

"Yeah." He clenched his fingers again. "If justice is served, the bastard will go to prison for a long, long time. Pardon my language."

"Given he's an abusive bastard, you're entitled to swear."

He snorted a laugh. Not so stiff after all. Way too easy to talk to. And a smile that went straight to— He cleared his throat and stood as the other women returned.

"Here we are." Deb carried a tray into the room and set it on an end table. "Detective, I hope you drink coffee, and we have homemade chocolate chip cookies."

"I sometimes take coffee intravenously. Much appreciated. The cookies too." Night hadn't yet receded when he wolfed down a takeout breakfast sandwich.

Miriam Littlefield hovered in the doorway. "Please *excuse* me, Detective. I have a video *conference* call with my stepson. You're in good hands with my granddaughter and my *ghost*." With a flutter of manicured nails, she disappeared down the hall.

Her granddaughter had probably finagled that departure, but again Miriam delivered a stunner of an exit line with a stage actress's flourish. He sat mute as Deb poured coffee. She handed him a blue pottery mug and returned to the chair beside Sheri's.

When she indicated the creamer and sugar bowl, he

said, "Thanks. Black is good."

"More efficient delivery of caffeine." Amusement lit Sheri's eyes. She stirred milk into her mug. "Go ahead and drink your coffee. Now that Miriam has given me permission, I'll answer the question you're itching to ask."

"Ghost?"

"I'm a freelance writer. She hired me to ghostwrite her memoir. Many clients want readers to believe they wrote the book themselves, so the typical contract has a confidentiality clause."

"But not this one?"

She tore off a small chunk of cookie. "The provision is part of this contract, but the confidentiality applies to the writer—me—not to the client. She just outed me as her ghost, so now I can tell you I am indeed here on business." She popped the treat in her mouth and leaned back, enjoyment lighting her face. "Delicious, Deb."

At first, he'd thought her merely attractive, but when she glowed with pleasure, she was beautiful. How would she look during— He cut off that thought and slugged down coffee.

After three cookies, Justin set down his mug. No reason to mention that the confidentiality clause wouldn't apply to police investigations. But she probably knew that, given her adherence to ethics.

"I'm ready to answer your questions," Deb said, cheeks pale. As she set down her mug, the pottery clattered on the tray.

"I do appreciate the refreshment and the chance to warm up." He leaned forward, elbows on his knees. Dammit, she was still rattled, and this might upset her further. No getting out of it. "I need you to go outside and walk me through what you saw and heard."

Chapter Three

AT DEB'S INSISTANCE, Sheri accompanied them. Detective Wylde had stared at her a moment before nodding permission. Dense lashes, as dark as his short hair, were such a contrast to his blue eyes. Riveting eyes. But as they set out, gone was the laughing smile of their earlier conversation. His chiseled features and gaze turned hard and closed. A cop face, she supposed.

She shouldn't notice such things about a police detective. She chalked it up to her writer's habit of observing people and kept her eyes on Deb's tight shoulders. She wanted to hear more of his baritone voice, too, mellow and evoking images of tangled sheets. She shook the thought out of her head. Where did that come from?

They left Comet in the mud room, moping. As they trooped out into the drizzle, she pulled up the hood her lined raincoat. And blessed Miriam for the loan of boots.

They stopped at the end of the drive, where a black state police SUV sat behind hers. A woman of about her five nine unfolded herself from the passenger seat, and Wylde introduced her as Detective Bess Peters. Her handshake and level gaze gave the impression of energy and purpose. Laugh lines softened wide-set gray eyes that would miss nothing. After pulling her slicker hood over the seal-black braid at her nape, she strolled along with them.

Sheri hung back, but close enough to provide support for Deb. The detective's gentle handling of her friend reassured her, but he couldn't shield her from stark reality.

The fog had receded toward the water so the yellow tape shouting *POLICE LINE DO NOT CROSS* stood out in relief against the muted granite. She saw no other official vehicles. They must have removed Adam Spear's body to the state medical examiner's office. Deb wouldn't have to see that part of the horror. Nor would Sheri. She shuddered in relief.

Deb's whimper of dread propelled Sheri ahead to grasp her hand.

"Sorry to put you through this." Wylde adjusted the hood of his black rain jacket. On the back, white letters spelled *STATE POLICE*. "I know it can be tough recounting violence. Keeping the fear inside is worse. Talking about it helps."

"He's right," Sheri said softly. "Retelling a terrible event drains away its power."

She saw in her friend's gaze the moment she remembered how Sheri had learned that, although no one, not even Deb, knew the whole truth about Noah.

Wylde withdrew a small digital recorder from a pocket. He zipped it into a plastic bag. "Recording the interview's more efficient than taking notes and more accurate than my memory." One side of his mouth quirked up as if in apology as he asked permission. Nothing deliberate to relax the witness, but more natural empathy. He then stated the time and identifying information for the recorder. "Begin with your arrival this morning. What time was that?"

"A little after seven thirty. I dropped the boys off at

school and came right over. Miriam's an early riser." Her lips curved in a weak smile. "I was coming here anyway to introduce Sheri. I arrived in time to take the dog for a walk. My grandmother will never admit she doesn't see like she used to, so I help out in bad weather." Inhaling deeply, she stared at the toes of her boots.

Years of interviewing people had taught Sheri not to fill silences. Deb's story would unfold in good time. The detectives also waited. When she looked up, Wylde nodded encouragement.

She straightened her shoulders and lifted her chin. "Comet and I walked that way, toward where the police tape is."

"Show me how far you went."

Deb squeezed Sheri's hand before moving ahead of the group, past the next-door neighbor's house and on another fifty feet or so to the house beyond.

"I stopped here to pick up after Comet. She started yanking on the leash all excited and jumping around. I followed her gaze and saw Spear on the cliff path. Well, it was the bright reflective stripes on his jacket that caught my eye. I didn't know who it was. I was too far away and the fog was thicker then. He was struggling with someone in a dark coat with a hood. And then he… he went over the edge."

Sheri peered at the house, another Victorian with a turret. No camera visible. Given today's technology, a tiny one could be tucked beneath the eaves. Like in the case she'd written about in Portland, the police would check for cameras. Perhaps they already had. Except for supporting her best bud, she would stay out of this case. One had been wrenching enough.

"What did you do next?"

Deb looked around, her brow crimped, as everyone inched onward. "At first I froze."

"How long?"

Fearing Wylde's increasingly terse questioning would further unnerve this tender soul, Sheri closed the gap between them by a step. A *back-off* shake of the other detective's head halted her. But Deb mirrored Wylde's sober expression and matter-of-fact tone. Perhaps straightforward and unemotional was contagious. A technique to file away for future reference.

"A minute. Maybe less. I don't know."

"What about the other person?"

"He climbed down the cliff. I wanted to help the fallen man—Adam—but I didn't know what the other person might do." She laid a hand on the neighbor's mailbox. "Then Comet wrapped the leash around this post and my ankles. I had to untangle her. When I looked up, I saw the other person coming back up."

She spun toward them, eyes wide. "I just remembered. He held something in his hand. It had a lighted screen. A cell phone, I'd say. Maybe he called 911?"

"I'll check." He exchanged a glance with Peters, who scribbled on a small notepad. His expression didn't reveal his thoughts, taking in everything but giving away nothing.

"I finally got myself together, but before I could make my feet move, he ran off."

"Did you see which direction?"

"On around the point. He disappeared in the fog." One shoulder lifted in a gesture of futility.

"A man? Can you describe him?"

"I said *him*, but I'm not sure if it was a man or a

woman." She chewed the corner of her mouth. "Adam Spear wasn't a big man, wiry and slim. The other person might have been taller. But with the hood and the big coat, I just don't know."

"Did you see a face?"

"He never turned my way. All I saw was the hooded coat. And dark pants."

"What about his hand, the one holding the phone?"

She lowered her head as if picturing the scene. "Dark like the coat. A glove, I think."

The population of coastal Maine boasted few people of color, but Sheri couldn't help asking, "Were you wondering about skin color?"

"Fingerprints," he said, mouth tight. "On Spear's windbreaker. Not the best surface but it was a possibility."

Everyone continued walking. The incoming tide rolled white-foamed waves onto the rocks. A hint of diesel fuel and the rumble of a motor drifted in from a lobster boat. Herring gulls cried and swooped through the fog. The sounds struck Sheri as mourning spirits.

As they neared the yellow barrier, Deb's shoulders stiffened and her pace slowed.

"Nothing to see but the tape and evidence markers," Wylde said in a gentler tone. "What happened then?"

"I shook off my panic and hurried to the cliff path. Comet was whining. She didn't want to go anywhere near there, and I had to drag her. I had to see if the person needed help." She drew a shaky breath. "He didn't move. Just lay there, twisted and broken. I didn't have my phone, so I ran back to the house and called." Her beautiful face crumpled as tears slid down her cheeks.

Sheri walked closer to the drop beyond the path.

"Don't get too close." Detective Wylde's smooth baritone came from close behind her. To protect her? The notion sent a little fizz of warmth through her.

She halted and gave him a nod over her shoulder. Colored tags marked the trajectory of Spear's fall. No straight drop. Spear had caromed off at least four boulders before landing a long way down. Other tags marked a different path, the one all officials would take so they didn't contaminate the crime scene, something she'd learned during the Portland case.

She returned and slid an arm around her friend, and they turned away from the cliff. Everyone made their way back toward the Littlefield house.

"Did you see anybody else?" Wylde asked.

"No." Deb's gaze bounced from one of them to another. "If only I hadn't been afraid. If I'd run out there, maybe I could've saved him."

"Don't think that. There was nothing you could've done to help Spear." He clicked off his recorder and tucked it away. "More likely you'd have put yourself in danger. Calling 911 was a good move. Did you cry out? Did the dog bark?"

"I couldn't make a sound, and Comet whined but she didn't bark. She rarely barks."

"If he didn't turn toward you and you made no noise, he might've had no idea anybody was there." From a jacket pocket, he withdrew two business cards and extended them. "I'll need your contact information."

Puzzled, Sheri stared at the card he'd passed her. Beside the MCU logo were the official Augusta address, his name, and two phone numbers.

"But I've told you everything," Deb said, her voice shaking.

Before Wylde could speak, Sheri put her arm around her friend. "You might think of something later, or he might think of a different question."

"Oh." She rattled off her mobile number, and he wrote it in his little notebook.

"You too, Sheri." His pen was poised, his eyebrows raised.

"Me? Why?" Her stomach jittered. It made no sense for him to think she was involved. What if he looked up her dad?

"You're a writer, an observant one. Humor me." His slow, crooked smile fanned her pulse.

Now he wanted her number? Was this about the Spear death or something else? Might that be attraction in those amazing blue eyes? She was here to work, not to flirt or anything else with this man, no matter how good looking or charming. She— Damn, she was dithering. She never dithered. Regardless, she had no choice.

She dug her brass case from her coat pocket. "My business card has all my information."

"Thanks." A rascal's grin on his mouth, he tucked the card she'd given him in one of the numerous pockets in his coat and turned back to Deb, his expression now solemn.

"We'll keep confidential you saw anything but Spear. Nevertheless, lock your doors and don't go out alone until we apprehend the person involved in Spear's death."

The possible threat to her friend punched Sheri in the chest. She stared into the fog. Could the assailant still be around, watching them? Waiting? She shuddered and turned away from the cliff.

****

JUSTIN SLID BEHIND the wheel of his state SUV, and Bess took the passenger seat, a tight fit because of the laptop shelf. His service pistol had gotten jammed between his hip and the seat, but he resisted taking the time to adjust his position. From her sly look and quirked lips, he knew where she'd take the conversation if he didn't jump in.

"We have fuck all to go on so far," he began as he reached for his notebook. "And I—"

"What's with letting the hot blonde go on the re-enactment with us?" No escaping her mocking tone. "What's the story with her?"

He schooled his features. Maybe he hadn't done so during their stroll in the damn rain. Bess was only getting started. She was always trying to fix him up with her single friends, of whom she seemed to have an endless supply.

"Sheri—" shit, he'd meant to use her last name but too late now "—was at the house when I arrived, and Delano seemed damned shaky, so when she asked if her friend could accompany us, I okayed it." He explained Sheri's ghostwriter gig, the reason for her presence. "She agreed to be supportive, but keep quiet during the interview. And she did. Both." He glared at his partner.

"So it's *Sheri*, is it? I saw the looks. And ooh, the exchange of phone numbers. Fast work for a tough guy who hardly finds time for dates, and who, after a couple loser babes, avoids relationships. You ask her out already?"

"Bess."

"What? She's not a witness. She's not a suspect. No reason you can't follow your inclination, Justin. And don't try to tell me you're not interested."

He was interested. More than interested. His reaction to her surprised him. On the job, he never let himself look at anybody even peripherally involved in a personal, let alone sexual way. Yet he'd had to drag his gaze from her more than once. What was it about Sheri Harte? Yeah, she was pretty, with eyes that seemed to notice and catalog everything and everyone. Sharp too.

When Bess cleared her throat, he shook off his thoughts.

"First, we can't be certain she's not a suspect. Second, I'm not discussing this with you." He dug the notebook from inside his jacket and flipped it open so hard he nearly tore the page. "The wife is next. What did Chief Galt's daughter tell you about her?"

Bess huffed and took out her notebook. "Was manager at a bank in Bayport. Described as prickly, has quite the temper. Another tech on the ambulance crew confirmed."

"Let's tackle her now before any more time passes."

"I co-opted one of Norman's officers to babysit her, keep her off the phone," she said. "If they're right about the irritability factor, she should be good and riled by now." She climbed out and hustled to her SUV.

They drove around the curve and parked in front of the Spear house. The drizzle had deteriorated, or improved depending on your outlook, to a mist. Justin exited into the cold and stared at the stone and glass structure. Adam Spear had done well for himself. Until today.

****

SHERI FOUND MIRIAM waiting for her in the library, seated in a burgundy leather armchair beside an antique cherry desk. On her other side, a tray containing a pitcher of water with lemon slices and two glasses covered a small table.

"I thought *this* might be a good place to work." She blinked as if she'd just wakened at the sound of steps. At eighty she probably needed rest after so much excitement.

"It's perfect, Miriam." Sheri set her laptop and digital recorder on the desk. The file she'd set up for the project was already open, so she keyed in her password. "I'll make notes as we talk, but recording will help me write with your voice rather than mine."

Violet eyes crinkled with pleasure. "Then let's *begin*. I was born in Boston in…"

Sheri let her rattle on for a few minutes. Her personality painted even the dry chronology of her birth and parentage in Dolby sound and 3D. Sheri itched to convey that lively voice in the book. When Miriam stopped to pour them both a glass of water, Sheri clicked off the recorder.

"Good start," she said. "But before we go further, let's consider what you want this book to contain and what exactly you want it to be—autobiography or memoir."

"I never thought about there being a difference. *Do* enlighten me." Miriam sipped from her glass, then tilted her head to one side, her gaze alight with curiosity.

"The difference can be fuzzy. An autobiography is history, with facts and dates. A memoir focuses more on how you remember your life, generally only significant parts, with anecdotes, feelings, impressions, life lessons, even conversations. Because you intend this book for family and not for publication, it can be whatever you want, one or the other or a blend of the two."

"Ah, I just blathered on about facts and dates." Her papery cheeks colored. "Not the *interesting* stuff. I want to tell more than *just* my experiences and choices, like what…" She fluttered a hand.

"What the experiences meant to you?"

"And how my choices shaped my life." Her smile dazzled, making clear how she'd attracted three husbands. "I want my children, grandchildren, and *their* children to *enjoy* my story."

Sheri keyed that in and punched on the digital recorder.

"Talk about events that mean the most to you and you most want to share. Don't worry about sequence. Start with whatever memory prods you, and I'll help you dig for the details. I'll ask questions to gather a lot more information than we can use, but the more I have, the better we can shape the narrative. We can work out later if and where to include dates and other facts."

Miriam nodded, clearly absorbing and analyzing. She rose, placing both hands on the chair arms to push up. When Sheri offered a hand, she shook her head. She strode with purpose to the orderly bookshelves and returned with a large book she placed on Sheri's lap. An old photo album covered in cracked black leather. A woven cord bound its pages.

"You probably don't *know* photo albums like this," she said. "Black and white pictures mounted on the pages by little glue-backed corners."

Sheri smiled as she opened to the first page, a snapshot of a brownstone town house.

"I sure do recognize this. My nana had a slew of these. Old family pictures and ones she took with a boxy

Brownie camera."

Neither Mom nor her brother wanted the old albums, so they lived in a box under her bed. She leafed through them sometimes when she couldn't sleep. A rotten shame Nana left this life before Sheri could write her memoir.

Miriam nodded her approval. She flipped pages, then pointed to a picture of a slender boy standing in front of the house. He pointed with pride to his bicycle.

"My twin brother Mitchell with his new Schwinn. It was our thirteenth birthday. I snapped this with my gift, a Brownie." Sadness dimmed her voice. "Just before his accident. Let's begin there. It's the day I decided to become a nurse. Well, I *wanted* to be a *doctor*, but back then times being what they were, I *settled* for nursing."

Chapter Four

SHERI AND MIRIAM worked until twelve thirty on the emotional story of the accident that left Miriam's brother unable to walk or ever again ride a bicycle. She covered her relationship with Mitchell and how seeing the dump truck strike him down affected her then and now. How that experience had led her into medicine. How it set the course of her life.

By the time Sheri heard Deb enter the house, the two women had soaked half a box of tissues.

"I bring Cape Cod chicken salad from Donna's Market. Made fresh this morning," Deb announced as she entered the library. She'd freed her hair to fall in a shining curtain across her shoulders. "My God, you two look like a mime disaster. This calls for emergency repairs."

Sheri didn't wear much makeup, a little blush, some mascara, so her repairs didn't take long. Moments later, makeup restored, they convened in the kitchen. Stamped-tin ceilings, white sheers on the nine-over-six windows, and off-white beadboard cabinets gave Sheri the impression of light. A complicated European-style coffee maker occupied a prime spot on the granite countertop beside a stainless-steel fridge. A pleasing blend of old and new.

"Sorry I was so late." Deb collected silverware and plates while she poured iced tea. "I had car trouble and had to call Buddy's Garage."

"My dear, what *happened*?" Miriam arranged placemats on the oak table, then sat.

"A freaky thing. When I left the house, the minivan was fine, but on the way to Donna's, the steering went wonky, making screeching noises and wobbling. It was a struggle, but I was able to pull over at the turnout after the Ridge Road. Buddy said the lug nuts on the front wheels were all loose. The back ones were solid. Super strange." Shaking her head, she passed around the food containers.

Sheri searched her memory. Nothing in there about lug nuts. The garage in Weymouth always handled her tire issues. She filled her plate with the salad, lightly dressed and seasoned chunks of chicken, chopped walnuts, and dried cranberries. "Is it drivable now?"

"Oh, yes." Deb spread butter on a French roll. "Buddy tightened everything and I drove on."

"Thank *goodness* it wasn't serious," Miriam said. "Or *expensive.* Let's enjoy our lunch."

After such a full morning, Sheri devoured a healthy portion of everything, including a lemon square, and so did her companions. She was glad to see Deb's appetite hadn't suffered. She asked what the writing team had accomplished that morning, but Miriam declared with a Cheshire-cat smile she'd have to wait for the book.

As they cleared away the dishes, Deb mentioned she'd bought enough salad to take to the Spears and asked if Sheri would like to accompany her.

She would indeed. She couldn't help wondering about Adam Spear's family. Her mom would call curiosity her biggest fault, but in free-lance writing it was a major asset. She waited for a reaction from Miriam.

"Much as I disliked *Adam*, I have no quarrel with *Angie*. Taking food is the neighborly thing to do. You girls go ahead. I have a few things to do *here*."

"Thanks, Miriam," Deb said. "We won't be long."

"A *stimulating* morning, Sheri," the elderly woman said. "We can work again when you return. Then we can both *rest* a little before everyone arrives at five."

Sheri barely prevented her lower jaw from hitting the floor. "I beg your pardon. *Everyone*?"

Miriam cast a silent reprimand her granddaughter's way. "I see my granddaughter *neglected* to tell you. Or *invite* you. I've arranged a *small* dinner party to introduce you to the family." One eyelid lowered in a sly wink. "The gathering may give you some *insights*."

Tamping down anxiety, Sheri went for calm regret. "I'm sorry, Miriam. I didn't plan on staying past five. I'd like to make it home before it's too dark."

She dismissed the demur with an imperious wave. "*Not* a problem. You'll stay the *night*. I have *plenty* of toiletries and extra pajamas. Then we can get an *early* start tomorrow. I'll show you to one of the guest rooms later."

****

AS JUSTIN ENTERED the open-plan office shared by all the MCU detectives, Bess Peters was hanging her slicker on a wall hook. He'd made a detour to the evidence techs. They'd just returned from interviewing Spear's widow and her sister, who was at the house.

Computers and printers hummed in the large, shared office, and male and female detectives near the windows argued politics. The lieutenant looked up from the potted palm she tried to keep alive. The plant's drooping leaves declared it needed life support. Other detectives hunched over laptops and rifled through file drawers.

"You want a cup?" Bess jerked a thumb toward the big coffeemaker in the corner.

"I came prepared for us both." He held up his insulated mug and a paper cup for her.

"My hero." She wheeled her chair over to his desk, and they settled, inhaling their caffeine. "So how'd your chat with the lovely widow go?"

"I had to tread lightly. Angela Spear, née Bissett, age fifty-three. At first I was afraid she'd bite off my head and swallow it whole, but she did answer questions." He flipped open his notepad. "Said she'd managed the branch of the First National Bank, but now just advises occasionally — whatever that means. Claims she and Adam had their arguments from time to time, but got along okay. No problems lately."

"The sister said different," Bess put in. "At first she said things were okay in that household, but when I pressed her, she admitted they'd had some arguments the past few weeks. She started to call them fights, but amended it quickly."

"Unless they aired their disagreements somewhere public, that'll be hard to verify unless Angela admits it." At her nod, he went through the rest of the interview and his impressions. "She agreed her husband had pissed off a lot of people in business deals and legal matters. Their son Stephen, age thirty-five—"

"Same as you."

He grinned. "I'll catch up to you yet."

A fake scowl from her. "Go on with the report."

"You're the one who interrupted. Stephen lives in Portland. She'd phoned him earlier. Claimed the DHP officer gave permission, bitched that he'd stood by listening."

"Permission? Angela probably threatened him with bodily harm if he didn't let her talk to her son. That it?"

"The officer verified that she'd told the son only that his father died on the cliff. That's it. What about Angela's sister?"

She consulted her small tablet. "Emma Tibbetts, age sixty. Their parents are deceased, and she seems to have taken on the mothering role. Cashier part time at the Hannaford supermarket in Bayport. Husband drives equipment for a contractor. Two children, grown, married, families, live in the area." She looked up, her expression gentled. "She showed me the grandkids' photos on her phone. Emma may be the big-sister bear protecting Angie, but she's not all bite."

"You going soft on me, Bess?"

"Caught me at a weak moment. I need more caffeine. And an energy bar."

He laughed. "Anything else?"

She shook her head, flung her braid back out of the way. "Not much. She didn't know the subject of their latest rows. If Spear's death is a homicide, I'll come down harder on Emma."

"I'd be surprised if the ME doesn't call it wrongful death. Maybe premeditated."

They sat in silence for a moment over their coffee before Bess went to her desk.

Justin booted up his computer and typed his report. When he finished, he started a search on Debra Delano. He ought to look up Sheridan Harte while he was at it. Hadn't he said to Bess she might be a suspect too? Doubtful. But looking her up wouldn't hurt. Rule that out. Open the door for him.

He pictured her humor at his cartoon tie, pictured her discerning brown eyes and wide mouth. Her long legs.

I wonder if she's still at the Littlefield house.

****

AS THEY WALKED along the Point road, Sheri averted her gaze from the garish yellow tape, drooping with the drizzle, and admired a seagull soaring overhead. Without Justin Wylde's guardian aura, the site of Spear's death seemed unbearably sad and ominous. Her friend also kept her eyes focused elsewhere.

They rounded the point on their walk to the Spear house, located about a quarter mile farther along. The fog and mist had shifted offshore, but the damp chill penetrated. She hugged her coat around her. Deb had left Len's slicker in the mudroom and wore her fleece.

The road sloped as the cliff fell away behind them, and the salt-rich breeze carried no traces of the morning's violence. A puffy duvet of fog in varying shades of gray hid the islands and the ferry rumbling toward Bayport. Sheri contented herself checking out the other houses—among the antique ones, a few newer ranch styles. Stacks of lobster traps occupied a few side yards.

Feel like you've been railroaded?" Deb said.

"More like flattened by a paving machine." Or maybe she was thinking of the detective's Wile E. neckwear. "So you were supposed to tell me about dinner?"

"Miriam framed that explanation to suit herself." Deb rolled her eyes at this apparently typical manipulation by the Grande Dame. "She told me to invite you, and I said not to bother with the dinner because you intended to return to Weymouth in the afternoon. Don't feel you have to stay."

Ah, but she did have to stay, despite the memories. "We've made such a good beginning on the notes I'd hate to disappoint her."

Sheri had contracted work and proposals going in various stages. She couldn't afford to limit herself to one project at a time, even to a project as large as Miriam's. Her article about bed-and-breakfasts in York and Cumberland counties was due next week. She could work on it after dinner. And spending the night meant she wouldn't have to pass Noah Tardiff's derelict house until tomorrow afternoon.

As they walked, this seemed a good time to ask about something else. "Miriam said Adam Spear cheated her son-in-law. Her daughter's husband?"

"That's right, my aunt Sydney's husband Gil MacRae. Gil owns a small contracting company. He was one of the subcontractors on the Spear house. Gil claimed Adam Spear shaved several thousand dollars off his final payment for bogus reasons. Hard to know what really happened. Gil sometimes jumps to conclusions."

"Did your uncle sue Spear?"

"Aunt Syd looked into the matter. I don't know if I told you, she's an attorney. She advised Gil that a lawsuit could cost him more than he'd recoup, so Gil ate the loss. But I think it festers inside him like a bleeding ulcer."

Sheri saw no reason to point out how Deb's uncle's dispute with Adam Spear gave him a motive for murder. If it was murder, Gil MacRae would be on Detective Wylde's radar. How many other people had cause to dislike, even hate, Spear?

As they reached the end of the point, their

destination loomed ahead. Sheri gaped. Multiple roof lines and formal landscaping—a sprawling leviathan. Three-car garage. Out of place in this neighborhood. "Seems Adam Spear was trumpeting his success."

"Ostentation pumped with testosterone." Deb tucked a stray hair behind one ear. "The property's been in the Spear family for generations. Five years ago, Adam replaced the great-great's two-bedroom Cape with this monster. Had to get dispensation from the planning board to build outside the original footprint."

"Bet that put some noses out of joint."

"Including Miriam's. Their first duel. She lost that one, but only because his house is on the side of the road *away* from the water. Then he wanted to install an eighty-foot-long dock. On the water side, of course. On that issue, she—and most neighbors on the Point— persuaded the planning board to see reason instead of permitting the blight. No reason for a private dock when the town has plenty of dock space that provides revenue."

Adam Spear seemed like a man who wanted his way or else. None of her business, but she couldn't help wanting to know more. Depending on how things played out, especially if Spear's death was murder, maybe she could get an article out of it.

"Tell me about the family. What sort of work did Spear do to afford this grandiose house?"

Deb chuckled. "Attorney. Must've charged damned high fees."

Another reason he could've made more enemies. "And his wife?"

"Bank manager. I heard somewhere she put Adam through law school. I don't think she works at all now.

These days I see her mentioned in the local newspaper chairing one civic committee or the other, cutting ribbons and presenting checks. That sort of thing."

High-powered society wife, more like a trout in this small pond. Counterpoint or complement to a husband who was a shark and perhaps a cheat?

Chapter Five

A MUD-SPATTERED white Subaru wagon sat in the Spear driveway. Sheri and Deb followed a flagstone path past azalea beds smelling of fresh cedar mulch to a side entrance.

A heavy-set, sour-faced woman dressed in puke-green sweats opened the door. Beneath tightly permed steel-gray curls, she looked down her broad nose at them. "Deb."

"Hey, Emma." Deb made introductions. The woman guarding the doorway was Angela Spear's sister. "Sheri used to live in D Harbor. You might remember her."

"Can't say I do." Small hazel eyes skewered her. "I know the name Harte though. Both my kids had your mom for English."

"Me to." Sheri offered a friendly smile.

The woman stepped aside for them to enter. "Angie's in the kitchen."

She accepted Deb's food donation but made no offer to take coats. Apparently their visit would be brief.

No mud room for this estate. From the tiled foyer they followed Emma into the kitchen. Its black and white décor was as contemporary and cold as the house's exterior. Gleaming stainless appliances, black granite counters big enough for TV's *Best Pasta Chef*.

Banging echoed from somewhere beyond, and an angry female voice shrieked expletives. When Sheri's nana died, she wept and buried herself in work. Noah's loss was another matter. More like Angela, though she hardly remembered the days immediately afterward. Everyone grieved in their own way, she supposed.

Emma stood by, her expression even more strained. Both hands clutched the salad container. Sheri feared for the fragile plastic.

Deb whispered, "Maybe we shouldn't have come so soon."

Angela Spear stalked barefoot into the kitchen from what looked like a small sitting room. When she spotted them, she stomped on the brakes. Emotion painted her cheeks crimson, and her breath came in ragged gasps. "Ah, hi, Deb. I didn't know anyone was here."

Sheri wouldn't want to be on the receiving end of the glare she sent her sister—her older sister, from all appearances—for not warning her that company had arrived.

Deb hurried to hug Angela and introduced Sheri. They both offered condolences.

Angela nodded in thanks. Hand trembling, she shook a long, slim cigarette from a pack in her pocket and looked around, likely for a lighter. Dressed in an orange velour warm-up suit, she stood taller than Sheri, close to six feet. Big boned like her sister but trim, with a swimmer's broad shoulders. A pricey stylist, not anyone at the village's Color and Curl, had created that perfectly layered almond-brown 'do highlighted with blond streaks. And genetics hadn't sculpted her blade of a nose and the taut skin over her cheekbones. Surgery or Botox or both.

Having found a lighter on the counter, one big enough to double as a flame-thrower, she lit up and paced back and forth in the kitchen, her gait stiff with residual temper. "Forgive me for not being a better hostess."

"I'm sorry we've bothered you," Deb began. "You must still be in shock."

Shaking her head, she waved away the apology. "I am, of course, but that's not the reason for the outburst. The state cops just left." She vibrated like a plucked harp string.

"They treated Angie like a suspect," Emma spat out. "Asked where she was and all. Like maybe Adam's death wasn't an accident, like she *killed* Adam or something."

An interview she interpreted as interrogation. Maybe she interpreted correctly. The spouse would be a logical suspect.

Deb uttered sympathetic murmurs. She was such a mom, nurturing part of her DNA. "How awful for you, Angie, after losing your husband this morning. Do you want to tell us about it?"

She exchanged a glance with Sheri. Yup, Deb knew she'd want the scoop.

Angela paced to a spacious breakfast nook, then back to the kitchen before returning to the glass-topped table. "Please have a seat. If you'd like coffee, Emma just made some."

Sheri registered a hazelnut aroma. Maybe Angela's body twitches were the reason Emma had switched from high-test stuff. Hazelnuts were tasty, especially covered with dark chocolate. But hazelnut *coffee*? A foul brew. Even if some called it coffee, it wasn't.

"Nothing for me, thanks." She unbuttoned her coat and slid onto a straight-backed chair. Cookbooks filled two shelves recessed into the wall beside her. Angela didn't strike her as a gourmet chef.

"I'd appreciate a glass of water." Deb chose the seat opposite her.

"Good you have family nearby to help out," Sheri said as Emma delivered the water in a wavy amber glass. "Deb said your son lives in Portland?"

Apparently too wired to sit, Angela stood beside Deb's chair. She sipped then copied her sister's earlier pose by holding the mug tightly with both hands as if it might try to escape. Diamonds the size of paperweights sparkled on her fingers and earlobes.

"Stephen's on his way home now. Like Emma says, the cops wanted to know where I was, what I knew. Which wasn't much. I was still in bed when Adam went out for his morning run."

Deb patted her arm.

"Hard to tell the police anything if you didn't speak to your husband," Sheri said.

"He's the early riser, not me. *Was*." Her voice wavered with just the right note of grief, but her eyes showed no ravages of recent tears. Her mascara and blush were perfect. Her demeanor evened to dispassionate self-assurance. "I don't know what time he left. I went back to sleep and the sirens woke me up. The bedside clock said seven forty-five."

"You got up then?" Deb asked.

"I was curious, concerned." Her gaze hardened. "Like my neighbors. When I saw the fog, I thought it might be a car accident. I threw on some clothes and went outside." Perfect white teeth closed over her lower lip. She lowered her gaze and a single tear slid decorously down her cheek. "Norman Galt met me at the foot of the drive."

Sheri watched as she took a moment to compose herself. Not that she appeared to need composing. No real distress, her facial expressions ranging from A to B. Maybe the Botox.

"Could he have planned to meet somebody on the cliff path?"

As if Sheri's question surprised her, her eyes widened and her shoulders hiked up. A dismissive wave of the cigarette. "I have no idea. The cops asked if Adam had enemies." She sucked in the nicotine again and laughed a bitter bark before exhaling smoke upward. She tapped ash into a crystal ashtray already smeared with ashes. "Adam liked a fight. His shrewd deals earned him enemies, but nothing serious. Maybe he fell because the rocks were slippery."

Another drag on the smoke before her gaze skewered Deb. "Wasn't it you who called 911? Did you see him fall? Was anyone else there?" For the first time, agitation edged her voice.

Unsure if the emotion was fear or anger, Sheri held her breath.

Flustered, Deb blinked. Her gaze flicked to Sheri and then down to her glass. "Oh, dear, I was walking Comet. Then I found Adam. I went back to the house to call. That's it."

How did she know it was Deb? Sheri slowly exhaled. Rather than keep Deb on the hook, she said, "He did have enemies, you say. Did you give the police names?"

"Adam pissed off a lot of people, including the board of selectmen and Miriam." Her lips pulled into a grim sort of smile, not the friendly one she likely went for. "But no one suspects her, of course."

Deb nodded at Sheri, and the two women rose to their feet. "We won't trouble you further today," she said. "I hope the police figure this out quickly."

"Not the way they're beginning." They left her sister finally stowing the salad in the fridge, and Angela escorted them to the foyer.

She stopped at an open closet and flicked on a light switch, illuminating the interior. In cubby holes on one wall, boots, hats, and gloves. On hooks, a yellow slicker, assorted windbreakers, and light jackets. She gestured at an empty hook. "Looking for evidence in the wrong place. They confiscated my brother's raincoat. He left it here last weekend."

"Interesting," Sheri said mildly. "What sort of coat was it?"

"A black hooded jacket. I threw it on earlier when I went outside." Another snort. "That female detective said if the autopsy indicated foul play, they had to move fast on the investigation. If testing showed the coat and gloves in the pocket were clean, it could help clear me. Like I *need* clearing."

Deb made sympathetic comments and they took their leave.

Once they'd left the Spear house well behind, Sheri breathed a sigh of relief, inhaling clean sea air free of tobacco smoke and outrage. "You did well in there, not letting on you saw the struggle on the cliff."

"Angie or Emma might broadcast it to the whole peninsula. You think the police really suspect her of killing her husband?" Deb said sotto voce, as if she thought Angie might hear.

"I wouldn't venture a guess, but it stands to reason

the detectives would need to rule out the wife first. Besides, it's the victim's home, a big reason to search." If it was wrongful death—a term she knew from the Portland case—they'd be back to conduct an official search. "Could she and Adam have argued on the cliff and she killed him by accident?"

"They've battled for years. A wonder the marriage lasted this long."

Sheri pictured Angela Spear's build. Visualized her marching into the kitchen, her neck and shoulder muscles flexing with fury beneath the stretchy knit. Judging from Deb's description of Adam, Angela had a few inches on her husband.

****

WHEN THEY RETURNED to the house, Deb headed home, saying she'd return with the family for the dinner party. Inside, Sheri found a note written in Miriam's graceful loops that she was resting and would be ready to return to work at two.

She welcomed a few minutes to herself, to catch up on email. She was settling at her laptop when her cell chimed.

Maine State Police, the screen read. She checked the card Justin had given her. The numbers matched. Her pulse did a little dance, and she swiped to answer. "Hello, Detective."

"Sheri. If I'm disturbing your work with Mrs. Littlefield, I can try again later."

Interesting. He'd given her an out. But she couldn't resist listening to that smooth voice. "I have a few minutes. What can I do for you?"

Had her own voice dropped to a lower register? Did she sound businesslike or seductive? *Am I suddenly fifteen again?*

"I'd like to meet with you later this afternoon if that's convenient. I have some questions to ask you."

She frowned and stared at the phone in her hand. "To ask *me*? I have nothing to do with whatever happened on the cliff. What is this about?"

"I don't have time to talk now. Please. How's four o'clock or so?"

She couldn't really refuse, could she? He *was* a cop. And spending time with him did appeal. Two hours with Miriam ought to be enough for the afternoon. "Sure, that's okay."

Nothing, only background office noises. Then, "I'll pick you up at the Littlefield house."

And with that, he disconnected, leaving her with questions. And nerves. Should she tell him about Gil MacRae's grudge against Spear? Or would that be just gossip—or worse, a betrayal of her position as Miriam's ghostwriter?

Whatever Justin wanted to ask *her*, she would tell *him* about Deb's narrow escape.

That decided, she concentrated on work. After answering a few emails, she reviewed her notes and began transcribing the morning's recording. Noting gaps and areas that could be expanded, she jotted down questions. Thank goodness she had this to take her mind off the day's events.

And off a certain state detective whose mere voice turned her on.

Or not. Wylde must have questions about her father's embezzlement. Or did he have a different interest in her? Or maybe she was projecting her own attraction to him. Not that anything could come of it.

****

JUSTIN SHIVERED IN the chill of the morgue, breathed through his teeth so as not to absorb too much of the odor of chemicals and the faint rotting-meat smell of death. Beside him, Bess hunched her shoulders. She popped in a second stick of spearmint gum.

The body on the metal autopsy table remained covered by a sheet while the chief medical examiner reviewed her notes on a tablet. Justin had met Megan Rosenberg, M. D., at his first crime scene after making detective. The Korean-American doctor, married to a rabbi, was about fifty. Black humor helped cops and forensics personnel deal with all the viciousness humans did to each other, but the dry wit uttered deadpan by this slight woman always caught rookies off guard. Including him ten years ago.

Rosenberg set aside her tablet and folded back the sheet to expose Adam Spear's head and shoulders.

"The crime lab won't have the full report on Spear's clothing for a few days," Bess said, reading from her tablet. "But foreign materials—granite, lichens, fungi, seagull droppings—were consistent with the site. Picked up on his way down. We're hoping you have something."

The ME's eyes were solemn as she swiveled around a monitor so they could see the crime-scene tech's photo of the body on the rough granite. "From that slab to this one. Rough trip."

Justin mentally chalked up a point for predicting her wisecrack.

Her shoulders wagged inside her scrubs, and again she consulted her tablet. "I can give you a preliminary assessment on the externals. Looks like multiple fractures to the limbs."

"Cause of death the fall?"

"COD indeed the result of the cliff dive, but he'd have died very soon anyway."

"What do you mean?" he asked.

"I'll get to that in a minute." She scrolled back to the crime-scene shot. "What do you make of the swastika pose?"

Justin hiked a shoulder. "Hard to say at this point. Can you tell if the limbs were moved pre- or post-mortem?"

Rosenberg pointed to the computer screen. "Spear was likely dead before he hit bottom. Boulders on the way down struck the fatal blow. I can give you more details later but his wounds are obvious. Skull meets granite, granite wins every time." She tilted Spear's head back, exposing bruising on the throat. "I doubt he had the strength to defend himself from either the attacker or the fall. His trachea and larynx were crushed."

Bess uttered a low whistle. "You're thinking the attacker struck first to disable him?"

"Takes a lot of strength to deliver a blow that hard," Justin said. Maybe more strength than a woman possessed, even a strong woman like Angela Spear.

"Not as much as you would think." Rosenberg folded back the sheet further. "Especially if you have one of these." She held up the metal object beside the victim.

"Brass knuckles?" Bess's eyes were wide.

"These are the steel ones from the crime lab's display case. Try them on for size." The ME held them out.

Justin fitted his fingers into the metal rings and held up his fist.

When Rosenberg smiled, he settled back for one of her teaching moments. "Metal and wood ring and knuckle style weapons have been used for centuries by criminals and by the military. They're illegal in most states, including Maine."

She swung the magnifier over Spear's throat. "Place that just above the suprasternal notch, please."

He held his armored fist to the bruising. Close match. *Son of a bitch.*

She continued, "Although the actual weapon had a slightly different configuration, the shape generally conforms to the contusions on the skin of the deceased. Such a weapon concentrates the force of a blow into a smaller area, making fractures more likely. Being hit in that vulnerable location would do considerable damage regardless of the size and strength of the owner. Spear couldn't cry out. He would've lost strength quickly. He couldn't inhale enough oxygen to survive more than a few minutes."

Rosenberg stepped back from the table and picked up a scalpel, preparing to begin the Y incision.

Justin stared at the brass knuckles, then exchanged a glance with his partner.

Bess murmured, "So the attacker came prepared."

Chapter Six

SHERI SPENT TWO hours that afternoon in the library with Miriam. Setting a course for the book apparently revived a barrage of memories. She came armed with notes. They covered the young Miriam Lange's pursuit of her R.N. degree — not common in the early 1950's — her courtship with medical student Isaac Littlefield, and her first experiences in Dragon Harbor as his office nurse before their sons Noble and Craig and their daughter Sydney were born. Sheri chuckled at the Boston girl's stories of her cultural shock in the isolated Maine village. Excitement about the project bubbled inside her. The humor and insights in the older woman's detailed anecdotes would yield a fascinating book.

Afterward, she had a few minutes before Justin Wylde arrived.

Resigned to spending the night, she fetched her kit of running clothes and toiletries from the car. Anxiety nagged her about the dinner. She knew some of the family but fretted about others. What would the reactions be to Miriam's working with George Harte's daughter? Probably nothing good. So much for the fizz of anticipation at seeing Justin. Um, Detective Wylde.

But she said nothing of her misgivings as Miriam showed her to an upstairs guest room with an attached bath. The puffy, flowered comforter on the four-poster bed matched the balloon-style curtains and coordinated with a dusty rose area rug.

"The bathroom has fresh towels and a hair dryer. Let me know if you need anything else. I'm going to freshen up and change. Everyone will begin arriving about five thirty." She handed Sheri the pair of lavender silk pajamas she pulled from an antique cherry bureau.

Sheri didn't mention her meeting with Justin Wylde. Miriam, like Deb, would turn it into more than it was. Nevertheless, Sheri would wash her face, brush her hair, and apply fresh mascara. But only in case she didn't have time afterward before the dinner party.

"These pj's are lovely. Now I won't have to sleep in my jogging suit."

"Or your *birthday* suit," quipped Miriam as she closed the door behind her.

****

"HOPE YOU DON'T mind riding in this," Justin said as Sheri buckled herself into the passenger seat of his truck. She wore the same outfit as that morning, but her dark gold hair was loose and curling on her shoulders. Touchable. But he gripped the steering wheel.

"Not at all." She eyed his chest as if checking for another cartoon tie on his denim shirt. "Does it mean you're off duty and won't be interrogating me like this morning?"

"I am off duty, but I can't make any promises. My brother says I probably came out of the womb asking questions." He cast her a sideways glance, catching a half smile. Was she teasing him? More likely nervous at riding in a cop's ride.

"I'm guilty of asking a lot of questions too."

Justin laughed, wishing she'd been the one amused. He wanted to hear that sexy liquid laugh again. He needed to know how deeply she was connected to this case, but for now he'd rather keep it light, the reason he'd arrived as a civilian.

"Okay if we head down the peninsula?"

"Sure. I have something to ask you about."

"Shoot." So maybe she'd thought of something else.

He turned left and proceeded slowly around the Point past the cliff's descent into the ocean on the left and the Spear house on the left. The F-150's engine rumbled evenly as he accelerated down the East Road. The recent tune-up had done the job.

He listened as she described her friend experience that morning. "Deb asked the mechanic who came to her aid how that could've happened. He suggested it might be the alignment. Or wear and tear, but he acknowledged the lug nuts weren't worn or rusted or the wrong size. Buddy's Garage and Bait Shop is a small-time business. Folks in D Harbor can rely on Buddy for a lube job or towing or fishing advice. But theories on automotive engineering? Doubtful."

"Likely Buddy was trawling for business. So you want to know more about the lug nuts."

"After what I've told you, don't you?"

He grinned. "You're as suspicious of coincidences as a cop."

"What do you think, Detective?"

She'd turned in her seat toward him, worry creasing her forehead. She nibbled on her bottom lip, and his eyes locked on her mouth. He jerked his attention back to driving just in time to avoid crossing the center line.

"Make it Justin, would you, Sheri? Changes in temperature can cause some loosening. But I bet you looked that up."

"Of course." Her shoulders twitched, but she didn't comment on how well he'd read her. "But we haven't had fluctuating temps. How loose would temperature changes make them?"

In his peripheral vision he could see Sheri watching him, but she remained silent, letting him think. Not a woman who felt she had to fill silences.

He drove on past an old Grange Hall and along a hillside on his right and a sheer drop on the left. When he saw a warning sign, he slowed, remembering the only other time he'd been here. On that case, another detective had been lead. Justin had been more of a gofer. He maneuvered around a sharp curve. Its nearly V-shape jutted outward to a sheer drop. Waves crashed on boulders big as his truck. The road continued ahead next to the ocean as far as he could see.

Finally he said, "Not loose enough to make her steering wonky like you described unless they were rusted or too flimsy for the vehicle. Neither is true according to the mechanic. Odd it was only the front ones, and odds are against it happening. It's possible somebody loosened them deliberately."

"Deb lives down that road." She pointed to a side road on their right. "She turned south here. When the wheels made it hard to steer, she found a wide space to pull off. If she'd headed north to Miriam's, she'd have had no place to go. The road stays close to the ocean for a few miles."

"I noticed. Great view."

"Yes, but the same feature making this section scenic also makes it dangerous."

"Especially that curve we just passed."

"Locals call it the Devil's Elbow." Sheri shuddered,

58

clasped her hands around the purse in her lap, and squeezed her eyes shut, which didn't ward off the image of Deb's minivan plunging off the Devil's Elbow.

"I'll add that to my inquiries. And I'll do some more checking on lug nuts. Okay?"

"Thanks." So would she. The lug-nut incident occurring the same day Deb witnessed what was likely murder was too much of a coincidence for her.

He kept the conversation light after that, asking about sights along the way—a house built of granite blocks, fields that swept down to the sea, islands off in the distance. He stopped at Donna's Market and bought them both coffees.

"Milk, right?" he said as he handed the paper cup to her.

Her cheeks warmed with pleasure. "Yes, thanks." When he continued driving, she explained that the market was where Deb had been headed when the lug nuts loosened.

He told her he'd been on the peninsula a few years ago for a case and pointed out the scene of a fire where now carpenters were framing a new house. The old Cameron farm, she told him. Deb had mentioned that fire to her, and the strange events surrounding it.

"I understand the road ends at a lighthouse." He smiled over his coffee cup.

"We're almost there. Glass Point Light, yes. Named for the first lighthouse keeper, Theodore Glass. There are still Glasses in the area. Old family. After the lighthouse, the road name changes to West Road and heads back up the other side of the peninsula." She pointed. "There's the road to the lighthouse, on the left."

He stopped the truck facing the lighthouse itself and

the broad stone slabs around it being battered by the incoming tide.

"My parents used to bring my brother and me here to picnic in warmer weather. At low tide, hermit crabs and small fish are left in the tidal pools. I loved to look for them back then."

"I'll bet in high school, kids came here for a different reason."

She laughed. "At night. Probably still do." A memory crept to the surface, of Noah and her and the moonlight, and she interred it again. Suddenly cold, she clutched her hot drink in both hands. "Why am I here? Am I under suspicion?"

"Whoa." He held up his hands in protest. "I came mostly because I wanted to see you. Off duty, remember?"

She took her time watching him, for subterfuge and, dammit, because she liked looking at him. Into those blue eyes as he watched her. In the middle of what might be a murder case, he went out of his way to seek her out? She'd planned to call him about the lug nuts, but that wouldn't have been social. Crap, *mostly* business. Not merely social. There was more. She knew there was more. "Mostly?"

He grinned. She felt the warmth of his gaze on her, and her mouth went dry. "You have me there. I can't move the needle on seeing you other than professionally unless I make sure you're not connected to the case beyond what I learned this morning."

Her pulse flipped a beat at the realization the attraction was mutual. "The case. Does that mean Spear's death wasn't an accident?"

"Can't say. The Major Crimes Unit will make an

official announcement soon."

"So how might I be connected?"

"I had to check your background. I saw you worked with Sergeant Atwood a few years ago, so I know you understand the importance of my search. Pete said you helped keep the little girl's story in the news and that made it possible for the police to find her and nail the creep that took her. Her uncle, as I recall."

"Pete's not a writer. He needed someone to shape the conversation." She bowed her head over the steam coming from her cup. "In the end, they found her too late."

"Pete said she'd been dead before he even asked you to help."

"That doesn't make it any easier, any less tragic."

"No, it doesn't. But knowing how you put yourself in the middle of that is another reason I wanted to see you again. The other is I wanted to hear you laugh again."

"Laugh? I think you're a little nuts, Detective Wylde. And you're trying to distract me."

"I should know a writer stays focused. What I need to ask about is your father's record."

"Ah. Dad, the embezzler." Forcing out the light words, sure didn't lighten the reality.

"Damned tough on a kid." He took her empty cup and set it in a holder.

"A shock, for sure." She wound her fingers together in her lap. It always tore at her to think of George Harte as an ex-convict. But he'd stolen from the town of Dragon Harbor and the school district. As business manager for both, he siphoned off nearly a million dollars into a personal account before an audit uncovered the loss.

"And that's what I have to ask you about. Could there be any link between your father's crimes and Adam Spear?"

"I can't imagine what. He wasn't Dad's attorney, but I don't know what connection he might've had with the town or the schools."

"None I could find." Justin's warm hand covered both of hers. "Must've been tough on you having to go to school and face your friends every day."

She shook her head. "It was tough, but not in that way. Mike was already away at college, and I was living with my aunt in Rhode Island. Mom bore the brunt of the disgrace before she took off for Boston. Most of the money was recovered. Dad pleaded guilty to spare us. He spent ten years in state prison."

"Did you know the Spear family?"

"Only Steve. He was in my brother's class, two years ahead of me. I'd see him occasionally with Mike's buddies. But that's all." She held her breath, hoping there was no more. He couldn't know the rest. Not all of it. *Oh God, Noah...*

She stared out at the waves. If Spear's death was murder, she'd have to tell Justin about Gil MacRae's dealings with him. People resorted to extreme measure to protect themselves. Would Deb's own uncle harm her? She blotted the question from her mind. For now.

When she returned her gaze to Justin, he was watching her. "Will you let me know if you find a connection to my dad?"

A little squeeze, and he lifted his hands. She wanted those strong hands to continue holding hers. "You'll be seeing me either way. You *do* want to see me again, I hope." His expression as he studied her wasn't even close to official.

Her pulse jumped. "You move right along, don't you?"

"A man in my line of work has to take action. When he knows what—or who—he wants, he has to make his move. So?"

She almost laughed, but he might take it the wrong way. "I'd like to see you again, yes. And just so you know, I don't do serious relationships."

"I like a woman who lets a guy know what she wants. I'll hold you to that." The gleam in his eyes made it clear he wasn't talking about just relationships. "Not serious works for me. The job makes it hard to maintain anything but casual."

He leaned closer, and she thought he might kiss her, but he only placed a palm on her cheek, leaving tingles when he withdrew. He wrote in his pocket notebook and tore out the sheet. "This is to my private phone. Unless it's police business, use that."

Her breath hitched, and she pressed her lips together trying to conjure that missed kiss. She tucked the piece of paper in a pocket. She'd add the number to her contacts later.

He turned the truck around and headed back the way they'd come. "Why did you leave town, leave your family?"

"I don't like to bring that up because it sounds like bragging. The school in Providence had a writing program for talented kids, and Mom wanted me to take advantage of that."

Which was true. As far as it went.

Chapter Seven

"AUNTIE SHERI!" DEB'S boys, eight and five, skidded down the hall toward Sheri. Comet raced around them, tongue flopping from her grinning mouth. The tow-headed whirlwinds hugged her around the waist before racing off, arms outspread in flight. They left behind little-boy smells of soap and wet sneakers.

Their father's half-hearted admonishment not to run in their great-grammy's house was lost in their jet-engine flight. Deb would've put a stop to the boys' antics, but not their easy-going dad. Len saluted Sheri from the living-room archway and mouthed *kitchen*.

She was only a few minutes late. She'd had to freshen up after returning from her outing. She shouldn't call it a date, not even in her head. Justin remembered she took milk in her coffee, so maybe he was really attracted to her and she'd see him again. He was self-assured, with an aura of power about him, but comfortable to be with. Casual, that's all she could do. Whatever else he uncovered about her, she'd deal with it.

Panting, the little dog gave up the chase and accompanied Sheri.

In the kitchen, she found the source of the dog's interest—not her company but food smells. Deb and her mom, Vera, were unpacking thermal containers. Aromas of rosemary chicken and a mélange of other mouth-watering dishes filled the kitchen. Comet sprawled in a corner on an old blanket, but kept watch for handouts or dropped morsels.

Vera emitted a whoop of welcome. She whisked over to brush powder-scented kisses on both cheeks and envelop Sheri in a well-padded hug. She had a massive soft spot for Vera, who had always offered comfort when she and her mother fell out.

The two mothers had once worked together at Dragon Harbor High. Sheri hoped Vera didn't ask after her mom. She'd rather avoid sympathy about their strained relationship.

"I'm so glad you're the one doing Miriam's memoirs." She lowered her voice. "I hope the interviews go well. She can be, well, demanding and opinionated."

Unfortunately, Sheri couldn't tell Vera about another client, a veterinarian who treated the pampered pets of Boston's Beacon Hill. He had the personality of a department-store mannequin but insisted she portray him as warm and folksy like James Herriot.

Sheri laughed. "Miriam doesn't come close to some of the trying clients I've had. She and I are getting along fine. Opinionated and demanding usually make for interesting reading."

"Now, Vera, leave the poor girl alone." Deb's dad set down the container he'd just brought inside and enveloped her in a warm hug. "She's no teenager. She knows her business." Spoken like a man who knew business, which Noble was as VP of Bayport Savings Bank. He inherited his barrel-chested build and blizzard of gray hair from his father, whose photographs Miriam showed her during their afternoon session.

His wife shoved a tray of canapés into his hands.

"Miriam's waiting for these." Vera shooed him away. To Sheri she added, "Jackie of Lupine Catering—that's Donna's daughter—prepared the food but she's home with her sick son, so we're doing the serving and clean-up."

Mouth-watering pies and fresh produce from Donna's Market came to mind. No surprise her daughter's business involved food. "Everything smells wonderful."

Sheri sidestepped Deb who carried a covered pan. She opened the oven door and slid it inside to keep warm. She'd changed into white wool pants and a lavender pullover. Very together as always, elegant yet casual.

Maybe Sheri's work attire wouldn't be too out of place. "What can I do?"

Vera handed her two baguettes and indicated a rack of knives. "Cut those into fat hunks and we'll put them in the oven to keep warm with the chicken."

While she sliced, Vera mixed pre-sliced and bagged veggies into salad greens in an enormous wooden bowl. Deb left with a stack of white linen napkins for the dining room table.

The rise and fall of voices overlapped in the living room. Sheri eyed the mound of salad. "How many people are coming to dinner?"

Vera rolled her eyes. "Ten or more family members and Lord knows who else Miriam might've invited. Deb's setting places for a dozen. Her boys can sit at a side table if necessary." She patted Sheri's shoulder "You all right? Sorry you had to step into this mess on the cliff."

"No biggie. Miriam and I managed to get started." She omitted mentioning that after her initial shock and horror, she found the tragedy intriguing. No way would she divulge her also intriguing hour with Justin. "Deb's the one affected the most."

Vera huffed, her mouth turned down. "Word was out early she's the one who found Spear. So many calls she had to unplug the landline."

"How could that happen? Detective Wylde assured her he'd keep that confidential."

"I don't know, but the *Bayport Chronicle* posted online by nine-thirty that it was 'a young woman walking a small dog.' Lots of people know Deb comes over to walk Comet."

Maybe a reporter talked to the neighbors or to the first responders. Or some busybody emailed the *Chronicle*. A village where everyone knew everyone's business. Or thought they did and spread it like lawn fertilizer. And an online news bulletin would broadcast it at warp speed.

Nine-thirty. Plenty of time for Spear's attacker to worry he might've been seen. Plenty of time afterward to loosen all the front lug nuts in Deb's minivan. The hairs on the back of Sheri's neck rose. She'd have to divulge what she'd learned to Deb or her mom. Or Justin would.

She didn't want any of this to be her business, whether or not she could write about it. But if Deb was truly a target, she was more than merely a bystander.

"If Adam Spear was murdered, could it have something to do with his law practice?"

"That would have to be an old grudge," Vera said. "He hasn't practiced law for, oh, about eight years." She leaned closer and lowered her voice. "Not everyone knows this, but being part of the local banking community, Noble has the inside track. Adam made a pile of money in a lawsuit a few years before he quit. He must've invested it."

Thus the extravagant house. According to his wife, he still maintained an office. If he no longer practiced law, what did he do? Boating or fishing? Not in April. Maybe he spent his days playing the stock market and checking on his blue chips. Even his wife said he had enem—

"How's Barbara doing?"

Vera's question snapped Sheri from her reverie. After her dad's downfall and the divorce, Mom had met and married an attorney in Boston. He moved his law practice to Salem, where they now lived.

"Mom's in her glory. She volunteers as docent at the Peabody Essex Museum, and Robert keeps her busy with social functions connected to his work." The life she'd hoped for when she married Sheri's father, but George Harte's love of the outdoors had plunked them in small-town Maine. Her frustrations had been burrs chafing and prickling Sheri's childhood. Mike's too, but less so. She didn't view her male child as an avatar for her stifled ambitions.

"I hated seeing you two argue over everything. Journalism club and track versus ballet classes. Eyebrow waxing or natural. I think she wanted for you what she missed in her life."

"I agree, Vera, but back then I didn't get it. To me, it was just nagging." Mom's constant comparisons to Sheri's blooming and curvy best friend could've driven a wedge between Deb and her but for Deb's generosity and lack of affectation. Some things her mother would never forgive, but distance helped.

"Mom and I get along better now. She's involved with the grandkids Mike and his wife have given her. I do have her to thank that I don't slump like lots of tall women."

Deb, who'd just returned, patted her shoulder. "Heck, if you slumped over more, we'd almost be the same height."

Sheri rounded her shoulders and bent so they were at eye level. "Not comfortable. Maybe you should do more yoga. Or stretch taller."

She smacked her forehead. "Never thought of that. I'll buy a rack tomorrow."

Good segue. "Speaking of torture, you didn't tell me the word was out about this morning."

Silverware rattled as she collected table settings from a drawer. She turned, the teasing glint in her eyes faded and her forehead creased. "Hard to keep secrets here. Friends called to offer sympathy, but mostly people were curious about what I saw."

"And…" Sheri prompted.

"I told everyone the police asked me not to talk about it."

That strategy was both good and bad. Good that she could get off the phone quickly and not reveal details. Bad that people might speculate even more. "You should tell Detective Wylde."

"I already called. We discussed the lug nuts, and he reminded me to be cautious. Len wants me to go out hauling traps with him tomorrow, not stay home alone. But I have too much work to do, contractors to line up for the cottages I manage, and…" She clutched the knives and forks against her chest. "I don't want to talk about this. Let's just enjoy Miriam's little party. Okay?"

Shoulders stiff, she marched out.

Vera turned toward Sheri, expression solemn. "You think she's in danger?"

"I don't know, but I'll talk to her about bringing her laptop and files here tomorrow." Len's lobster boat had no internet, but Miriam's house did. And Deb wouldn't be alone. That Justin had already followed up with Deb on the lug nuts eased Sheri's tension. A fraction.

Vera nodded, apparently satisfied. A few minutes later she tossed out a major change in topic. "Deb says your father's in Florida?"

The inflection in her voice meant she wanted more than a one-word answer. Any inquiry about Sheri's dad tightened her stomach but she couldn't hedge with Vera. "Dad captains a charter fishing boat in Tarpon Springs. That's on the Gulf coast." A raised eyebrow pushed her to add, "He's clean. No get-rich-quick schemes."

"Good to know George is doing all right," Vera said.

"Everything's ready here," Deb said. "Let's introduce you. Miriam's so excited about this."

****

SITUATED IN THE front of the house, the living room also had a fireplace. Comet trotted ahead of them through the open archway, similar to that of the library. When Sheri entered with Deb, conversation shut down as if she'd hit the Mute button. Half a dozen gazes homed in on her, some welcoming, some skeptical, all curious. Thankfully, only two faces were new to her.

In the far corner, the little boys lay on their bellies, their thumbs whirring over small electronic games. Vera joined her husband on a green-and-rose-striped loveseat by the gas fire. A fiftyish woman opposite on the matching loveseat gazed at Sheri with speculation. Based on her dark hair and generous figure, she had to be Miriam's youngest, Sydney MacRae. Miriam had told her that missing would be the middle child, Craig. The only one of the Littlefield siblings to enter medicine, he was an emergency room physician in New York City.

Comet nudged Sheri's leg as if in support, and she bent to pat the silky head. Leaving her side, Deb crossed the room to whisper to her husband before she took the armchair beside his.

Len sent Sheri an exaggerated wink as he ambled toward a beverage cart beneath a window. "Ladies, what can I get you?"

Vodka martini on the rocks would've been her preference, but given the circumstances, she chose something with lower alcohol content. Something more genteel. A moment later, she and Deb held crystal goblets of white wine.

Dressed in a rich purple knit dress that fell to mid-calf, Miriam rose from a sofa in front of the street-side window. The man seated next to the sofa began to stand but she waved him off.

The papery skin of her slender hands felt cool as she gripped Sheri's in welcome. With a smile, she linked their arms. "Most of you know her but I'm doing this *anyway*. Meet Sheridan Harte, my *ghost*. Be *nice* to her or I'll *trash* you in my memoir." Her peal of laughter covered the grumblings and forced chuckles. Almost.

Sheri felt out of place at best. On the spot at worst. She schooled her features into a pleasant smile.

"Good to see you, Sheri. It's been a very long time."

The deep male voice behind her sounded familiar. By the archway, the wing chair's height had concealed its occupant. She turned to see a tall man in a loose-fitting fisherman-knit sweater pushing to his feet with the aid of a carved wooden cane. The sight of his beak nose and thick auburn hair summoned an old image in her memory.

A little older, Reed Keniston had been part of the pack that ran with her brother. His parents' unfortunate choice of given name fit his spare frame only too well, leading to the nickname "Reedy." The same year her dad's crime was discovered, he lost both parents in a car accident. In all the drama over her dad's trial, Sheri'd forgotten about his tragedy. And him.

"Reed, I'm glad to see you too." She extended a hand, which he took in a firm grip. A broad smile split his pleasant features. "So you're part of this family?"

"Great-nephew," Miriam clarified. "My brother's *grandson*. Back *home* after many years." Ah, the loss of Reed's parents meant Miriam's brother had suffered more tragedy beyond the crippling bicycle accident.

"Like you, Miriam." Reed turned gray eyes back on Sheri. "Skiing accident a year ago made me rethink priorities. I left my job at a west-coast company and bought a house here farther down the peninsula."

"I'm sorry about the accident," I said. "I hope the cane's not permanent."

One shoulder hiked up in a self-deprecating shrug. "The knee will never be the same. Mostly stiffness now. Just call me Tripod. I manage just fine, though at a tortoise's pace. Join me for drinks sometime and we can get caught up."

She said she'd enjoy that, and he returned to his highball glass, atop a delicate candle stand beside the wing chair.

Miriam led her to the man who tried to assist her

earlier. "Gil MacRae's my *son*-in-law."

He was the contractor Adam Spear cheated. Or not.

Gil stood, a little unsteady, a tall, muscular man with heavy-boned features. Drops splashed from his glass— scotch or bourbon on the rocks, likely not his first. He offered a broad, callused hand. "Don't believe everything Miriam tells you about the family. You gotta give us a chance at censorship."

"No one censors Miriam, honey. You ought to know that by now," called a feminine voice from across the room. Sheri'd guessed correctly, the woman on the loveseat was Miriam's daughter, Gil's wife.

"Sydney has *that* right. I'm telling it *all*!" Miriam chuckled as Sheri escorted her back to the sofa. She took the middle cushion, nudging Sheri toward the end near Reed Keniston. Comet flopped down at her mistress's feet.

Miriam the matchmaker?

Reed raised his glass in a silent toast to her. Something gleamed in his eyes. Male appreciation?

Sheri would have to rethink his offer of cocktails and catching up. Not that he wasn't a nice enough guy, although rather bland. But she was here to work. How was it possible she'd been there less than one day and already *two* men were hitting on her? An exaggeration, but still.

She sipped her wine, regretting she hadn't opted for the vodka.

Chapter Eight

"HOMICIDE?" ANGELA SPEAR said through the cloud of smoke she'd just exhaled into her kitchen. "So somebody really murdered my husband. How do you know?" She tapped her cigarette over the crystal ashtray in her other hand. The falling ashes barely missed the goblet of red wine on the kitchen counter.

"Sorry, Mrs. Spear, we can't divulge those details during the investigation. Detective Peters and I figured you'd rather hear this much from us before the official announcement." The aroma of roasting beef made Justin's mouth water. Starting the discovery of the body and his other child abuse case, this had been a long day, with little time for sustenance. But apparently grief hadn't dimmed the widow's appetite, only the color of her warm-up suit. This one was blue.

"You know who did it?" She sucked on her smoke, her expression wary.

"Ma'am, not yet. At this point in the investigation," he said, "everybody and nobody's a suspect. We're just gathering information. Your son's not here? We'd like to talk to him."

"He had to go back to Portland to pack a bag." The oven timer dinged, and she punched buttons. "*One* of the neighbors had the consideration to bring pot roast, not some tasteless mystery dish. I detest casseroles. My supper's ready, detectives. Stephen will return tomorrow morning. You can talk to him then." She started toward the front door.

Revealing the determination of homicide and nothing else only poked the woman with a sharp stick. He worked his jaw, revving up to do more poking.

"We'll do that. But since this is the home of the victim, we need to conduct a search. Every minute counts in a case like this."

That stopped her in her tracks. Her eyes narrowed and she turned, planting her feet. "Are you looking for something specific?"

"You did say your husband had enemies," he said. "Business connections, town issues, and such. A search might give us insights into reasons someone would dislike him enough to harm him." Including family, but he'd keep mum on that. For now.

"It's not enough that you took my brother's coat, which he'd like to have back. But now you want to tear apart my *house*?" She jabbed out her cigarette and reached for another.

"The lab's almost finished tests on the coat. We'll return it as soon as possible," Bess Peters said, her tone woman-to-woman apologetic.

Angela ignored her and drilled Justin with smoke. "Don't you need a warrant for a search?"

He hadn't smoked since college but now and then craved that kick. Not today. This female chimney was a turn-off. "You did consent to a partial search earlier. If you want to rescind permission, we would need to obtain a warrant."

Bess shot her cuff and checked her watch. "Almost six p.m. Judge Nadeau won't be in his office again until tomorrow morning. He doesn't like his evenings disturbed."

Justin rubbed his nape. "Here's the situation, Mrs. Spear. We'd need to secure the house until we have the warrant in hand. That means you'd have to leave. Be a shame to let that beef get cold." He offered a remorseful twist of smile.

She stiffened, reached for the cigarette lighter. He could see her weighing how refusal might be viewed. "You might as well go ahead."

"Thanks," he said. "We'll try not to make a mess." Pulling on latex gloves, they left behind a steaming Angela Spear.

****

AN HOUR LATER Justin and Bess convened in the upstairs office. He consulted his spiral notebook. "I don't have much on the wife, Bess. You?"

"Norman's daughter Genie, the EMT, cleans house for the Spears."

Justin grinned. "So *Norman* shared info? I see." Maine was a small town, and cops all knew each other. Maybe that was all, but probably not, given the chief's rep. Second time this possibility had come up. "Very chummy, you two."

She sniffed. "It was Genie I spoke to, not Norman. And it doesn't hurt to butter up the local force. Norman Galt is no Barney Fife."

He took that and the warning in her eyes to mean he should butt out. "So what did his daughter have to say?"

"Angela Spear splits her time between the Seaside Resort's fitness club, various civic committees, and the Bayport community theater. Genie said people respect her for her charity work, but don't much like her overbearing manner. She said her friend, who works at the bank Angela used to manage, and other employees found her hard to please. Plus she coerced a few young tellers into blind dates with her son. About Adam, she implied he'd pissed off people from one end of Bay County to the other. Including his wife."

"I love a case with an endless list of suspects." He sat on the padded desk chair.

Walnut cabinets and golf trophies, traces of new leather and Old Spice. Polished cherry desk with clean modern lines. Silver pen in a green marble holder. New model, slim laptop on the desk pad. Adam's domain.

"Living room, dining room barely look lived in." Bess opened a louvered closet door. "Too much like one of those design-magazine houses where nobody'd dare leave shoes lying around."

"Master bedroom's like that too." He held up a plastic evidence bag. "Picked up Adam's cell phone. And it was Adam's room. Angela's is farther down the hall."

"Separate. Doesn't surprise me," Bess said. "Another interesting thing. Only ashtrays in the whole place are the one Angela's filling and another in a small office off the kitchen. Household bills in a letter holder. Looks like her space."

He swiveled the desk chair. Ergonomic. Pretentious word for comfortable. Seat cranked lower to suit Adam's height. Drawers glided open at a mere touch. Pens, pencils, other junk, but no keys, no list of passwords. He felt beneath the desktop, beneath the drawers, the seat. Zip. He lifted the laptop lid. A screen icon asked for a password. Like the phone. Damn. Maybe the tech people could get into it. Or Bess. Or maybe Angela knew the password. A big if.

"You think Adam didn't approve of her smoking?"

"I'm thinking he banned it. Now the grieving wife is making up for lost time." She closed the closet door. "Filing cabinet's in here. Drawers locked."

"On Adam's bureau, car key fob with attached

house key and what appear to be the keys to the office he shared with Quentin Frost. No other keys. None here either."

Bess dived into the lower cabinets while he searched the walnut shelves above them. Tucked into the wall behind law volumes as fat as suitcases was a small safe.

"Where would he hide the combination?" he said to himself.

"Same place he hid the keys?" Bess said from inside a cabinet.

"Smartass."

Replacing the law books, he checked the back wall. Plaques and framed appreciations for civic shit, pictures of Adam in gray pinstripes beside other suits, including a woman in pinstripes. Damn ego wall.

He gingerly lifted the larger frames and felt behind each one. *What's this?* He lifted down a photo of self-satisfied men holding golf clubs. Taped to the back was a small white envelope.

"What do you have there?" She stood and straightened her jacket.

"Not much. If this once held the safe combo or the filing cabinet key, it's gone now."

"Check out these photos on the side table," she said. "Formal family one of a smiling Angela—if you can believe it—Adam, baby Stephen. A few other candid shots. Everybody looks happy. Anything strike you as odd?"

Justin studied the silver-framed portraits, pursed his lips. "None of the son older than ten."

She nodded. "I saw more recent photos on Angela's office wall. Even a couple more studio portraits. One of only mother and son."

"Something more to ask the guy about tomorrow." He wrote in his pocket notebook. "We need more about the grieving widow than what Genie told you."

"I'll pay a visit to that bank branch for starters." Bess tapped keys on her tablet. "I'd like to know if Angela's quick to anger and then cools off or if she holds grudges."

"Or has violent tendencies." He tucked the laptop beneath his arm. "Time to face the dragon. Get her to sign the release for this and the phone."

"Norman recommended a take-out place on the way to Bayport. Good lobster rolls, he said. If she yields the safe combination or the file keys," Bess said sweetly, "I'll buy supper."

"You got it, but I'd be safer betting on the Red Sox."

****

SHERI TIGHTENED THE laces of her New Balance running shoes, belted on her water bottle, and pulled a fleece hat down over her ears. She'd fastened her hair with a scrunchie at her nape. The overnight wind had swept the inclement weather out to sea in favor of a brisk blue April day. She shivered in the briny morning breeze, counting on the exertion of the run to warm her, and set off across the road to the cliff path.

Last night she'd taken her car out for a spin to plan her route. If she turned left, she could avoid the crime scene, but that direction would take her back toward Noah's house where too many memories haunted her. One of these days she would make herself go there. Not today. A right turn it was.

Running Adam Spear's fatal course felt way too creepy. In her mind she saw Deb's frown when she'd told her she planned to run this morning. "Go run somewhere else," she warned. Unlikely Adam Spear's murderer would be lurking on the Point, but Sheri's nerves hummed like a high-voltage wire. She had her phone and pepper spray in her pockets.

She sped ahead to put the crime scene behind her. The shell bits on the cliff path crackled beneath her soles.

Last night's gathering at Miriam's had been enlightening in more than one way. Deb's brother Todd and his family and two other couples who were neighbors on Echo Cliff Point joined the gathering. After introductions, everyone sat down to dinner. Miriam seated Reed Keniston beside Sheri, leaving no doubt about her matchmaking intention. Sheri resolved to be courteous but nothing more.

The sizeable crowd meant the children were relegated to their own table in the kitchen, overseen by Todd's wife. No one brought up the subject of Sheri's jailbird dad. Instead, to Deb's dismay, the topic of conversation among the adults turned to Adam Spear's death. The police hadn't yet said it was homicide, yet theories as to the killer zoomed around the table at the speed of fiber optics. The wife, the son, the business partner, and more. Gil MacRae shoveled in his food without adding to the discussion.

"So many enemies, so many suspects," Reed whispered to Sheri as he passed the bread.

He'd proven wittier than she expected, though his jokes seemed forced, almost planned, she thought now as she jogged the Spear house. An older pickup took the place of Emma's muddy car outside the garage. Steve's, Sheri guessed. How terrible, losing his father to violence.

Shortly she turned onto the East Road. She breathed more easily, leaving behind the cliff and the notion of a boogeyman jumping out at her. What little snow remained had been pushed off to the side, leaving a wide shoulder. In spite of the hard-packed dirt, she stumbled a couple of times. Darn that distracting view of sunlight glinting on the blue-green water.

Soon the road turned away from the cliff and inland with only distant views of the water and closer ones of fields and old farmhouses. She felt more confident and in the zone. She cruised to her two-and-a-half-mile turnaround and turned back.

Not long after the Devil's Elbow, she heard her name called. Despite her jacket and the sweat from her run, a chill lifted the hairs on her arms. She grasped her phone with one hand and the pepper spray with the other as she slowed to look for the owner of the greeting.

Reed Keniston leaned on his cane on the side porch of a white Cape. He beckoned with a coffee mug. "Sheri, I thought that was you. Take a breather and join me. Coffee's fresh."

No boogeyman. She slipped her devices back into her pockets and waved as she debated.

She had two miles to go, but he seemed so eager. Nothing against Reed, but she had to be careful. Fewer conflicts of interest or instances of personal animosity could arise if she separated work and socializing. Having her best friend set up a contract with Miriam meant she was already dipping a toe in the conflict pool. Avoiding more personal links with the family seemed the wise course. But perhaps a brief chat on the porch would fulfill her drinks obligation.

"Thanks, Reed, milk, please. I can stop for a minute or two, but I need to keep moving," she managed, panting and slowing to a trot. She jogged in place on the walk while he went inside to fetch her a "cuppa," as locals would say. As she'd have said if she'd remained in town.

Reed returned with a steaming mug for her. His smile crinkled lines beside his eyes and mouth, adding warmth to his long countenance. "Sure you don't want to come in? I have cinnamon cookies. Bought them at the grange bake sale."

She shook her head and, halting her in-place jogging, warmed her hands on the mug. "I appreciate the break, but I can't stay long. Miriam will be ready for our morning session." And she'd need time to shower and dress, organize more breakfast than a cookie.

He leaned against the porch post. "Interesting evening last night. Apparently the whole county is overflowing with people who held grudges against Adam Spear."

"Something out of a mystery novel." She sipped her coffee. Not enough milk. "Except it's all true. Or speculation. What can you tell me about Adam Spear?"

"I didn't know the man" he said. "Anyway, you have me to thank for rescuing you."

What? His odd segue startled her. "Rescue from what?"

He chuckled. "From whom, you mean. From Sydney. If I hadn't sat between you two, she'd have pounced on you. She didn't say anything to the group, but she's worried about you fleecing her mother. She'd have tried to finagle a way to see the contract."

It wouldn't be the first time a family member questioned a ghostwriter's credentials or felt threatened by what a memoir client might divulge, like family secrets and teenage rebellion. Her skepticism could be due to Dad's embezzlement or maybe personal issues between Sydney and her mother.

"If she doubts my credentials, she can easily check me out. But showing her the contract would be up to Miriam, not me. The amounts and a schedule for payments are quite specific."

"I wouldn't worry about it. Miriam will handle her." Using his cane for support, he came down the steps and joined her. "Syd isn't the warm and fuzzy type, but she's fierce as a mother bear when it comes to family. After my parents died, the MacRaes took me in. She and Gil helped me through it so I could return to MIT."

The year of his parents' accident he'd been about nineteen or twenty. "I'm really sorry, Reed. That must've been so hard for you, your whole life changed overnight. I'm trying to remember. Your dad had a landscaping business?"

His gaze darkened. "And lawn care. In the winter, he plowed snow. Mom answered calls and did the billing. Dad started drinking and lost everything. I don't know if alcohol was to blame or if he deliberately drove the car into that oak tree." His face remained a placid mask but every word came out taut as strung wire.

Sheri made sympathetic comments, felt more ill at ease. "What a terrible tragedy."

Reed squeezed her forearm. "Some people don't understand, but I know you do. You've suffered tragedy too—Noah's suicide."

Whoa. Time to go.

She'd known it was only a matter of time before someone brought that up and the trauma for her as his fifteen-year-old girlfriend. But hearing Reed state it so bluntly hit her hard. Mumbling something he could construe as agreement, she eased away. "Thanks for the coffee. I'd better get back to Miriam."

Not the best exit she ever made, she thought as her shoes hit the road. She looked back as Reed waved goodbye.

"I'll phone you soon about that drinks date," he yelled.

Chapter Nine

SHORTLY AFTER JUSTIN and Bess Peters had
reported the ME's assessment to their lieutenant, the
MCU released an official statement that Adam Spear's
death had been ruled a homicide. Kept confidential were
the assumption of premeditation and the brass knuckles.
The ME had shaken her head about tracing the origin of
the brass knuckles, which were for sale all over
cyberspace.

After that, the investigation kicked into a higher
gear. Bess drove to Bayport to interview Spear's law
partner and the bank manager who had replaced Angela.
Another detective was conducting more extensive
background checks. Justin had to dodge reporters with
cameras as he bought coffee at the general store. The
Bangor Daily News and P*ortland Press Herald*, along
with the *Bayport Chronicle*, carried stories of the case
complete with photos of Echo Cliff and the police
barrier. Local TV channels covered it too. Maine had a
low crime rate, so a sensational murder garnered a huge
audience.

Now in the Spear kitchen, Justin linked his fingers
behind his back as Angela Spear railed against police
harassment in general and him in particular. Along with
invectives, smoke spewed from her mouth. After all, this
was *Dragon* Harbor.

Justin hadn't expected a warm welcome, but

returning her brother's black coat should've earned him at least a thank you. What he got was a fire-breather protecting her cub, or whatever a baby dragon was called. Stick with cub. He pushed aside his annoyance and suspicion in favor of a bland expression while he studied said cub.

To one side and behind her, bulldog chin clenched, Stephen Spear stood, arms folded in a tough-guy pose. Taking after his mother's side of the family, he was a couple inches taller than her. Wrinkled khaki cargos hung low, and an untucked, stained, green T-shirt stretched over his belly. As Justin's sister would put it, Stephen Spear was more flab than fab. His gaze locked on the kitchen window, then skittered to the tiled floor, the microwave—anywhere but on the cop here to interview him. Worried about a chat without his mom's backing?

"I'm Stephen's mother," Angela Spear was saying. "I should be able to remain in the room while you interrogate him." She crushed her cigarette butt in the ashtray.

Enough venting. Any more and *he'd* need to vent. He kept his tone measured. "If your son was a minor, Mrs. Spear, you would have that right, but according to the Maine Bureau of Motor Vehicles, Stephen Adam Spear is thirty-four. And this won't be an *interrogation*. I just have a few questions. As I told you yesterday, I'm gathering information."

She sputtered, and before she could speak again, he directed his gaze to Steve. "If we can't speak in privacy here, we can have our conversation at MCU headquarters."

The color drained from the man's face as his gaze

lifted to Justin's. He swallowed, touched his mother's arm. "No problem, Mom. I don't mind answering questions."

Angela snatched her cigarette pack and the ashtray from the table. "Well, I *do* mind. But it seems a mother has no say." She huffed, headed toward the adjoining room, but turned back. "Detective, if you harass Stephen or make accusations, I'll have my husband's law partner put a stop to your so-called questioning. Do I make myself clear?"

"Perfectly, ma'am."

She stalked out, slamming the door behind her.

Justin pulled out a chair at the table. "We might as well be comfortable."

Steve lumbered to the table and sank onto the opposite chair. "Sorry about Mom. She's pretty upset about my dad."

Upset didn't begin to describe her attitude but the cause was unclear. Secrets, fears, anger? Or general habitual bitchiness? He set that conundrum aside. Both mother and son had the size to throw someone smaller off a cliff, and both could've had motives and opportunity.

"Understandable, her grief." The bereaved son might freak and call for Mommy if Justin started the recorder, so he flipped open his notepad. "I advise you to tell the truth and share as many details as you can. Do you understand?"

"Yeah, sure."

"Your parents were close?"

Justin knew the answers to his preliminary questions, but going over those sometimes allowed him to focus on what subjects *didn't* say. And sometimes they said something helpful. Assessing this guy's state of mind would make it easier to lead him into riskier issues. A delicate exercise.

The other man shrugged a shoulder. "Close? I guess. I haven't lived at home in a long time. Left after high school."

"A shame you weren't here when the chief of police informed your mom about your dad. She'd have appreciated your support. How did you find out?"

"Mom called my cell."

"When was that?"

"I dunno. Maybe about eight, eight-thirty." His Adam's apple jumped as he swallowed, and his brows knitted together. "She said he fell after some argument. But now they say some dude killed him?"

"Evidence indicates he didn't just fall."

Steve blinked furiously. He lowered his gaze to the table. After a moment, he lifted his head but said nothing. A guy of few words.

Not hostile but either previous experience with cops had taught him not to volunteer information, or someone had coached him. "Where were you exactly when you learned of your father's death?"

"In my truck, headed to Kittery with a delivery. I drive for Coastal Courier Services in SoPo."

Justin flipped to previous notepad pages. "That's interesting. After your mom mentioned your employer yesterday, I gave their South Portland office a call. The manager there, a Mr. Dayton, said he let you go last month. Something about drinking on the job." He'd also mentioned that Steve was a high-school dropout, but no point in interrupting their tête-à-tête for that. "Still on a courier run to Kittery yesterday, Steve?"

Sweat beaded on Spear's temples. "The drinking thing is bogus. Dayton doesn't like me. I had a cold. He smelled cough meds on my breath. He was looking for an excuse to get rid of me and hire his brother-in-law."

"Why lie about it now?"

"Shit, man, you see how Mom is. Ellie—that's my girlfriend—she's helping me with interviews and stuff like a résumé. Soon as I land another job, a better job, I'll tell Mom. She doesn't have to know now. I mean, you won't rat on me?"

"It's just between us guys." Justin nodded in agreement, stifling his scorn at the immaturity and shiftlessness sitting across from him. His cop radar said there was more going on with the guy and with this dysfunctional family. After letting Spear babble thanks at his complicity, he asked, "So if you weren't on the road to Kittery, where were you between the hours of six and nine yesterday morning?"

Steve's broad forehead scrunched as if searching his memory. Finally he said, "I got up around seven. Had breakfast, then drove around Portland. When Mom called, I was on the Eastern Promenade. I parked by the kids' playground to answer the phone. I don't see my mom that often, so when she calls, she talks forever and I have to pull over."

"Can anyone other than your mother verify your whereabouts?"

Steve's face fell. "You mean like an alibi? No, man, I was just hanging out until I could meet Ellie during her lunch break. 'Course, that never happened. I came here instead. But I phoned her, if that helps."

"I'll talk to her." Justin held his pen poised over a clean notebook page.

"Ellie Stone. She works at a law office in downtown Portland. One of those with a string of names. I can't remember. She does filing and stuff. Paralegal it's called." Steve looked at his phone and rattled off her cell number.

Justin made a note to check with both mother and girlfriend on the calls. Sometimes little details led somewhere useful, sometimes a dead end. He'd need more cause before the state attorney would issue a subpoena for phone records. "Tell me about your dad, about your relationship. What kind of guy was he?"

Steve bent forward, relaxed now they were buddies. "Everybody will tell you, so I might as well say it. My dad was a hard-ass. He pissed off plenty of people in this town, in the courtroom, in his business dealings."

"Was he tough on you?"

"Sure as shit, but it was just his way." Steve's shoulders jerked, a swaggering gesture, but his gaze slid away. "Made me tough. Most of the time we got along. Understood each other."

Made him tough—maybe. Or resentful. Or both. "You sure about your relationship? I saw no recent photos of you in the upstairs office, only kid ones."

Steve looked away, seeming to process Justin's statement. Had he never noticed? "No big deal. It was his home office, mostly for his awards and golf shit."

Justin probed a little further about the relationship, keeping the discussion conversational, before ending the interview. No full-court press, with Mommy Dearest nearby. Hell, Angela probably had a recorder mic against the keyhole.

Some of Steve's answers didn't jibe. The guy answered in partial truths. Or just plain lies.

****

SHERI SPRINTED THE last mile back to the Littlefield house, passing a familiar state SUV parked at the Spear house. *Justin*. Or was that wishful thinking? She should be working out how to let Reed down if—*when* he called about going out for drinks. She'd have to lay it out, her conflict-of-interest rule. Miriam would hear about it, but she'd have to understand.

At dinner last night Reed had told her about his career as a software engineer. She didn't understand much except that his investments and a settlement from his accident set him up here. His job became managing his investments—not unlike Adam Spear. Bank branch manager wasn't the same thing as investment manager. Angela might not be up to it.

After showering and dressing in yesterday's outfit, Sheri ate her usual breakfast of banana and a mix of yogurt and granola, provisioned by her friend. Deb hadn't been happy about having to lug her laptop and files to Miriam's for the day, but after her mom leaned on her, she gave in.

Sheri found Miriam in the library, Comet snoozing at her feet, a stuffed squirrel toy beside her. Sheri mentally crossed her fingers Miriam wouldn't mention Reed. The woman had likely alerted him she'd be jogging past his house.

"You must've had a long morning walk." Sheri poured coffee for both from the insulated carafe on the side table. "Comet's worn out."

The elderly woman's lips curved in an indulgent smile. "She *should* be. She spent the last *hour* chasing *real* squirrels in the backyard. Now, Sheri, *do* tell me. What's going on at the *Spear* house?" She leaned forward, apprehension creasing her brow.

Sheri wanted to launch into the questions she'd prepared, so she'd be sure to keep to their schedule and head home by four. But apparently her client had other ideas. At least her topic *du jour* wasn't about Reed. She booted up her laptop and keyed in her password.

"All quiet this morning. The pickup parked there might belong to Steve." Thinking she was scared, Sheri chose her words carefully. "Are you worried the person who attacked Adam Spear might be hanging around?"

Miriam shook her head. "No, I hoped the *detectives* were back. I want them to solve this quickly. Deb is *frightened* the killer will guess she saw him. And so am I, for *her*."

The same concern had crossed Sheri's mind more than once. Okay, once an hour. But Miriam needed calm, not shared fear. "Don't worry. Deb will be all right. Only the police know she saw more than Spear's body."

Sheri started the digital recorder. "Let's return to the anecdotes we discussed yesterday."

"Stephen Spear's *only* luck seems to be *bad*."

Sheri depressed the stop button. No deterring Miriam. "What do you mean?"

"I was living *abroad* when you young people were growing up, so I don't know Stephen well. He walked Comet for me a couple of times. Last night *Vera* said he could never *please* his father. Angela doted on him but Adam came down *hard* on him."

"He lives in Portland now. Maybe he's moved on, is doing better."

"I would be *surprised*. When I walked Comet one day around Christmas, I saw him and his father arguing in the driveway. Adam yelled he was *never* to come back again. Then he threw a bag at his son, one of those soft bags, a gym bag, I think." Her brow crinkled again. "I *wonder* how Stephen *feels* about his father's death."

A tragedy, such animosity between father and son. And not just butting heads like Sheri and her mom, but cruelty. If Adam wrote off his son, disowned him, the rejection had to affect Steve's entire life.

"Whatever happened between them in the past, I'm sure he mourns his father now." She wasn't sure at all, but the platitude seemed politic. She scrolled to see the questions she'd added. "I loved your accounts of your early days in Maine. More details would improve the part about your first winter on the coast."

Comet yawned and stretched, and Miriam bent to pat the dog's head. "I wonder if they've scheduled the *visitation.*"

Chapter Ten

SHOULD HE OR shouldn't he? Justin gripped the steering wheel with one hand and his phone in the other. He glared at his phone screen. It glared back.

Hell, Sheri'd intrigued him ever since he met her. More since their drive yesterday. He pictured those brown eyes that saw everything, the thick, dark-honey hair he wanted to run his fingers through. She probably wasn't in any danger, but it didn't hurt to check.

He placed the call.

The phone rang on her end three times. His dashboard clock read one thirty. She was probably busy with the old lady. Bad timing.

"Hello, Justin. Since this is on your state phone, does that mean you have more questions about my dad?" Her tone was mocking but with a hint of worry.

"None. It's about your personal safety. I saw you jogging this morning." From the window by the Spear's front door, he'd watched her long legs eat up the lane and the way her running gear hugged her perfect ass. "You might be taking a risk running alone like that."

"With a murderer on the loose, you mean. Deb's husband informed her he heard the announcement on the radio while he was out hauling."

"The small-town telegraph probably spread the word faster than the media. Yes, homicide, a reason to take precautions."

"I had my phone and a can of pepper spray. You looking out for me, Detective?"

"Clearly Mrs. Littlefield couldn't stop you."

"She gave me the pepper spray. You were back at the Spears'. Questioning Steve?"

"You know I can't tell you."

She chuckled, the sexy note making him shift in his seat. "It doesn't hurt to ask. Never know what I might learn."

"Same here, as you already know."

"So you called just to warn me to be careful?"

"I did more research on the lug nuts issue. No way more than one loosened like that in this situation. The odds are astronomical. I've already spoken with Deb Delano."

"Good. So did I. She had to go to a cottage she manages to check on some cabinets, so I persuaded her to wait here at Miriam's until her husband could go with her."

"Good move. I'm sending techs to check for evidence. Doubtful they'll find much now that Buddy's worked on the van, but it can't hurt."

"That's great. I'll tell Deb. And I'm happy you phoned."

She sounded as if she was ending the call. He didn't want their conversation to end, but his phone buzzed with an official call. He advised her to be careful and said good-bye.

The other call was Chief Galt saying he was back in his office and ready to meet with him.

Justin never stepped over the line between professional and personal. But Sheri wasn't involved in the Spear case except peripherally. She'd cleared up his concern about her father, and he'd found no link between the man and Spear. The lieutenant might call Justin on pursuing something with Sheri. But he perceived no hard line he shouldn't, couldn't cross. He was interested. Sheri was interested. So why the hell not. Something casual, no big deal.

****

"WHY DID HE really call?" Sheri whispered to herself. She smiled, replaying Justin's smooth baritone. He could've phoned Deb directly to explain about the lug nuts and sending police techs. Surely he couldn't have really been worried about Sheri's safety. Or maybe he was or maybe it was more. He'd said he'd like to see her again. And she'd said the same. What was next? What did she want to be next? Casual, that's what next *had* to be.

After Deb left with Len, Sheri returned to the library and Miriam. She was able to steer Miriam away from the Adam Spear intrigue and back to the memoir. After they filled in the needed details, she expected another anecdote about Miriam's early life in Dragon Harbor, but she leaped ahead to a touching story about nursing in Africa. *Africa?* Okay, Sheri'd told her she didn't need to proceed in sequence. But to see how to balance the narrative, she needed a time frame. Miriam obliged.

She summarized the years of her three marriages. She worked as her first husband's office nurse through the births of their children. When she lost Isaac to heart failure, she struggled to support her school-age children on a small inheritance and a part-time nursing paycheck.

Eight years later, an empty-nester, she transferred her nursing experience to a Peace Corps assignment at a small clinic in Kenya. There, she married Whitley

Keane, a British surgeon. They worked together there for ten years before he died of dengue fever.

Comforted and courted by widower Radford Woods, the philanthropist who funded Keane's clinic and others, she married for the third time. They lived in England and traveled the world, including visits to her family in Maine. She helped him oversee clinics and raise funds until his death. She and his two sons then managed the philanthropy until her return to Dragon Harbor.

"My step-sons and their children are perfectly *capable*, so *here* I am," Miriam finished. "But I'm still on the board of directors. I like to keep my *hand* in." Ah, the reason for yesterday's video conference call.

When Sheri left for the day, she was smiling. That life story helped her appreciate this amazing woman a whole lot more. She'd overcome adversity, taken charge of her life, and come out on top, managing a major non-profit for the past several years. No wonder she couldn't resist taking charge of her family here too.

She stopped at the Dragon Harbor General Store to buy provisions for supper. The small lot was full but luck provided a space being vacated by a tiny car whose only visible occupant was a bear-size Newfoundland dog.

The yellow frame store had been an institution on the peninsula since the beginning of time or, according to the sign over the door, since 1850. Back when Sheri was small, it was a cramped and creaky store, offering mostly canned goods including locally packed sardines in mustard sauce, a favorite of her dad's she couldn't stomach. Over the ensuing years, a succession of owners gradually added on and modernized the place into a bright and welcoming establishment stocked with fresh, frozen, and locally grown foods.

As she entered, the jingling bell over the door turned the checkout clerk's head her way. "Come on in, *deah*," the woman said in a heavy local drawl. "Beef stew's hot, and we just got a delivery of scallops. Fresh and sweet outta the Gulf o' Maine."

Sheri smiled and thanked her, and she immediately returned to her conversation with a hefty man and a red-haired woman.

"I saw it on *Bayport Online*. Adam Spear's death weren't no accident. The police announced it was homicide."

Sheri had thought as much when she saw how far down those rocks Spear had tumbled. Or been pushed. Who hated—

Stop it, Sheri. Great, just great. Now *she* was doing it. Was there no escape from the hot topic of the past two days? She didn't want to be sucked into the life and times of D Harbor. Too many memories. Too many of them awful. She snagged a shopping basket and scooted down the produce aisle.

Scallops would be tasty but required more culinary effort than she would have in her after the drive to Weymouth. Beef stew could be reheated. She gathered salad fixings on the way to rear of the store, the source of the rich beef-and-vegetable aroma.

There more shoppers gossiped. A tiny gray-haired woman in denim overalls tapped a gloved finger on the butcher counter. "I saw a state detective goin' into the police station with Chief Galt."

"Maybe they got a suspect," a long-faced woman in a plaid wool jacket added. "Not many folks much liked Adam, but who'd hate him enough to kill him?"

"I can think of a few," replied her friend. "Police chief'll know 'em all. Maybe Deb Delano saw more'n she's sayin'."

So folks did know who found the body. Talk about a prophecy coming true. Deb's husband had better stick to her like paint.

The bald and pencil-thin butcher handed each woman a package and they shuffled away, continuing to chew on the gossip like kids savoring a new bubblegum flavor. He donned new sanitary gloves and peered at Sheri over the glass front. "Can I help you?"

She placed her order with the sour-faced Ichabod Crane, nothing like the butcher who used to slip Mike and her peppermint candies from behind the counter. Just as well. She didn't need or want a reunion with anyone here.

He handed her a quart container of stew, and she hustled to the checkout. The coast there was clear. No murder gossips. After adding a bag of ice, she paid and hurried to her vehicle. She stowed her purchases in the cooler she kept in the wayback. Hoping to make it home without further delays, she closed the back gate.

"Sheridan Harte?"

Damn. What now? She turned toward the gravelly voice. "That's me."

A large man in a tan Carhartt jacket strode toward her. The man who'd been talking to the clerk. A wide grin gleamed white inside a reddish beard. "I knew that was you in the store but you didn't recognize me behind this thicket." He flapped a beefy hand at his beard.

She recognized the eyes beneath a tangle of ginger eyebrows. "Boyd. Boyd Rankin, of course." She let herself be drawn into a bear hug that took her breath away.

Boyd had been Noah Tardiff's best friend and was nearly as devastated as Sheri when he hanged himself. Boyd played football in high school. The smell of fish and salt water emanating from his stained work coat told her how he was keeping that muscle these days. She preferred to avoid a reunion with Boyd, but to quote Jagger, *"You don't always get what you want."*

"Boyd, it's wonderful to see you, in spite of the thicket."

"Almost ready to shave 'er off. Keeps me warm in winter but itches somethin' fierce as the weather heats up." He scratched beneath the luxuriant growth. "I heard you was in town, writin' a book with Miriam Littlefield. The murder happened just down the road from her house. You must've seen the goings on?"

Oh, boy. Gossip had spread word of Sheri's presence along with Deb's involvement. "I arrived too late to see anything but police cars, thank goodness. A terrible thing in this peaceful place."

Boyd nodded, his expression darkening. "Can't say I'm sorry Adam Spear's dead. Son of a bitch tried to force the fishing co-op to shut down so's him and his rich friends could buy up the shore frontage. It's a working harbor, not a fucking condo resort. No secret in town him and me had some shoutin' matches. I figure the state detectives'll be talking to me soon."

Shit, more than she wanted to know. When would it stop?

He brightened. "Enough about all that. You're probably anxious to get home."

"I am, but tell me, how's Doreen? Any kids?" They'd been high-school sweethearts too, like— She

100

squelched the thought.

His expression turned blank. "No kids. Doreen up'n left me last year. She's down in Florida now with some guy. They have a new baby."

"I'm sorry things didn't work out, Boyd."

"Yeah, me too." He patted her hand. "Hey, drop by the co-op sometime. I'll treat you to some lobsters, go to my house, and cook 'em up. We can get caught up."

"Thanks, Boyd. I'll see about that." She clasped his big rough hand. "It's great to see you."

She opened her driver's door and watched him stride to his pickup. Get caught up? Maybe. But more likely further conversation would lead to reminiscences. Things she couldn't forget and didn't want to discuss. With anyone. She would avoid the fishing co-op. And Boyd Rankin.

As she turned on the engine, her cell jingled. "Hey, Deb. You home safely?"

"Along with all my guys," she said. "No baddies slinking around today." Her normal optimism had returned. Sheri hoped that didn't mean she would let down her guard.

"Thanks for letting me know you're okay. I just picked up supper at the general store. Oh, and I ran into Boyd Rankin. He invited me to drop by the co-op—free lobsters."

"You should take him up on it. I'm working at the counter there two afternoons a week, filling in for somebody. You could stop by and keep me company sometime. Kinda quiet, but at least I can take my laptop."

"Tell your guys hi for me. I'll see you tomorrow."

"But we didn't get to the reason I called. Miriam wants—"

"Don't tell me. Another dinner party?"

"This time the guest of honor is Chris Hemsworth."

Sheri chuckled. "Given Miriam's connections, I don't doubt she could manage to snag Chris. If it's true, count me in and seat me next to him."

"Sadly, no hunky Chris. Here's the real reason I called. Angela Spear's sister told me Adam's body will be released tomorrow. The visitation's Friday afternoon at five. I should attend, be a friendly face for Angela. Will you go with me? You can bug out after."

The whole peninsula and half of Bayport would turn out, not out of grief over Adam Spear but nosiness and a chance for free food. She saw only one way out.

"I'd go but I hate visitations almost as much as funerals. Too depressing. You understand, Deb. Too stark a reminder of seventeen years ago."

"I know, hon," Deb said, sympathy in her tone. "You don't have to stay long. But it's what Miriam wants. She insists we both go."

Chapter Eleven

THE WEDNESDAY MORNING sun sharpened the contrast between the clear sky and spring's new growth. "Nowhere greener than a golf course even in April," Justin observed as Bess exited her state SUV, parked beside his, at the Bayport Golf Club.

She sniffed. "Ground'll be mush."

He'd take trout fishing in a cold drizzle any day over knocking white balls around in sunshine. No matter how he changed his stroke, the damned evil spheres sliced into the rough. "Good thing we're not here for nine holes."

Yesterday afternoon they'd finished a canvass of the houses on Echo Cliff Point. No surveillance cameras except outside the Spear house, a single lens over the garage. That camera showed Adam starting out on his run. Nobody else around. No cars passing. Dead end there. They left the DHPD police chief armed with a lengthy list of individuals to interview. People with grudges against Adam Spear and others he'd crossed for whatever reason. They would divvy up the list after this first one.

Bess had finagled her way into Spear's phone and came up with some interesting revelations. Including a reason or two to re-interview his law partner.

"I see our quarry over there on the practice putting green." Bess locked up. "Like his office manager said, you can't miss him."

"Ouch, not in those pants." Solid color jacket and plaid pants in what some would call preppy orange. More like warning-sign orange. He grimaced as they crossed the parking lot toward the attorney. The grounds smelled of new grass and money.

She grinned. "The man must've dressed in the dark."

"Reminds me of my mom's comments about my clothes when I was a teenager."

"Bet yours weren't as coordinated."

As their footfalls swished across the grass, Quentin Frost straightened from putt position. In his fifties and of above-average height, he looked solidly built, a man who worked out. Wide-set brown eyes perused them with shrewd intelligence.

"Detective Peters, I thought we completed our discussion yesterday." His gaze slid from one to the other.

"This won't take long," she said equably before introducing Justin.

"Counselor." Justin didn't expect the offer of a handshake and got none. He stood slightly to the left and behind his colleague. They'd agreed she'd carry most of the questioning because Frost had been cooperative and pleasant with her. His brusque opening didn't bode well for today's interview.

"The others in my foursome are waiting. Tee time is in ten minutes." Frost tucked the gleaming putter into his golf bag.

The whacks of clubs hitting balls drifted to them. Justin counted four small groups on foot towing wheeled carts like Frost's. Club must've banned driving carts on the new grass. Not a bad turnout for a Wednesday this early in the season.

No golfers were milling around on the first tee. They had time to lean on Frost.

Bess opened her pocket notepad and clicked her pen with enough force to explode it.

Justin bit back a grin. She hated these walk-and-talk interviews because balancing a tablet while typing was impossible. Had to resort to old school.

"I have a few questions about issues that didn't come up in our meeting," she said. "We have information Adam Spear intended to dissolve the partnership. How did you react to that?"

Frost's expression continued to suit his name, but something shifted in his eyes. "Where did you obtain that information?"

"Surely an experienced attorney like you knows better than to ask such a question. I will tell you we have documentation. What was your response to the dissolution of the partnership?"

Frost heaved a theatrical sigh. "I saw no reason to end our relationship. We got along fine, had no financial disputes. But I respected his decision."

"Did Spear give his reason?"

"Only that he wanted to be independent now that he had a new focus apart from practicing law."

"Which was?"

"It's no secret. Investments. Sometimes people simply want to move on."

"When Spear ceased practicing law, what happened with his clients?" she asked.

"A few with active cases came to me, upon agreement by the clients. Adam and I consulted on those."

"And the rest?"

"He retained the files. I can tell you no more." His mouth thinned, reinforcing his statement.

"As you said yesterday, Spear covered the litigation part of the practice." She tilted her head and smiled brightly. "The big money. You deal in corporate law, estates, bequests, and such. Turning over a few cases to you must've been lucrative. What effect does his death have on your arrangement?"

Frost shifted his stance, and the furrows in his forehead deepened. "Those matters will be worked out between his widow and me."

"Like a buy-sell agreement? With provisions should a partner pass away?"

"Surely an experienced detective like you knows better than to ask such a question. Obtaining any documents will require a subpoena." He gripped the cart handle and swung his golf bag around.

Justin stepped forward. "Word is you and Angela Spear are involved romantically. Could've made things complicated between you and her husband. Even tense."

If the color darkening the attorney's pale cheekbones was an indication, Justin's drive just shot the ball straight down the fairway. "Gossip, Detective. Angela and I are just friends."

Justin watched the attorney stride toward the first tee, where his friends waited. "Shit. Without more reason to suspect him, no prosecutor will issue a subpoena."

"And don't even think about a warrant to search a law office. We'll have to rely on Spear's home office."

Not only had Angela Spear claimed not to have the file cabinet keys and the safe combination, she'd refused their locksmith request.

Justin said, "Get the judge on the horn so we can order up the can opener."

****

AS SOON AS Sheri entered the packed funeral home on Friday, she regretted giving in to Miriam's request. Correction, *command*. Memories crashed through her mind — Noah's mother weeping in her arms, their friends clutching each other, a waxen Noah in a flower-draped casket.

Her stomach clenched but she lifted her chin, assuring herself she didn't have to stay long. She needed to get on the road to Weymouth and sleep in her own bed.

Mainers didn't dress up for these events, and she and Deb wore what they considered business casual. Sheri in coffee-dark pin-striped pants and a dark turquoise turtleneck, what she'd worn to work with Miriam today. Deb in black pants and a mauve twinset, the cardigan's fluttery edges on the *edge* of fashion. The day was warm enough that they each left their jackets in their respective vehicles.

They weaved through the crowd to greet Angela and Steve. Overweight, as Sheri remembered him from school, but not sullen. He even thanked them for coming. His mother appeared strained and jittery.

Next was the refreshment table, followed by a memory display. Photos of Adam Spear with golf trophies, on the podium at civic luncheons, at the wheel of a Mercedes sports car. All chosen by Angela, Sheri assumed, but none of him with his wife and son.

She moved off and sipped overly sweet punch served in a plastic cup while Deb signed the guest book.

Sheri recognized a few people but they'd changed in the intervening years as much as she probably had. No other Littlefield or Delano family members. The police chief, taller than most and imposing even in street clothes, surveyed the crowd from a position near the door.

Beside him stood Justin Wylde, a dark sport coat framing his lean build and broad shoulders. He surveyed the room with a flat-eyed expression that must make suspects quiver with fear. On the job, hoping to spot the murderer. *Sure, that was a likely outcome.*

When his gaze landed on her, he dipped his head a millimeter and the corners of his eyes crinkled as one side of his mouth lifted in a half smile. The overall impact quivered her insides. She returned the smile, well, not *that* smile. She wanted to fan herself.

She swung her attention back to the family. Steve had strolled away to the refreshment table. Angela was speaking to a fiftyish man with a comb-over and dressed in a charcoal suit and red bow tie. She leaned closer to make herself heard over the babel. "Who's that with Angela?"

Deb handed her the pen. "That's Quentin Frost, Adam's law partner."

Angela clamped a hand on Frost's forearm. Her pinched expression could've resulted from feet jammed into the dagger-toe heels matching her blue suit. Or from whatever the two of them were discussing. His features tightened, and he peeled her fingers from his worsted. He took a step back and spoke sharply before moving away.

"Word is they've been having an affair. No sweet talk now. Looks like an argument," Deb whispered. "Money or murder?"

Sheri sputtered into her punch. *Leave it to Deb.*

108

"Shh, someone might hear you."

As she bent to sign the guest book, someone knocked into her. The pen flew as she stumbled. The remnants of her drink sloshed onto the table's white linen runner. She caught a whiff of whiskey and rancid body odor as the man pushed away from them. He headed for the middle of the room.

"You okay?" Deb kept a firm hold on her arm.

"Fine." She dug tissues from her handbag and mopped up what she could of the punch. Luckily none had splashed her or the guest book.

A black-suited funeral home attendant whisked over with a towel and a new linen runner. He waved off an apology and performed quick repairs. Sheri signed the book and joined Deb, who'd backed away to make room.

"That was Walter," she said, clutching her cardigan around her.

"Who?"

"Walter Bates, the man who jostled you. There, in the middle of the room. Poor man, he lost his son in an accident two months ago. He's been going downhill ever since."

Hard to miss him, wide shouldered but stooped and unkempt, wiry brown hair standing in tufts. Unfocused dark eyes were sunken in his lined countenance. Other mourners gave him wide berth. The poor man hovered there as if he didn't know why he came.

Sheri didn't know why she'd come either and couldn't wait to leave. "You ready to go?"

Deb hooked her arm through Sheri's. "I need to see Adam first. I must get the image of his mangled body out of my head."

"Sure, go ahead. I'll wait here." Or better yet,

outside.

Deb shook her head and laid a hand on Sheri's arm. "When was the last time you attended a visitation or a funeral?" When Sheri didn't answer, she went on. "Noah's, right? None since."

Not even her nana's funeral three years ago. Admittedly, her excuse had been then and still was lame. She was in Florida with Dad. Deb had reminded her more than once that airlines flew regularly between Tampa and Portland.

"Call it desensitization. There's a lot about Noah's suicide still locked inside and tormenting you. Some reason you blame yourself. I'm here when you want to let it out."

"I know. Maybe someday. You're the best, Deb." Sheri nodded toward the dais—and the casket. "But you know I didn't want to come in the first place. Don't make me—"

"You need to do this." Said in her best mommy voice, gentle but firm.

She was right. Sheri told herself this was a step toward closure. She let her BFF lead her toward the dreaded sight of another person dead by violence, stitched together, made up and dressed in his finest, on display. A ghoulish doll. Mercifully, no one she knew or cared about.

A small group clustered around, blocking the view. Three women bent to read the cards attached to the floral sprays. When a young couple in matching black leather jackets moved aside, Deb dragged her forward.

The man who'd bumped her jostled her again. Walter Bates shoved between them to the open casket, so close his jacket crimped against the brass rail.

His arms hung stiffly at his sides and his hands flexed in jerky motions. Shoulders hunched and breathing labored, he stared at the deceased. From what she'd heard about Spear's business and personal dealings, very few mourned him. Why was this man so affected by his death?

Bates withdrew something from his pocket and turned it over in his thick, callused hand. Maybe a memento to place in the casket. A snap and a jagged blade sprang into view.

Sheri gasped.

He raised the knife above Spear.

No! She grabbed his arm with both hands and reared back. "Don't! Help, somebody!"

The women nearby scooted away. Deb gasped and reached for his other arm, but he elbowed her aside. People cried out but no one else came to Sheri's aid or to stop the atrocity.

As if shooing a fly, Bates shook her off. He plunged the knife into Spear's shoulder. He bent to peer at the embedded blade, then at the dead man's face. Seemingly satisfied, he yanked out the knife and flicked it closed. "Good."

Exclaiming in horror, people moved out of the way as the man turned to leave.

Sheri grabbed his arm again. "Help me! Stop him!"

Above the commotion, she heard a booming voice. "Police! Move out of the way! Coming through."

The next seconds were a blur of action and noise. Bates tried to pull away. Sheri let go as Justin tackled him. He fell to his knees. The knife tumbled to the carpet.

"No!" Bates roared. "Fuckin' son of a bitch killed my son!"

Galt added his weight and helped Justin push the struggling man to the floor face down. "Walter, you're under arrest. Quiet down. You'll hurt yourself."

Bates continued to struggle but he was no match for Justin's strength and the other man bending his arms behind his back. The snap of handcuffs deflated him.

Chapter Twelve

POLICE OFFICERS HERDED the last few remaining mourners toward the parking lot. A DHPD unit pulled away down the circular drive with Walter Bates slumped in the backseat.

Justin buttoned his jacket against the cooler air of a day winding into dusk. Police officers herded the few remaining mourners toward the highway and their vehicles. Sheri's Rav4 and Delano's van were parked beside the broad porch, brought around by one of the DHPD officers.

"Don't usually hear of excitement at funeral homes," he said as Galt, finished with supervising, climbed the steps.

"Not like this, for sure," the chief said. "Walter Bates used a folding hunting knife, nice L.L. Bean serrated blade."

Bates, one of the names on the list Galt had given Justin earlier. Blamed Spear for his son's death a few months ago. Justin had spent the day tracking down people on that list. Too bad he didn't make it to Walter Bates. "Trying to jump to the front of the suspect list?"

"Or get himself eliminated as a nut job." The chief flipped open his notepad. "He's facing a pile of charges — abuse of a corpse, use of a weapon in commission of a crime, disorderly conduct. They don't amount to much time but may get him into counseling."

Class D crimes were DHPD jurisdiction. Justin wouldn't overstep. "If it's all right with you, I'd like to talk to him later."

"Give him time to settle down, sober up. Let me know when you're headin' to the county jail. I'll call ahead so they set him up in an interview room." Galt's mouth edged up. "While I smooth the funeral director's feathers, you can get details from the witnesses. I've already spoken to them."

Justin glanced to where Deb Delano and Sheri Harte huddled in parkas on a wicker settee. They cradled white china mugs with what he hoped was coffee. Maybe he could wangle some.

"Both women tried to stop the attack," Galt said, "but Deb's pretty shaken up. Understandable. You can probably get more from her friend. Ms. Harte has a damned good memory for details."

Justin thanked the chief and made his way to where the women sat.

"I can't say I'm surprised to see you here," Sheri said. "This murder must have you working long days. I saw a different SUV on the Point this morning. Was that Detective Peters?"

"Enough legwork in this case for us both." Bess had been re-interviewing some of the neighbors. "And my long day just got longer, thanks to what happened here. Chief has your statements, but since this impacts my case, I'd appreciate hearing from you directly."

Deb paled and clutched her mug closer to her chest. No doubt shaken up. For the second time. Plus the sabotage on her van. Tough for anybody, especially a gentle woman like her. This case had more victims than just the deceased.

"Oh, um, well," she began, her voice breaking.

Sheri touched her friend's arm. "You stay here so Galt doesn't think we left without his permission. I'll go over everything with the detective. He looks like he could use a cuppa." As she rose from the seat, her raised eyebrows seemed to ask if that arrangement would suit him.

The dark aroma of java wafted from the mug she held. He inhaled, but the smell wouldn't contain enough caffeine to keep him going. "Fine. And coffee'd be great."

The reception room now contained only stacks of folding chairs and a table off to one side. A few floral tributes remained where the casket had stood on a dais. The faint scents of flowers and lemon hung in the air. He imagined minions whirling through cleaning and spraying.

Sheri poured him a full mug from a carafe on the refreshment table. She gestured at his neckwear. "A superhero? You must have quite the collection of ties."

"Gives my mom and sister something to shop for." Justin swallowed some of the fresh brew. "No kid to see today. Only twenty somethings. Thought it might put them at ease."

"A conversation starter."

"There you go." Her hair was loose again, brushing her shoulders as she moved, a casual look. He wanted even more to touch it, let it run through his fingers. She might slug him.

"I appreciate you letting Deb off the hook just now. She's frightened enough already. We both want this over with. Did you find anything on her van?"

"Evidence team checked it over. Driveway too. I'll

get the results soon." He swallowed a slug of coffee. Stronger than he'd expect here, just the way he liked it. "So how'd you end up in the middle of that man's attack?"

"*He* was the one in the middle." She flapped a slender hand in dismissal and set her empty mug on the table. "How much detail do you want?"

"Beginning to end, as much as you got. Your impressions might be as important as exactly what happened." Whether it meant anything for his case remained to be seen.

She closed her eyes briefly before launching into her narrative. She led him first to the small table where Bates had bumped her as she signed the guest book, then to the dais. Details, impressions, insights, very thorough. And brave. Or foolhardy.

As she finished with the police chief and him tackling Bates, he said, "You took a chance grabbing him the way you did. You could've been hurt."

"I didn't think so at the time. He seemed intent on carrying out his mission and leaving. He barely noticed Deb's and my interference." A slight shiver rocked her shoulders. "You and the chief would've stopped him soon anyway, but he plowed into the crowd. The knife in his hand was closed." Her words trailing off, she bit her lower lip.

"Galt was right about you having a good memory." If only all witnesses could give such clear and precise descriptions. Then something she'd said earlier clicked. "All the state police SUVs look alike. How'd you know the one on the Point this morning wasn't mine?"

A wash of pink crept up her cheeks. "Different license number."

He grinned. "Not just a *good* memory. You one of those people who remembers every day of their lives?"

She withdrew a clip from a pocket and fastened her hair back. "Nothing like that. It would be an incredible burden. But I can recall in detail specific images and objects, sometimes conversations. Most people call it photographic memory. The technical term is eidetic memory."

She was clearly uncomfortable sharing this about herself, likely to avoid being considered a freak. Grinning, he said, "Remind me not to play poker with you."

"Blackjack's more my game." Her shoulders relaxed and she smiled, not the liquid laugh he preferred, but beautiful. As they walked outside, she asked, "What will they charge Bates with?"

"Minor crimes. Would've been worse if he'd struck a live person or kept resisting arrest."

Chickadees chattered in the branches of a juniper bush. All DHPD police cars had left. Deb Delano sat hunched in her van, looking like she hoped to avoid any more questions and involvement. Only Justin's and Sheri's vehicles and the ones belonging to the funeral home remained on the grounds. Bates's truck was gone, likely towed.

"He didn't seem the type to be a fan of *Charade*." Sheri took out her key fob as they descended the steps.

"Charades? Why do you say that?"

"Not the parlor game, the Cary Grant, Audrey Hepburn movie *Charade*. Sorry, I'm a classic move buff. In the first scene, a man wants to make sure Hepburn's husband is really dead. He stabs the corpse's hand with a hatpin." She pursed her lips. "He does it with calm deliberation, not the anguish and anger of that poor man today."

"Poor man?"

"I know only the little Deb told me. He *is* poor, ekes out a living by clamming and odd jobs. Worse, he lost his son recently. He—" Her gaze slid away. She clamped her lips together and swallowed hard before continuing. "Maybe you already know this, but he blames Adam Spear for his son's death and was arrested not long ago for threatening him."

What had she been about to say about Bates's son? Something powerful choked off her words. Maybe the memory of her boyfriend's suicide. That had to warp you for life. Otherwise she seemed fine. More than fine. He scratched his chin. He ought to tell her he'd learned about that death. But not now.

She stood there quietly, her gaze unsettled. The question there prompted him to say, "He makes a compelling suspect. Be nice to end this so neatly. We'll see."

"As much as you can say about an investigation, I know."

"And more than I usually say. How do you do that? Is that *look* how you get clients to share their secrets?"

"I don't know what you mean. But most of my memoir clients hire me because they *want* to divulge their secrets." A smile pulled at her lips. "Except for those who lie."

"Not that different from interviewing witnesses—or suspects." Or family members who kept dark secrets for too long.

"I expect so. Unless you have more questions, I'll send Deb in."

She held out her hand and he took it, savoring the warm press of her palm.

"Thank you for your help. I have enough. Deb can go on home." When she began to pull her hand away, he held on. "Are you in a rush or do you have time to join me for a drink?"

****

SHERI AND JUSTIN maneuvered through the Seaside Resort's darkened bar. She wanted to lean closer as he placed his hand on the small of her back. How long had it been since a man escorted her this way? She had no answer, instead let herself enjoy the attention. They took the empty table in the corner. She'd have one drink and then be on her way.

The barstools were full, their occupants laughing and chatting with the bartender. Couples and groups occupied several tables. A Billy Joel song played over the sound system.

"This is a better choice than Dragon Harbor's Wheelhouse Bar and Grill," Justin said as they took their seats. "Quieter and probably a better brand of poison."

"We'd have been under a microscope there." She shuddered at the thought of the Friday-night crowd of fishermen and other locals speculating on whether it was interrogation or date.

"Word would've spread through town faster than a Nor'easter."

"A storm's a good analogy. We're less likely to run into D Harbor people here. This is more of a tourist spot. Well, not this early in the season."

A server glided over to their table. Hard to discern her age because of her heavy makeup. Her mouth turned down at their order, maybe too tame for her. A white wine for Sheri and a draft IPA for him.

"You hungry? We could order food too. It'll be late before either of us makes it home."

She had some leftover beef stew in her fridge, but her stomach was empty now. All she'd had since lunch was punch and coffee. "Sure, great idea, thanks."

When their drinks arrived, they ordered the house special pizza.

"The Wheelhouse a favorite hangout?" He lifted his beer glass and took a long drink. She watched the movement of his Adam's apple in his strong neck.

"Not for me. Mostly a male hangout. When I was a kid, my friends and I considered that bar a den of iniquity and hot older guys. One Friday during happy hour, three of us sneaked in. Deb and another girl and me. We thought if we wore enough makeup, we could pass for twenty-one."

"How old were you?"

"Fourteen. We made it past the first row of tables. My dad was sitting in the second row. He marched us outside."

Justin's hearty laugh rang out. He clinked his glass against hers.

Her dad told them to go home and wash their faces. All evening she kept waiting for the other shoe to drop, but punishment never came. He never told on her. Not the first time he protected her from Mom's over-the-top reactions.

The pizza arrived and they dug in. The first bite exploded in her mouth—black olives, artichokes, and pepperoni over feta and mozzarella and a spicy sauce. As they ate, she coaxed from him why he wanted to be a detective.

His dad was an attorney, he said, wanted all three of them to go into law. None did, to their dad's dismay, but two were in law enforcement. The oldest, Thomas, was a game warden. Annie, the youngest, was a journalist. He was a cop because justice and protecting the weak were more important to him than money and power.

"And truth," he said in a near snarl. "Truth is important. I hate lying and secrets. As a detective I ferret them out. Lying can destroy lives."

Wow, a powerful statement. Something was buried there. She said mildly, "You're all seeking truth and justice. Admirable."

His mouth full, he nodded his thanks.

A memory trickled up from a few years ago. "Your sister is Annie Wylde, the journalist?"

"That's her."

They talked about the big story that put Annie's name in the news. On a canoe trip in northern Maine, she and her now-husband, Sam Kincaid, caught a notorious serial killer. Justin told her he'd played baseball with Sam during a post-high school year at the Maine Central Institute.

He mopped pizza sauce from his chin. "Sam played for the Red Sox until he got injured. He's batting coach for their Triple-A team now. He and Annie live near Boston."

"That story, and her book, gave her a boost. I've seen her byline in the *Globe* recently."

"Can't stump you. Enough about my family. What about you?"

"My brother and his wife have a ten-year-old daughter and live in Portland." She told him about her dad's charter-boat fishing and that her mom had remarried, but didn't mention the strained relationship between them. She summed up her writing career, first for magazines, and then easing into freelance.

When they finished the meal, she offered to split the bill, but he insisted on paying because he'd invited her.

On the way out, she spotted two familiar silhouettes at the restaurant's entrance, grasped Justin's arm, and hustled him outside.

"I like a woman who takes charge," he said, covering her hand with his as they jogged to the parking lot. "Making our escape?"

"Avoiding the microscope. Miriam's daughter and her husband were waiting to be seated at the restaurant."

"If memory serves, she's an attorney. Imagine the questions she could've asked."

"I'd rather not. And I assume you'll be questioning them both soon, or at least Gil. I know, you can't tell me if Gil MacRae's on your list." She lowered her head and drew a deep breath. "Listen to me. I'm a terrible gossip. I didn't intend to betray anything about Miriam's family."

"I won't ask you to. But while you're on that peninsula, keep your eyes and ears open. You can tell me anything that doesn't conflict with your work. Will you do that?"

"That much I can promise to do." Especially if it might end this and keep Deb safe.

He drew her along the aisle to their vehicles and out of the lights' glare. "Now that we have a bit more privacy, I need, want to tell you something."

She angled her head. "Sounds ominous."

"When I met with Chief Galt, he told me about Noah Tardiff and that you were the one to find him. I'm so sorry." He placed a hand on her shoulder.

She went still, except for her heart rate zooming to mach speed. "I— It… was a long time ago." She blinked away the memories. "Sometimes I see him like it just happened."

"Something you'll never forget. I can't forget my first homicide case either—a grisly murder—and it was a stranger. I can't imagine how it is for you."

His tone was gentle, his gaze soft. She looked up at him through a thin veil of tears.

"Thank you. And on top of being inundated with those memories, I'm worried for Deb's safety. Spear's killer knows where she lives. He must've sabotaged her wheels there. He might even know she works at home. Alone." Putting the danger into words hit her in the solar plexus.

"She should still take precautions," he said, "but five days later, word in town is that she didn't see Spear's attacker. He may be feeling secure."

She blinked away her tears. "I hope that's true."

For a long moment, he said nothing, then pulled her close, and she placed her hands on his chest. He was lean but all solid planes and muscles, hot against her palms. They fit together well. His heat warmed the chill that had invaded her body.

When she looked up, he bent his head and kissed her. She stiffened, but when her arms found their way around him, she relaxed and leaned into him. He took that as an invitation and with one sinewy arm clamped her against his body. His free hand skimmed her nape and his fingers tangled in her hair, the sensation sending shivers through her. His lips were warm and firm, and he was all hardness and heat and an earthy scent she couldn't identify. When she kissed him back, a hum deep inside his chest vibrated through her, and her senses struggled to keep up.

"Well, this is a cozy scene."

Chapter Thirteen

THEY BROKE APART. Justin stepped in front of Sheri. Who was this guy?

Just what she needed. She eased to Justin's side. "Hi, Reed. Out for the evening?" A bland greeting, but in a forced *happy to see you* tone.

The man approached them, his wooden cane tapping on the parking lot blacktop. He looked to be about Sheri's age, but stooped, a beak of a nose in a lean face. His sharp gaze flicked between Justin and the woman man tight against his side. "I'm joining Sydney and Gil here for dinner."

"Nice. We're, ah, just leaving." Justin squeezed her arm to remind her he was here. She added, "Reed Keniston, meet Justin Wylde."

Justin and Keniston each took a step forward, shook hands, and returned to their corners of the ring.

Keniston's eyebrows rose in his high forehead. "You're the state detective. Seeking evidence?"

"Winding down after a day of gathering information." Justin bared his teeth in what some might call a smile.

"Then I'll leave you to it." The other man nodded to Sheri. "Have a nice evening." He turned and made his way into the resort.

"Best laid plans." Justin chuckled. "We might as well have gone to the Wheelhouse."

"Being seen together amuses you, but gossip about me could affect my relationship with Miriam." She explained Reed's connection to the Littlefields. "First thing he'll do is tell Syd and Gil. I don't know him well, so I don't know how many others he'll tell he saw us... um, close."

"I bet Miriam will laugh about it, and a little gossip might open some doors for me as I question people."

"Well, then, I'll buck up." A laugh bubbled from her. "Thanks for dinner. And for... well... Now I really need to get on the road."

"And I have an interview to do at the county lockup."

As she dug in her bag for her keys, he stopped her with a hand on her arm. "You were worried about danger to your friend, and I took advantage. But I won't say I'm sorry for a kiss we both enjoyed. If I'm not mistaken." This with a lift of one eyebrow and mischief in his eyes. "A shame if it was the last time."

****

ON MONDAY NIGHT at the Bayport Blues Club, the quartet was tight, and the singer's full-throated styling reminded Sheri of Ruthie Foster. Aromas of burgers and fries and beer swirling around them, she boogied with Deb and Len amid the crowd on the dance floor.

When she stood at intermission to leave, Deb said, "We're staying until the last song. It's so hard to find a babysitter on a Monday night, we're taking this opportunity."

"Tide's too low in the early mornin'," Len added with a wink. "I can sleep in a little before I head out to haul traps."

For a lobsterman, sleeping in meant five a.m. rather than three. Sheri laughed and waved goodbye as the singer sashayed back to the stage for the next set.

She was happy to escape. Deb kept pestering her about why she hadn't wanted to invite Reed to join them. Matchmaking seemed to be a Littlefield family hobby. No way could Sheri tell her Reed had seen her Friday night in Justin's arms.

Justin. He was kind and funny, protective and fiercely dedicated to his work. He'd used humor to reassure her after Reed had confronted them. Being held by him, even though it was because she was upset, felt so good. And not just his words and his devastating kiss showed he wanted her. Before he turned and got in his car, the heat in his blue, blue eyes nearly incinerated her. Nothing might materialize but like he'd said, it would be a real shame if something didn't.

On the outskirts of Bayport she pulled into a gas station to fill up before the drive home. When she started the flow, the pump clicked off immediately. Crap, a broken lever. She didn't mind pumping gas, but hated having to grip the damn nozzle and inhale the fumes. She zipped her parka against the night air and held on tight.

The hoo-hoo hoo-hoo of a barred owl carried over the rumble of the few vehicles on the road and the hum of the station's neon signage. All was dark except for halogen lighting over the automated pumps. No one around but Sheri.

Screeching from somewhere startled her into nearly dropping the nozzle. Another yowl and a yellow cat streaked around the building's corner and disappeared.

Sheri gulped and willed her racing pulse to ease up. Last week's events still had her jumpy. She glanced at the pump gauge. Still only half. This had to be the slowest gas pump in the state of Maine.

Inside the car, her cell phone rang its familiar chime, but she had to let the call go to voice mail. Who would call this late anyway? Some scammer with a cruise offer or a wrong number.

After an interminable time, the fill-up completed, she climbed back in, and started the engine. She cranked up the heater before checking the missed call. Miriam's name and cell number appeared on the screen. She sometimes called with a request for the next day or a question, but never this late. She went to bed earlier than Sheri did.

When Sheri was working with clients, she set the phone for their missed calls automatically to go to voice mail. She selected voice mail and listened to the message. Muffled voices. Then thuds, thumps, and muted cries. A repeated sharp sound. Barking? A metallic clunk. Noises, but nothing she could identify. Then a click ended the call. She stared at the phone screen a long moment.

Her fingers trembled as she put through a call to Miriam's cell. No ringing. Straight to voice mail. She tried the landline next. Six rings and her lilting voice asked the caller to leave a message. "Miriam, please answer."

Calling Deb was the next option. But would she hear a voice, any voice over the cranked-up sound system? Should Sheri call 911? Both moves were premature. Maybe Miriam had been walking Comet and the dog took off after a skunk or a cat in the trash cans. Something simple. She'd call again in a few minutes.

Sheri increased the volume and listened to the

recording again. Barking, that was definitely barking, distressed barking. All week she'd never heard a yap from Comet.

She couldn't shake the sense something was wrong, that something had happened to Miriam. But why phone *her* instead of one of her family or 911?

She peeled out of the gas station back toward Dragon Harbor. Twenty-five minutes later, she swung into the Littlefield driveway.

No lights illuminated the Victorian's exterior or glowed in the windows, not even the one in Miriam's bedroom, which overlooked the driveway. Her habit was to turn off all lights when she retired for the night. Great. If nothing was wrong and she'd gone to bed, this abrupt arrival would frighten the poor woman. She'd be the one calling 911 to complain about a trespasser.

When Sheri opened her door, she heard the barking. Frantic cries, somewhere inside the house. Not little woofs or yips but deep baying—deeper than she'd expect for a smallish dog—broken by prolonged howls. Her phone's flashlight guided her way down the drive.

She couldn't swallow past the wad of paste in her mouth. Dread stiffened her gait as she traipsed to the side door. Unlocked, thank you. Maybe an intruder? This was a safe town. No one locked doors, or had need to. Despite the Spear murder, why would Miriam be in danger? Should she call 911? Should she call Justin? Was she overreacting? She shook off her misgivings and entered the mud room, then proceeded to the dark hallway.

No other sounds came to her over the dog's alarms resounding from upstairs. Shut in a room? Miriam's bedroom? An image flashed in Sheri's mind of her elderly client on the floor, unable to get to her feet, her phone somehow out of reach.

She found the light switches by the kitchen door. Blinking in the sudden glare of the overhead fixtures, she hurried forward. Halfway along, she froze.

At the foot of the staircase, Miriam Littlefield lay, pale and motionless.

****

THE GRANDFATHER CLOCK by the staircase chimed midnight as Justin strode into Miriam's library and sank onto the sofa beside Sheri. A car started up outside, the DHPD officer leaving.

Yawning, Sheri straightened from her slumped position and slid down glasses from the top of her head. "My eyes were too gritty to tolerate my contacts any longer," she said, her voice raspy.

"If I wore contacts, I'd take them out too."

On her lap, Comet sighed as she sank more deeply asleep, the sheltie-spaniel's furry body gently rising and falling with her breath. He'd pet her, but the touch might wake her.

"Poor girl is exhausted. So am I, but I doubt I could sleep anytime soon."

"Any word from the hospital?" Justin asked, his voice also raspy, the result of exhaustion.

"I talked to Deb a few minutes ago. Miriam is unconscious and they're trying to stabilize her. The family is waiting for reports on the X-rays and other tests." Her chin firmed against the trembling he'd noticed. "I hope I haven't dragged you here for nothing. You were probably off duty."

He jabbed a thumb toward his tieless neck. He wore jeans and a gray V-necked sweater over a collared shirt. "Observant of you. But not a problem. I was on the way home from my folks' place in Cape Elizabeth. Important dinner. My brother and his family were there too for an announcement from my sister and her husband. We knew Annie was pregnant, but the news was it's twins. Can't imagine Annie chasing after one baby, let alone two." Still blown away, he grinned.

"Congratulations to them. I'm learning more about you every day. Well, night in this case. Maybe you won't think my input nutty after all. I appreciate you coming to hear me out."

"You saved her life, you know. Calling 911 and covering her with a blanket to hold off shock. Great presence of mind."

"Thanks, but I probably wasted too much time dithering about her strange phone message. If I'd only arrived here sooner, maybe—"

She smoothed a palm over the dog's fur. The animal didn't react. Too deeply asleep. "Comet's the heroine of the night. Hearing her barking over the phone is what worried me enough to return."

"A shame you weren't here to prevent the injury, but you usually leave by five. Your friend Deb said you didn't want to spend nights on the peninsula."

His comment was met with a pregnant pause the length of the coast of Maine. And a hurt look in her eyes. Shit, he knew damn well why she didn't want to stay here. Hadn't she cried in his arms only a couple days ago? How could he fix this?

"You know my history here," she said, head held high and chin firm, "so you should understand that my last memories of this town aren't happy ones."

"That was tactless. I'd blame it on being tired, but that's no excuse. I apologize." He leaned toward her, propping his forearms on his knees. "Running away from the past doesn't usually work. Miriam Littlefield obviously intends to revisit hers in her memoir, maybe even uncomfortable parts. Moving on can be easier once you confront the past."

"No one's past is all roses and laughter. Including yours, I bet."

"We're ranging far afield here." He shuttered his expression. She'd probed right back, good way to shut the door on him. He scraped fingers through his hair. "The DHPD sergeant thinks Miriam's fall was an accident. What prompted you to phone me?"

Comet lifted her head, her brown gaze accusing them of disturbing her rest. She arched off the sofa and sprawled on the oriental rug.

"I'll show you while I tell you." Sheri pushed to her feet. "Reminding myself Miriam is alive gives me the nerve to go through this. I didn't go with the family to the hospital so I could take time to formulate the reasons I believe she was attacked." She swallowed, then bowed her head briefly.

They walked into the hall, where the scent of lemon polish belied the recent violence.

"At first I was afraid she was dead. To my relief, I found a faint, erratic pulse in her wrist. I managed to tap in the emergency number. Calling Deb came next. I directed her to the Bayport Hospital because by then the D Harbor ambulance had arrived. Your cell was my third call."

He took out his digital recorder and raised an eyebrow.

She nodded. "If you hadn't asked, I'd have insisted."

He clicked it on and stated the requisite identifying

information before clipping it on his belt. He was counting on Sheri's photographic memory and penchant for details.

Shoulders stiff, her beautiful face taut as marble, she stood at the foot of the staircase. It'd be unprofessional to wrap his arm around her shoulders and might interfere with her recounting what she'd observed. He stepped to the side of the stairs.

"Several things about the fall bother me," she began. "First, the house was dark when I arrived. Miriam wouldn't walk up or down the stairs without turning on the lights. As you can see, they all work. No bulbs burned out."

"Point taken." He schooled his features and maintained a noncommittal tone so as not to influence her. He jotted notes as he trailed her up the stairs.

She showed him the first step below the second floor, where the stair carpet was bunched up beside a loose edge. It looked like the toe of Miriam's shoe caught there and tripped her, causing the fall. Exactly what the DHPD sergeant believed had happened.

"I went up and down the staircase at least three times today and noticed nothing wrong with any of the treads. No lumps or loose edges. If you examine that step, you'll find the carpet was deliberately pulled up. And recently."

Chapter Fourteen

BACK DOWNSTAIRS, SHERI addressed the issue of Miriam's shoes. The one that came off during the fall and its mate lay with her cell phone on the nearby credenza, where the emergency techs had put them.

Justin walked closer and peered at the shoes. No touching, she observed, in case they might be evidence. Good. "Three-inch heels. Anyone could stumble on worn carpet, especially an eighty-year-old woman."

He had to play devil's advocate, she understood that, but she still wanted to pick up that damn mauve pump with its tiny pink bow and give him a good whack. And this, about the man whose kiss Friday night had nearly buckled her knees.

She drew a deep breath and let it out slowly.

"Not Miriam," she said. "Sturdy and steady, confident. High heels are a typical part of her wardrobe. Which brings me to another point. She wasn't dressed for bed and stayed up for a reason. Miriam dresses up for company." She slanted him a pointed look. "Now we've established our working relationship, she no longer considers me company. When I left her earlier this evening, she had on sneakers, French terry pants, and a matching pullover. Tonight she wore a skirt and a silk blouse."

His mouth thinned as the implication sank in.

Yes! She continued, tapping a sequence on her

phone. "Her position on the floor bothered me. I doubt my memory works as evidence, so I'm sending you the photo I took. Afterward I covered her with the afghan from the library and waited by her side for the emergency crew."

His phone vibrated and hummed, announcing the photo's arrival. He studied the image, turning the screen this way and that. "Okay. She's prone, sort of spread-eagled. One shoe off, one on, cell phone on the floor beside her. Fell from her hand or a pocket. What else?"

"The sergeant said Miriam was *face down*. Not precisely. Her head's turned to the right." She pressed her hands together in prayer fashion. "Confession time. I played sports in school, mostly ran track, but basically I'm a klutz. I've hit the dirt countless times. Once when I was a kid, I fell down the stairs. Anytime I landed like Miriam, it was literally *face down*. In one fall, I chipped a couple of teeth." She left off revealing that her pearly whites had caps.

The corners of his eyes crinkled with what might be humor before his expression shuttered. She refused to think about how either made him even more appealing.

"She might've sustained facial injuries at any point in the fall. But given the odds, the head position is possible. Especially if she was unconscious and not moving purposefully to protect herself."

She wanted to growl at his skepticism. She touched the screen image of the blouse. "She looks too neat, too put together for someone who had tumbled down nine steps with enough force to continue past the landing and down nine more steps. Her blouse is perfect. In what universe does a violent fall *not* cause a blouson top with a banded hem to ruck up to at least bra level? Someone pushed her, hard, and then—" Unable to continue, she jabbed a finger at the picture.

"Straightened her clothing." Justin's brows snapped together in a scowl as if he'd just made the connection. "Shit." He pocketed his phone. "Sorry for the language."

"Not a problem. I've said that word a lot tonight." She managed a half smile and waited, hoping he'd explain his reaction, but was disappointed. She'd described the odd call and played the voice mail for him and the DHPD sergeant earlier but played it again now. They bent their heads over her phone. "Listen closely to the end."

Hearing the appalling sounds of Miriam's descent, Sheri clenched a fist behind her back, dug her nails into the palm. When the message ended, she could breathe again. "I can't identify the muffled sounds, but there's a gap in the downward trajectory before she tumbles the rest of the way. I think she was pushed. And I think the last click means someone—not Miriam—ended the call. I picked up the phone. It was turned off. I wasn't thinking about fingerprints then."

The skepticism on his face earlier had slid away, replaced by acceptance. And perhaps respect.

"I'll need your permission to obtain the voice mail from your carrier, but for now forward the message to my cell, and I can have our techs get started enhancing the recording. Maybe they can give us more answers."

Us. He was starting to accept her argument. Unless he meant his partner.

"I have more," she said. "The dog. When the sergeant arrived, he checked the upstairs, and then I joined him to get poor Comet, who was locked in the en-suite bathroom. She'd stopped howling by then, thank goodness. I can't imagine Miriam would shut her in like that."

As soon as she'd opened the bathroom door, the wide-eyed little dog hurled herself into her arms. Sheri carried her, trembling, down the stairs, then snapped on her leash to keep her away from the EMT crew. No more barking but she'd whined, watching them secure her mistress to a gurney.

"I can think of at least one possibility. She heard a strange noise, an intruder, and wanted the dog out of the way." When Sheri started to object, he held up a hand. "Hold on, Detective Harte. Let's look at all possibilities before you object."

"Detective Harte?" She grinned for the first time since she'd found Miriam, and a little more hopeful Justin would accept her *evidence*, she shook her head. "I do have more clues."

"Then we're back to the question of why the lights were off. You have direct evidence of a visitor?"

"This way." She headed down the hall.

The kitchen's air held traces of chamomile tea, apples, and spices. "When I left, Miriam was emptying the dishwasher and putting away the clean dishes. She might've made a pot of tea to serve her guest. Maybe offered cake. Used teabags are by the pot on the counter and there's leftover apple cake in the fridge." She indicated the teapot, washed and in the sink drainer, before reaching for the dishwasher door.

After a look inside, he straightened. "Two mugs, a small plate, and two spoons."

"I didn't touch them, only the door, like now." She folded her arms and watched as he paced the length of the kitchen.

"Sheri, you make a convincing argument that someone pushed Miriam Littlefield down the stairs. Deliberately tried to kill her."

"But *why* would anyone want to kill her?" She was torn between elation she'd made her case and horror at the threat to Miriam. "Could it be connected to the murder of Adam Spear?"

Something flickered in his gaze, but his mouth thinned. "The timing is striking. I don't much believe in coincidences, especially concerning homicide."

"I can't imagine Miriam inviting Walter Bates for tea and a chat, but I have to ask. "What about that man? Is he still in jail?"

"I questioned him Friday night. He's been bailed out now." Justin turned back a few pages on his pad. "Released to his attorney, Sydney MacRae."

"How strange." She gazed at the dishwasher and kept silent. Gil MacRae's dispute with Adam Spear would have to come from someone else. She'd brought up his name Friday night, and that would have to suffice. For now.

"Adds another angle to this mess." Justin added notes to his pad. "Small towns, everyone's connected in some way. "I wonder why Walter blames Adam Spear for his son's death."

"You want to know what Deb told me about Walter and his son?" She raised an eyebrow.

"Sure. It might fill in gaps in what I already know."

"Walter's wife died of complications from diabetes when their son Travis was fourteen. That's six years ago. Walter hasn't worked steady since. He does odd jobs, digs clams, when he's not too far into a bottle. His sister lives in Bayport, but Deb didn't know what their relationship was."

"The sister told Peters she's tried to help out but he blows her off, says he's fine."

"Hard to help someone who won't admit he needs help. His downward spiral did no good for Travis. He got into drugs and alcohol, dropped out of school and got arrested for minor offenses. Six months ago, he took a joyride in Adam Spear's sports car. Spear left it unlocked, keys in the ignition, outside a Bayport restaurant."

"Probably figured no one would dare steal his baby," Justin said.

That fit what she'd heard about him. "Travis acted on impulse, high on something. He passed out tooling down the East Road. The car jumped a ditch and got stuck in a field. He was okay. Walter swore he'd straighten out his son, begged Spear not to press charges."

"Let me guess. Spear said no dice."

"And he wanted full restitution for the repairs, which neither father nor son could put together. Then in January when Travis was out awaiting trial, he got drunk and drove his beater of a pickup into an old limestone quarry filled with water. It broke through the ice. By the time the Bayport Fire Department fished him out, it was too late. It might've been an accident." The thought of it being suicide churned her stomach.

"So naturally, Travis's father blamed Adam Spear," Justin said.

"Something occurred to you when I showed you Miriam's position, didn't it?"

He nodded, his expression wary.

"Remember what Deb said about Spear's attacker

coming up the cliff with his cell phone? I took Miriam's picture. What if that's what the attacker did? Was Spear moved, posed for a photo? Like Miriam?"

He leaned against the sink and massaged the back of his neck. "Pete Atwood was right about you having an analytical brain. Yeah, Spear was posed, his limbs moved after he landed on that granite slab. And about the cell phone, your suspicions and mine match. All of this must remain confidential. I'm asking you not to reveal what we've discussed to *anyone*."

Unnerved to have her guess about the pictures confirmed, she wrapped her arms around her middle. "Certainly. I do know how to keep a secret."

"Given the strictures of your work, I'm sure you do."

"But why posing and why take pictures? And why would the person who killed Adam Spear want to harm Miriam?"

"Believe me, I want answers as much as you do. I'll know more once the state crime lab processes the evidence. If it gives me a lead, I'll have you to thank. And so will Miriam."

Sheri pressed a hand to her mouth and blinked away tears. Of hope, this time. Dammit, she hadn't cried this much in years. Not since… "I just—"

"Hey, chill." At her distress, Justin's expression softened. He crossed the floor and pulled her into his arms. "You've done your job. Now let me do mine."

Twice he'd comforted her, and twice she'd let him. His breath was warm and tickly against her hair. She liked his soothing voice, and she rested her head against one broad shoulder. "I'll let you do that. I'm too tired to do anything more."

"No wonder. Tonight put you through the wringer. Where are you staying tonight?"

She looked up, taken aback. "It's so late, I thought I'd stay here. In the guest room upstairs."

He stepped away, at once all brisk and official. He tapped his phone screen.

"Not possible, Sheri. This house is now officially a crime scene. The sooner the Evidence Response Team can get here, the better. Their work could take all night. Once a tech takes your fingerprints, you have to leave. Probably not a good idea for you to be here at all, not after this."

"A crime scene. Of course, I should've known that."

The scrape of claws on the floor announced the dog's arrival in the kitchen.

Sheri crouched to scratch beneath the furry chin, and a warm, moist tongue kissed her hand. "What about Comet?"

Chapter Fifteen

TUESDAY MORNING, JUSTIN filled his insulated mug from the thermos Bess Peters brought to the Littlefield house. After downing a long slug of the strong brew, he joined her at the kitchen table. "You're a life saver, Bess."

Bess gave him a thumbs-up and slid her braid off her shoulder. She sipped coffee while she sorted through papers in a file folder. "Got the ME's report." She slid it across the table.

Their years of working together had taught her to give him time for the caffeine to kick-start his brain. After the techs had left early this morning, he caught a few hours' shuteye on a recliner in the library. Slept like the dead until eight, when Bess rang the doorbell.

He sipped coffee and waited for the hot drink and the breakfast sandwich to sharpen his mind. Shit, he'd hated having to send Sheri away. Not every place would take a dog, but a phone call located a room in the village. He was tough on her about the old lady's attack. An attack, no accident. But she stuck to her guns, and damn, if she hadn't laid out her case like a prosecutor.

He remembered that night at the Seaside Resort, her soft mouth opening for him. The kiss said they'd damned well see each other again. Regardless, he should apologize for pushing her tonight. Soon.

That decided, he skimmed the ME's report on Spear.

What they had so far wasn't much.

The information didn't add significantly to Rosenberg's initial findings. Blunt force trauma to the frontal and temporal bones, intracranial bleeding, extensive internal damage, no drugs in his system, only orange juice in his stomach. Justin's gut tightened at the long list of bones broken in the fall, some but not all post mortem. She suggested the body landed in a position close to a swastika, so the attacker didn't have to move the limbs much to complete the pose. Too soon to draw any conclusions on symbolism or the lack thereof. In a homicide investigation, it paid to look beyond the obvious.

Too many people had motives to dislike or hate Adam Spear. Too many knew about his early-morning jogging route because the man had liked to brag about his fitness regimen. Justin still didn't know where the attacker had waited and watched for Spear, but had an idea how he kept out of sight. A path through the woods behind the houses created by residents living on the Point—a place to exercise their dogs or enjoy nature. Dozens of tracks and shoeprints.

Bess and he had attended Adam Spear's funeral on Saturday. Misty drizzle, appropriate. Showing up at victims' funerals was respectful and occasionally helpful, but this graveside service offered no surprises and nothing new. No crowd, only immediate family. Walter Bates was a no show. So were the MacRaes.

"Okay, I'm ready." He turned pages in his notepad and began with yesterday's frustrations. "I talked to more on our list, need to corroborate their stories." He described the events leading to Travis Bates going into the quarry.

A gleam lit his partner's eyes. "The kid took his Benz? The one in the Spear garage? The 1993 Signal Red 500SL Roadster?"

He should've known this sports car lover would have the details locked in her memory. "The very one."

"So naturally, Travis's father blamed Adam Spear," Bess said.

"Chief Galt said that twice afterward Bates threw rocks at the Spear house and shouted 'murderer.' Galt felt sorry for him and kept him overnight in the DHPD holding cell rather than stash him in the county jail."

"Bates had motive and opportunity. Maybe means. Said he has no computer, but he could've used one at the library to find brass knuckles. Only a land line, no cell. Claimed the only cell phone was Travis's. It went in the quarry with him. At that point, he broke down and sobbed."

Mouth tight, she shook her head. "Hard to untangle the dysfunction from the denial. What about this attack on Miriam Littlefield? Could that be Bates?"

"Something to check on. Let's see if Walter Bates is home." He pushed back from the table and grabbed his coat. "Let's take my wheels. I can go over last night on the way."

Outside, wood smoke laced the brisk breeze chilling Justin's neck. He squinted in the bright sunlight and tugged up his zipper as they walked down the drive. Before he pulled away, he phoned Deb Delano to let her know the forensic techs had finished and the family could come in and straighten. She said she'd let Sheri know.

He turned left onto the East Road. As they headed farther down the peninsula, he detailed his walk-through with Sheri and the techs' work. Monday's cool winds blowing down from Canada dried out the weekend's puddles so neither the mud room nor the carpet contained evidence of tracks.

"Guy was pretty thorough," Bess said. "He could've deleted the phone call, but that would've ruined his accident scenario. Neither does posing the vic for a photo op, but maybe he figured we wouldn't tumble to that."

"Smarter-than-cops mentality. Exactly how criminals trip themselves."

She tilted the phone screen for a closer look. "He messed up about the carpet."

"Sher— Harte said the cleaning service came on Thursday, so surfaces were dusted and polished only a few days ago. I know better than to count on fingerprints or DNA on the tea things. Unless whoever Miriam had tea with wasn't the guy who jumped her. Maybe she said goodbye to her guest and our guy slipped in later. Apparently Miriam doesn't always lock the door." Mainers were too trusting. He locked up—*all* the doors.

"No notes anywhere about a visitor?" Bess asked. "A senior citizen might need a reminder. My folks have appointment and to-do sticky notes all over the house."

"No stickies, no note on the kitchen calendar. Nothing in the library desk. The appointment calendar from the little desk in her bedroom contains appointments and social stuff, but nada for yesterday. I'm waiting for the phone records." He flexed his fingers on the steering wheel.

"I can't work out how the would-be killer managed to stay undetected by the dog, at least until Comet was stowed away. Why didn't she bark when he entered and snatched her?"

"She doesn't bark much. The reason hearing barking on the voice mail worried Harte. Maybe Comet didn't become alarmed until she heard her mistress fall."

"Or the dog's familiar with the guy," she suggested as they turned in beside a rusty mailbox. "I wonder if Comet knows Walter Bates."

****

AFTER A FEW hours' sleep, Sheri arrived at the Bayport Hospital amid the clacking of breakfast trays. She made her way along the warren of corridors to the Intensive Care Unit. In hushed tones barely audible above the whoosh and beep of monitors, a nurse directed her to the family room.

Earlier, Deb had told her most of the immediate family stayed through the night, except for her brother's wife, who remained at home with all four young kids. Syd and her husband and Noble left after Miriam's physician met with them. Miriam suffered cracked ribs — painful but not serious — and a broken right hip, which would require replacement and therapy. Her most severe injury was a subdural hematoma, bleeding between the membrane covering the brain and the brain itself.

That news kept Sheri tied in knots.

The waiting room door swished closed behind her, shutting out the smell of cleanser and the squeak of rubber soles. Walls in a soft blue and furniture upholstered in a coordinating plaid struck her as appropriately soothing. The only occupants of the room were Deb and her mother, slumped against each other on a sofa. Both turned toward Sheri with heart-breaking hope in their red-rimmed eyes.

"Only me," she said. "I'm hoping for good news

too."

"Oh, Sheri." Deb rushed toward her and clutched her. Deb's tears wet her cheeks, and Sheri held on before being passed to Vera.

Was it only eight days since the last time Deb had needed comfort and since Sheri first met her grandmother? In that short span of time, Miriam Littlefield had become dear to her.

Vera released her. "The neurologist is keeping Miriam under sedation while they monitor the head injury for swelling and bleeding. Awake, she'd be in a lot of pain that could complicate the treatment for the head trauma. Recovery will take a long time but the prognosis is good."

Her wobbly smile shrank the cannonball in Sheri's throat to manageable size. "Thank God."

They took seats, the two of them on the sofa and Sheri on an armchair, and passed around a big box of tissues courtesy of Bayport Hospital volunteers.

"Thank God and thank *you* for going to her rescue." Vera blew her nose. "She would've died from shock. You saved her life."

Sheri waved away her praise. Miriam wasn't yet out of danger. "Will they send her to Portland? Maine Medical Center might have a specialist or—"

"He's here," Deb interrupted. "Sorry, the neurologist there also works here. He feels it might be more damaging to move her at this point."

"And you won't have to travel as far to be with her. That should help her heal. Detective Wylde said you could go back into the house today if the crime scene techs were finished."

"He phoned this morning with the all-clear. And he

wants me to see if anything's missing." Deb shook her head. "How could anyone do this to her? To *Miriam*?" Her voice broke on the name.

Sheri had no answers. "The detective promised me he'd do everything possible."

Tears welled and Vera swallowed hard. "Wait. Into the house, you said. No one's there? What about Comet?"

Sheri patted her hand. "Comet's in my car. When the police took over the house, I had to leave, along with her. I discovered the Eastward Inn is pet friendly." She didn't mention Comet had refused the dog bed the night manager provided. The sweet little thing slept beside her on the queen-size bed. They needed each other's solace. Except she got more rest than Sheri. "At breakfast I learned Comet is a favorite inn visitor. Miriam often takes her along for tea."

Asking now about the memoir project would seem crass but Sheri needed direction. She'd have to drum up more clients or write a lot of articles fast to make up for the income if she lost this contract. Approaching the subject from an oblique angle seemed best.

"Deb, shall I drop the pup off at your house before I head home to Weymouth?"

Deb's brow wrinkled. "That won't work. My two kitties are terrified of dogs, even little Comet. They hide and tremble. You'd think a wolf was after them."

"I guess I could leave her at Miriam's house instead." She should return the three boxes Miriam had entrusted to her yesterday. Carrying them out to the SUV was the reason she'd been up and down the stairs so much and knew the carpet hadn't been bunched up before night.

Vera shook her head.

Uh oh. Before going indie, Sheri'd worked at *Greater Boston Journal.* She saw that same *open wide for bad-tasting medicine* expression on her editor's face preceding an expansion of assignments without a corresponding expansion of her bank account.

Deb licked her lips, and she and her mom exchanged a glance.

"Sheri, we were all here a long time last night. The subject of the memoir came up. We don't want you to stop working on the project." Vera rushed on when she started to interrupt. "Miriam *will* be all right, but her recovery will take months. You have notes to get started on the draft, and you can stay at the house with Comet and interview people."

"Get their impressions and stories about her," Deb put in, "some from the old days and some from now. You could even talk to her other family in England. Little anecdotes you can add between my grandmother's dictated ones. Flesh it out more, you know."

"Noble and Deb have Miriam's power of attorney," her mother said. "Anything you need, any access to documents, just ask."

Their gazes were overly bright. Forced optimism. They wanted the memoir finished in case Miriam didn't make it. They trusted Sheri to complete the job if she could not.

Oh, God, how could she turn them down? Continuing now would mean moving in, albeit temporarily, spending every night in Dragon Harbor. She'd been handed the perfect excuse not to, but smaller freelance jobs couldn't cover the painting and repairs her house needed. If she didn't agree, she'd have a tough time managing.

Her own heartbreak and guilt haunted her still, and being forced to *live* there for weeks faced with reminders of her first and only love and her part in his tragic death would flay her daily, slicing her apart piece by piece. Odd, but she could no longer conjure up Noah's face. Or why she'd loved him. If she stayed, perhaps she could come to terms with the past and face her future—not unburdened with her guilt, but stronger.

And she couldn't abandon Miriam's memoir and Deb's fears.

Sheri blinked away the image that flashed in her mind — Miriam sprawled on the carpet, almost lifeless. "Of course I'll stay."

Chapter Sixteen

AFTER SHERI LEFT the hospital, she drove home to Weymouth to meet with the painting contractor, a woman recommended by friends. Sometimes she wished her nana hadn't bequeathed her that damn duplex. Except that the *Greater Boston Journal* went digital and eliminated positions, hers included. Freelance was all she had now.

A hundred years old, the big house had been divided in half some thirty years ago. Nana did little or no upkeep for the last several years. The exterior was chipped and peeling, and the interior was more to her taste than Sheri's, but that could wait.

Comet sniffed beneath the shrubbery while the painting contractor enumerated options. Finally she got to what she'd likely intended to suggest from the start. Stain rather than paint. "Have to scrape it down for either, but stain'll last wicked longer."

Sheri nearly keeled over when she said they had a cancellation and could send a crew to start on Friday. A filler, she judged, because such immediate scheduling never happened. They agreed on a light gray that would be easy to find because the color was ubiquitous in coastal Maine.

Proceeding with Miriam's memoirs would give her carte blanche to be nosy. Maybe she could learn something helpful to Justin. No one in D Harbor appeared to care anymore about her dad's disgrace, something she'd experienced only indirectly. To her he was still Dad.

She spent Wednesday packing and organizing her side of the house. She hadn't been home for meals, so the fridge was nearly empty. Her endlessly tolerant tenant in the other half agreed to oversee and keep her posted on painting progress.

Thursday morning, she loaded up the car with reference materials, her laptop, more clothing, and purses. People were addicted to many destructive things, but her handbag addiction made her happy without harm. Except occasionally to her bank account. She liked a nice pair of shoes, but handbags were more utilitarian. That was her story and she was sticking to it. Three handbags, favorites to buoy her spirits about spending weeks in Dragon Harbor, went into a tote. She'd carry her hobo with the YSL logo, probably a knockoff, but she liked it. No way could she afford the real thing.

She picked up the last suitcase. She'd fed and walked Comet only a little while ago, but the dog trotted around her every time she headed to the door with a load. This time was no exception. Ears flying and tail high, she pranced at Sheri's feet.

How could she resist those brown eyes and big doggy smile? "Sweetie, next time out I'll take you with me, I promise." She edged out and closed the door on the saddest little face.

How many trips had she made? She should've pulled out of the garage and turned around to back into the driveway so she had a shorter trip to load up, and closer to the house rather than nearly in the street. But she'd been thinking about other things—like Justin and if they'd found fingerprints at Miriam's house. At least the street in this neighborhood was now mostly empty of traffic, so she should have no trouble backing out.

She opened the rear gate with her key fob and stuffed in the suitcase next to the three heavy boxes Miriam had sent home with her. She shoved aside her set of weights, necessary for her fitness regimen.

The packing looked like she was moving out forever, not just for a few weeks. Shaking her head, she closed the gate.

When a high-powered engine revved and tires squealed nearby, she turned toward the noise. A huge black pickup truck sped down the street her way. What an idiot! Why—

The truck veered toward her driveway. And her.

She stared in disbelief, frozen. White noise in her ears competed with the roaring motor. The gleaming chrome grille filled her vision. She half ran, half dived around her fender. Her keys flew from her fingers.

The engine rumbled so close she felt the truck's heat on her back.

She stumbled and slammed to the pavement.

Before she could move, a rush of air and exhaust fumes swept over her.

The pickup raced away.

Sheri rested her forehead on the cool concrete and inhaled a calming breath, and then another and another. When her heart had settled to less than mach speed, she rolled to a sitting position.

She pushed to her feet, but needed to lean against the car for support. The knees of her leggings were shredded. Her palms were bleeding. They stung, as if she'd stuck needles in them.

Was that unintentional? Maybe distracted driving? Or he was drunk?

Inside, Comet was barking frantically, just like—

No accident. *That guy aimed right for me*. She had to call the police. And Justin.

****

WHEN SHERI OPENED the door to Justin, he wanted to grab her and hold her to him. She looked okay — better than okay —in an orange pullover and jeans. And sexy bare feet. A little red on the toenails, a surprise. On second glance, that wasn't polish, but blood dripping from her left hand onto her bare toes. The reason she was holding a box of bandages and a wet washcloth.

"You said you were okay." He closed the door behind him.

"I'm mostly fine, but I could use some help." She thrust the bandages at him and pressed the cloth between her palms. "I managed the knees, but I couldn't deal with scrapes on both palms. My renter's at work, and the officer who was here paled when I asked for his help."

The fresh-faced Weymouth PD officer wouldn't last long on the job if he couldn't handle a little blood. But Justin kept it to himself.

Comet wriggled up to him, lobster toy in her mouth, and he knelt to ruffle her fur.

"The uniform came outside as I pulled up. I left him checking on the hit-and-run truck's license plate number." He rose to his feet. "Let's go get you patched up."

"You came pretty quick. You have a private jet or something?"

He laughed. "I was already in Portland. Something to do with the Spear case."

"I know, you can't tell me." She huffed. "Powder room's back this way."

He enjoyed the swing of her ponytail and her sweet ass as she led him through a living room, past a galley kitchen, and to a tiny bathroom.

While he applied antibiotic ointment and bandages to her scraped palms, she described the hit and run. "I'm sure it was deliberate. He swerved toward me, into the driveway. Why me?"

"If we can find the owner of that pickup, we may get an answer." He had his doubts. "There, all bandaged." Because she looked so worried and frightened, her beautiful face tight and her lush mouth a straight line, he kissed her lightly and pulled her into his arms.

She released what seemed a pent-up breath and laid her head against his shoulder.

This hug was all he had time for today. He had more work to do in Portland.

He'd come south searching for Stephen Spear's girlfriend. Calling the number Steve had given him resulted in a "Number Not in Service" answer. Steve claimed he couldn't reach her on the phone either. No run-ins with the Portland PD for an Ellie Stone or an Elizabeth Stone, but a search had found one Portland area address for Ellie Stone and three for Elizabeth Stone. Just before Sheri's phone call, he'd eliminated the Ellie Stone address. The woman who'd answered the apartment door was old enough to be his grandmother.

When the Weymouth officer announced his return, they separated.

"Thanks, Justin," Sheri whispered. "Guess I needed a hug."

"Anytime. And I mean that, anytime." He brushed a

155

kiss across her lips, wishing this embrace could last longer.

In the living room, they found the officer standing at parade rest, Comet at his feet. Standing guard? As soon as they entered the room, the dog ran to Sheri.

"What've you got, Officer DiMaggio?" Justin asked.

The officer rubbed his nape. "The license plate number came back belonging to a red 2017 Dodge Ram truck."

"That's impossible," Sheri said. "This truck was black, not red." She closed her eyes briefly. Justin had seen her do that before when searching her memory. "But it *was* a Ram. The word was on the grille."

DiMaggio's eyebrows arched, and his brow creased. "Ma'am, are you sure of the color and the number?"

"Positive."

"You can be sure Ms. Harte gave you accurate information," Justin said. "I suggest you contact the owner of the truck those plates belong to. You may find they've been switched."

The officer colored. He nodded to Sheri. "I'll get back to you when I know more."

"Keep me in the loop, would you?"

"Yes, Detective."

"Oh, and Officer DiMaggio," Sheri put in, "I'll recognize the grille of the truck that tried to mow me down. It's missing two chrome crosspieces."

When the officer had closed the door behind him, she sank onto the sofa. Comet jumped up and snuggled next to her. Sheri stroked her head, keeping her injured palm lifted.

Justin sat beside the dog. He didn't like where this

was heading. Not one damn bit. On face value, how could this attack be connected to Spear's death and Miriam's assault? If it was, what did that mean for Sheri? Why Sheri?

"You're damned impressive," he said. "You were almost road kill, and you can recall not only the license number but the flaw on the grille. And even get snarky with the local law."

"Thank you, I think." She dipped her head and smiled.

He spread his arms on the sofa back. "Nice house, and I like the furniture, contemporary but comfortable. But some of this—" he jerked his chin at the walls "—doesn't seem like you."

Comet climbed farther into her lap. Justin could go for that too. He contented himself with toying with a strand of her hair. Even better that she let him.

"Furniture's mine, so thank you, but the flower-and-scroll wallpaper is definitely not me. My grandmother left me the house on the condition I live here for three years before I can sell. The main reason I returned to the state."

"Think your grandmother manipulated you?"

"Most definitely." Her expression turned somber. "Could this attack on me be connected somehow to Spear's murder? Or could someone not want Miriam's memoir written?"

"Questions I've been asking myself." He had more, but he'd ask just one. He turned slightly, rested his arm around her shoulders. "If it's not linked to either of those, could anyone have another reason for wanting to harm you?"

"I have no idea. I've made no enemies that I know

of. I'm hiding no state secrets." Her brow knitted, she tilted her head. "Justin, you once told me how you hated secrets, one reason you became a cop. To ferret out secrets. Why is that so important to you?"

She wasn't the first to ask him that. She deserved more than his stock answer, but not the whole truth. "A long time ago, someone entrusted me with a secret that could tear apart my family. Keeping the confidence gnawed my gut like a rat chewing me from the inside out. Sometimes it still feels that way. So yes, I hate secrets."

"What a horrible feeling." Her gaze shimmering, she reached toward him. Her hands floundered a beat and then rested palms up on his knee. "It seems unfair to put you in that situation. No wonder you feel the way you do. I have no secrets that could harm anyone. I can think of none of my clients' secrets that could be dangerous either. But someone wants me dead. The driver of that truck tried to kill me. I'm lucky he roared off and didn't get out to finish the job. I wasn't in any shape to fight him off or run away."

"You didn't move, so he might've thought he'd succeeded." He shuddered, thinking how close to reality that was. "Honey, we can't assume the threat is past."

Chapter Seventeen

FINALLY, SHERI HEADED north. Thank God for
Justin, who'd been a rock, bandaging her and holding her
while she trembled, and then showing he believed her
memory about the pickup. He wanted her to give her
hands some healing time before returning to Dragon
Harbor, but she was all packed up and ready. Driving
would settle her, she told him. He followed her car on I-
295 until she'd exited toward Bayport. He'd had to return
to Portland for whatever he was doing on the Spear case.

First he'd called her honey, making her feel all
squishy inside. Did he sprinkle the term of endearment
on all the women he knew, or because they were what,
an item? And now he'd escorted her — her private police
escort. *No, stop.* She shouldn't care. Whatever was
between them was casual, had to be only that. She'd
made her pact long ago. Nothing could change it.

As soon as she turned onto Echo Cliff Point, Comet
sat up in the passenger seat and whined. Sheri's throat
tightened. "Yes, me too, girl. I'd love to see your
mistress greet us at the door."

Inside the house, the dog raced from room to room
searching before finally returning to Sheri in the kitchen.
Comet was clearly asking where Miriam was.

Sheri set down the heavy box she'd just carried in
and winced at the sting in her hands. She knelt to hug the
dog. "I wish you could understand, sweetie. We have to

hope your mom gets well soon."

Her ears perked and her tail swished on the carpet as if that made sense to her. Sheri unlatched the doggy door to the fenced backyard. Comet shot through and chased some surprised squirrels up a tree. Around and around she raced, eyes bright with excitement, distracted from worries. If only such simplicity of spirit could switch off cares and woes for humans.

While the pup wore herself out in the yard, Sheri organized her books in the library. This was what she was being paid for. Unpacking her clothing could wait. The pen holder, calendar, and phone on the desk were askew. She'd probably left them that way because she'd been in a hurry to pack up her laptop. She shrugged it off.

The room was chilly, so she took her laptop to the couch. She'd move the desk tools later when the room heated up. Before she started on the memoir notes, she opened the DD file. *I almost died today. Would you care if you knew? I hope you don't hate me too much and would care at least a little. Here's what happened..."*

Engrossed, she jumped when the landline phone on the desk rang.

The number on the answering machine wasn't familiar, although a local D Harbor number—unless it was a scam call. In case it was someone in Miriam's family, she answered.

The silence after her greeting lasted so long she thought the call got disconnected. Or the robocall recording didn't start.

"Sheri! Wonderful to have you back in town!" Reed Keniston's voice boomed and she had to hold the phone away from her ear.

"Hi, Reed. How are you?" What could he possibly want, especially after that awkward encounter Friday night? He always seemed to be trying too hard.

"On a beautiful day like this, I'm great. Sydney tells me you're staying at Miriam's with the dog and continuing the memoir. That should please her when she wakes up."

Perhaps, and she hoped Miriam would get well enough so she'd find out. "I hope so."

"They're not letting visitors in to see her. Any word on how she's doing?"

"I spoke to Deb last night. Her condition seems to be stable, but they're still keeping her sedated." She crossed her fingers this was his reason for calling. It was mid afternoon and she wanted time to herself—and with Comet, who needed attention and reassurance. "Thanks for calling. I'll be sure to say you asked about her." She started to say good-bye, but he spoke again.

"That's okay. Sydney told me the same thing this morning. I thought you might have something newer." The hum and clink of a refrigerator dispensing ice into a glass. "I really called to invite you to dinner. Of course, now I'm back in Maine I have to call it *suppah*."

She slumped. She was in no mood for socializing. "How nice, Reed. I'd love to some other time, but I really need to stay here and get settled."

"Are you sure? I'm making my world-famous lasagna with garlic bread and Caesar salad. Well, not *world* famous, but my friends in California enjoyed it. Syd and Gil insisted on you coming. Tell me you have something cooking on the stove and I'll let you off the hook."

For all she knew the fridge held only leftover cake

and days-old chicken. If she cried off now, he'd hear the lie in her voice. The mere idea of lasagna woke up her taste buds. Interesting that the MacRaes insisted on her presence. Likely Sydney wanted to confront her about her contract with Miriam. But perhaps she'd learn more about Gil's dispute with Adam Spear.

"You have me there. I'd love to come. What time?"

****

CONCERN FOR SHERI interfered with Justin's concentration all afternoon as he went over reports at his desk. Maybe it was because they had zip in both cases. Correction, all *three* cases, now that Sheri had been attacked. Every time he dug into what they had, mostly the lack of evidence, he saw the scrapes on her hands, the fear in her pretty brown eyes.

Dammit.

He looked at the techs' reports again. No good leads on the Spear case. Nobody liked the man, except maybe his law partner, who was rumored to be having an affair with Angela Spear. Some hated him, but few had strong alibis. No fingerprints on the mugs in Miriam Littlefield's dishwasher. No DNA. Rinsed and wiped. A clue, but not helpful. No fingerprints on Deb Delano's wheels or on the van, no tire tracks, and too many family footprints on top of each other everywhere in the gravel driveway. Bess kept reminding him it was less than a week since this began. Didn't help.

And Sheri was in the middle of it all. That attempt on her life was connected. But how?

Was she safe in that big old house in Dragon Harbor?

Dammit. He picked up his personal phone, and dialed her. "You okay?" Shit, he was such a prick. "It's

Justin, Sheri. Sorry I couldn't go with you. I wanted to check you made it okay."

"I'm fine. Thank you for the police escort to my exit. It calmed me down after, well, all the excitement."

He could hear a smile in her voice. Okay, then. "Be sure to keep the doors locked in that antique house. No alarm system I could see."

"I will. I've lived in cities for too long to feel secure otherwise. The family is having stronger locks put in."

"Good for them. I expect to be on the Point again soon. I'll stop by, okay?"

"Yes, yes. I might have something for you by then." She chuckled, the sound almost as sexy as her laugh. "I mean, about the case."

"Sheri, when I asked you to keep your ears open, I didn't mean you should play detective."

"I know, but Reed invited me to dinner tonight. The MacRaes insisted, he said. I might learn something about Gil's dustup with Adam Spear."

He pictured Gilbert MacRae's height and strong build. How his face had darkened with anger during Justin's questioning. Dammit. "Be careful. I'm told he has a temper."

She agreed and ended the call, saying Deb had just arrived.

Just as well. He'd have kept her on the phone all afternoon just to hear her voice. The MCU office in Augusta meant he was too far away to protect her, but neither could he let himself get too close. Eventually she'd disappoint, like the others. Still…

****

"YOU'RE RIGHT ON time."

Sheri stepped inside Reed's house out of the

gathering fog. The aromas of spicy tomato sauce and garlic greeted her in the kitchen. "Fabulous you decided to come! Gil and Sydney are in the living room."

She'd braced herself for a comment about seeing her with Justin, but he said nothing, and seemed jovial, even exuberant. Maybe he'd said nothing to the MacRaes after all. She followed the tap of his cane down the hall. While he hung her coat in a closet, she covered her nerves by smoothing her crocheted tunic over her slim jeans.

Reed ushered her into the living room, its small size typical of antique Capes. "Last but by no means least," he announced.

Gil, glass in one hand, rose from a tan leather sectional and pumped her hand. "Let me know if you need anything while you're at my mother-in-law's."

Both surprised and pleased at his affability and his offer, Sheri thanked him and nodded to his wife, seated and expressionless. Both hands gripped her wine goblet. Any tighter and the delicate stem would break. No chance of a friendly handshake there.

Sheri pasted on a smile. "How nice to see you again, Sydney. You must be relieved now the doctors have upgraded your mother's condition to stable."

"Indeed I am. Though we're still concerned about her blood pressure. Thank you for going to her aid. We might not have her with us otherwise." She swallowed a healthy amount of the red wine as if expressing appreciation had scraped her throat raw.

"I'm grateful I could be there."

Reed laid a hand on her shoulder. "Have a seat, Sheri, and I'll fix you a drink. What's your pleasure? Syd seems to like the Tuscan Sangiovese I'm serving with dinner, or would you prefer a cocktail?"

Given Sydney's legal-shark attitude, Sheri wanted fortification. "I'd love a vodka martini, if you have the ingredients. Very dry, on the rocks, please."

He winked. "Coming right up."

Muttering about freshening his drink—whiskey again—Gil followed him to the kitchen.

Sheri settled on the armchair beside the leather sectional. She set down the macramé Sak bag that matched her coral top. Looking anywhere but at her adversary, she surveyed the room. A storage unit held a flat-screen TV. The shelves beside her were stuffed with books, some spine out and some stacked in no particular arrangement. She scanned titles—histories, and texts with esoteric titles, likely on computer engineering, Reed's former profession. Small tables, contemporary and spare that must've come with him from California. In this room papered with faded cabbage roses, incongruous, as the high-end kitchen appliances had also seemed.

"What happened to your hands?" Sydney said.

Sheri'd hoped no one would notice. She'd put fresh bandages on her palms, not the wrap-around kind Justin had applied. "Took a tumble while I was jogging. It's nothing."

The other woman gave a sharp nod. She set down her glass and folded her arms across her breasts. "You might as well know. I am not in agreement with my family about your continuing the memoir."

The clink of bottles and glasses in the kitchen meant no one was coming to Sheri's rescue. She'd faced skeptical family members before, but none had been an attorney. "I'd like to understand your misgivings. Is it me you object to or the memoir project itself?"

"Certainly not the memoir. My focus is protecting my mother's interests."

"Noble has a copy of my contract with Miriam. I'm sure he'd allow you to examine it. For now, I'm organizing notes and outlining, not writing chapters. If Miriam wants me to postpone the rest until she's well, I have no problem with that. I do have other projects I can turn to." None as lucrative, but no reason to share. While Sydney appeared to mull that over, Sheri slipped a business card from her bag and pushed it across the coffee table. "My website has a list of former clients who will answer any questions you have about me and my work."

She tucked the card in her handbag—the black striped luxury brand one Sheri coveted. "I suppose that will have to do. For the time being."

Maybe Sydney was the one who'd been in Miriam's house earlier today, but asking her now would seem an accusation, no matter how Sheri framed it.

"Here we are, ladies."

She accepted with thanks the brimming rocks glass. If only Reed had arrived with it a few minutes earlier. He sat in the chair matching hers.

An equally full glass in hand, Gil lowered himself to the cushion beside his wife.

They chatted about mutual acquaintances and the larger Littlefield family. Gil and Syd expounded on the accomplishments of their daughter's son, who at seventeen was completing his first year at Bowdoin College. Reed asked about Sheri's other writing projects.

She was happy to talk about the bed-and-breakfast article, ecstatic to leave aside the question of the memoir and the Spear murder. If anyone knew about the damage to Deb's van, they didn't say. Drinking half the martini took the edge off, and she set her glass on the table.

Soon everyone convened in a dining room also furnished in a contemporary style. Syd sat across from Sheri at the table as the men took seats opposite each other. Sheri hadn't eaten much all day and her mouth watered at the delicious aromas.

The pasta, savory and cheesy with sausage and ricotta, exploded on her tongue. After her first bite of it and of the garlic bread, she raised her goblet to Reed. "Your California friends are right. This lasagna is delicious. It *should* be world famous."

The others seconded the praise. Reed beamed and lifted his glass toward Sheri.

"Gil, Deb tells me you're renovating a kitchen at one of her rental cottages." She served herself a hunk of garlic bread. She shouldn't indulge, but she'd have a salad tomorrow. "How's that going?"

He slugged down whiskey and nearly dropped the glass as he set it down. "Supplier screwed up, sent the wrong cabinet hardware. Couldn't reorder in time for delivery tomorrow because of that damn cop takin' up my time." The liquor thickened his voice and his Maine accent.

Thank you for the segue. "Cop?" Sheri angled her head to indicate fascination.

"Really, Gil." Syd laid a hand on his arm. "No one wants to hear about your interview."

He bit off a hunk of garlic bread as if chomping down on the cop. Either Wylde or Peters. Sheri crossed mental fingers he'd ignore his wife and spill all.

"But we do. Go right ahead," said their host as if reading her mind. "Unless Sheri'd rather not hear such

167

things. Don't want to spoil your appetite for dessert."

"No, no, it's fine." Aiming for a sympathetic tone, she said to Gil, "You're clearly upset."

Gil brushed off Syd's hand. "Interview, crap. A damn interrogation. It was that Detective Wylde. Cops ought to catch Spear's killer instead of harassin' people. Sure, the man cheated me, shaved four grand off the bill. Said the granite countertops weren't the right color. Pile of crap. They were exactly what Angela picked out." He shook his head like a bull about to charge.

"But that was a few years ago." Sydney's words spilled out in a rush. "The experience changed how Gil does business. Now the contracts have more detail and customers sign off at all stages of the process. Tedious, but necessary."

With Sydney representing the defense, Sheri wouldn't be getting more. "Surely Gil's not the only one who had a grudge against Spear."

Reed held up the wine bottle. "Exactly. I'm sure the police are talking to everyone who had problems with him. No stone unturned."

Sydney held out her goblet to Reed for refilling. "Everyone has a story about his sketchy dealings. My colleagues considered him an ambulance chaser. He quit practicing law several years ago after a big win in a civil case. One of the paper companies suing another, for what I don't recall." She turned to Gil. "Do you, dear?"

"Something about cuttin' trees on the other's land." His gaze shifted to Reed. "Wasn't it Spear who tanked your dad's business?"

"He may have been one of several." His gaze untroubled, Reed sipped his wine. "Hell, it was so long ago. I was just a kid, so I barely remember. I've moved on."

Syd lifted her glass to him. "Yes, the past is past. Leave it there."

"Would anyone like more lasagna? Then I'll serve dessert."

Everyone praised the meal but opted for dessert. He reached for his cane, and Syd waved him to the kitchen while she cleared the plates. Her consideration for Reed's leg softened Sheri's feelings toward her. She should've gotten to her feet to help too, but their departure gave her time with Gil.

"I see what people mean about Spear having enemies. You have no reason to worry about your interview. You must have an alibi, of course."

His cheeks ruddy in his broad face and his brows beetled, he leaned toward her over the table. In a deep, measured tone, he said, "Where I was and what I said to the cop is none of your fuckin' business. You'll get yourself in deep shit making accusations."

Her heart rate shot into the stratosphere, and white noise roared in her ears. She scooted back and threw up her hands as meager protection. "Please, I meant no offense."

Gil shook himself as if only just realizing how he was behaving. He subsided. His chest heaved as he backed off. "Shouldn't have got so worked up. Sorry."

Sheri nodded, unable to form speech over the clattering of her pulse. Not that he'd apologized for what he said, only for overreacting. She hadn't expected this kind of attack, an implied threat. And out of left field.

She reached for her wine with a trembling hand. No, she'd had enough. Instead, she lifted her water glass. She could blame the alcohol for her bold tongue, except an

Susan Vaughan

inner voice reminded her she'd accepted the invitation for the explicit purpose of quizzing Gil.

They sat in silence, both calming, thank God, until the others returned a few moments later.

Sydney passed around slices of chocolate torte, her contribution to the meal. The kitchen was only across the hall from the dining room, but Gil's verbal attack probably hadn't been loud enough for them to hear. In any case, neither remarked on it. Gil's countenance always seemed to have color, but Sheri's cheeks flamed in the aftermath of…what, fear? Reed and Syd chattered away about a mutual friend's divorce as everyone stuck their forks in the torte. After coffee, Sheri took her leave and drove home in the fog and in her own fog.

Hours later she lay awake, Comet snoring softly at the foot of the bed. Gil had no reason to dislike her, regardless of his words. So what was that all about? Clearly, the liquor stoked his temper, and he did rein it in quickly. Gil was just lashing out because of Justin's questioning. But his hatred of Adam Spear, even dead, was palpable. Had his resentment festered and built to the level of violence? Had Gil met the smaller man on the cliff that morning? Remembering his balled fists and twisted mouth, she fumbled with the bedside lamp. She needed light.

What had she gotten herself into, playing detective? Justin had warned her, hadn't he?

Clearly she was a better interviewer and observer than interrogator. She vowed to do as he'd said, keep her ears and eyes open, but leave the actual detecting to the professionals.

170

Chapter Eighteen

THE NEXT MORNING, Sheri arranged appointments with two of Miriam's oldest friends — in age as well as relationship. The nurse who'd taken over for her at her husband's practice couldn't see Sheri until five. The retired minister's wife was busy with garden club and committee meetings until seven. Sheri had reviewed her notes, but how far could she progress without Miriam's input? Unless…

She brought into the library the three boxes Miriam had sent home with her. The writing in marker on top said only *Décor*. Cardboard flaps folded them closed. Under crumpled newspaper Sheri found notebooks. Dozens of them, at first glance. Not musty, they smelled faintly of Miriam's fragrance. She lifted out one, bound in faded red leather and fastened with the kind of tiny brass lock typical on old diaries. She pressed the button, and the catch released. She gingerly opened the cover and read the old-fashioned cursive on the first page.

This is the property of Miriam Alice Lange. Private. Keep out!

Sheri could almost hear her voice. The date below the words meant Miriam had been thirteen.

Sheri's heart pounded and she grinned. "Thank you, Miriam."

This was how she'd been able to come up with details about long-ago events. While Comet snoozed by the fire, Sheri spent the morning sorting the diaries—yes, diaries and journals, all of them—into chronological order. Early ones all leather bound, then stiff cardboard and spiral notebooks with blue-lined pages, and finally leather again, in red. One for each year. And she'd entrusted them and their contents to Sheri. A treasure trove. Humbling. And challenging.

Comet stretched and came to her. She rested her chin on Sheri's knee and beseeched her with liquid eyes.

"Had enough lying around, have you?" Sheri gave her soft ears a scratch.

She needed reviving and stretching her legs too. She changed into her running shoes and clipped on the dog's leash. The rain had stopped, but the April breeze chilled her neck, and she zipped her jacket up to her chin.

They hit the cliff path. All evidence of Adam Spear's death had vanished as if the violent attack never happened. Comet trotted happily along, her tan tail swaying like a plume. More than once she strained toward robins and red squirrels hopping about on greening lawns. Sheri turned back after a mile along East Road. She wasn't sure how far to push the little dog.

Or was she avoiding Reed's house on the off chance he would waylay them? He was nice enough, but she wanted nothing but an acquaintanceship with him. She concentrated on Comet sniffing a twig rather than ask herself if she wanted to get involved even with Justin, who made her pulse riot. Short term was all she could give. All she deserved.

Soon their feet again crunched on the cliff path's crushed shells. "Good puppy. What a trouper! I think we both needed that."

Comet started tugging Sheri across the road, and she

172

looked for what attracted the dog's attention. Steve Spear was carrying a cardboard box from his parents' house.

"He a friend of yours, Comet?"

Apparently spotting them, he took a step backward. He looked Sheri's way, then toward his truck, then back into the house again. He backed up, but as Comet dragged her up the Spear driveway, he continued outside. He closed the door behind him.

"Hi, Steve," she called with as much cheer as she could muster. "Comet insists on saying hello. Hope you don't mind."

He set his load in the truck bed beside a second box. "No prob, Sheri. Comet and I are good buds." As Comet reached him, he knelt. Ear and chin scratches, and the dog wriggled all over. Steve heaved himself upright, puffing with the effort. He zipped his sweatshirt over his belly and flipped the hood onto his head. He glanced aside at the truck. "Um, good to see you."

"I'm sorry about your dad. How are you doing?"

A shrug of his hunched shoulders. "Okay, I guess."

"And your mother?"

His gaze shifted to Comet, who was investigating a stain on the driveway. "Mom's having a rough time. 'Specially since the cops said somebody murdered Dad."

"I heard. That makes it worse."

He looked up sharply. "Oh, hey, what about Mrs. Littlefield? She gonna be okay?"

"I hope so. I'm staying at the house for a while to work on the memoir. Did you see anything that night? Maybe someone on the Point who shouldn't have been here?"

"Oh, no, I'm not staying here. Monday night my girlfriend was helping me work on my résumé. I'm looking for a better job." His broad forehead crimped into a frown. "How can you write the memoir without Mrs. L?"

Sheri's smile was probably more wistful than cheerful. "It'll be hard, for sure. But Miriam—" An idea hit her and she coughed as cover for her lapse. "Sorry. I hope she'll be able to help soon. For now I'm interviewing family and friends." Comet's nose nudged her leg. Her cue. "I'd better get back to work. Take care, Steve."

"You too."

Comet led her away from the Spear property and they continued toward the Littlefield house. A few moments later, Steve drove past them. Sheri returned his wave and watched the truck pick up speed.

"An odd encounter, Comet." Steve had seemed furtive, taciturn. Maybe he'd always been that way. She'd hardly known him years ago. Angela didn't seem to be home. Did Steve not want her to know he was taking away boxes? Something of his dad's, she guessed, or maybe his own. She remembered what Miriam had told her about their Christmas argument. A sad relationship, that one. She hoped that was all it was.

She'd stopped herself from blurting out the existence of the diaries. It stood to reason that if Miriam kept a diary or journal for sixty some years, she must have been writing in a current one. Neither Vera nor Deb had mentioned the existence of journals, so maybe no one knew.

Especially her attacker.

"Comet, let's see if we can find that journal."

An hour later, she plucked her phone from her jeans pocket. What she'd discovered made sense to her, but what would Justin think? If only she had something more concrete.

****

JUSTIN LEANED BACK in his desk chair as his partner entered. Bess removed her slicker and shook it as another detective came by carrying a mug of coffee.

"Watch it, Peters." The guy recoiled, lifting one elbow as a shield from the flying raindrops. "Some of us would like to friggin' stay dry."

She draped the slicker on one of the wall hooks. Her death-ray glare nailed the stocky detective. "And some of us actually leave the building to investigate cases, downpour or not."

The man mumbled something in reply as he stalked to his desk.

Justin passed a hand over his mouth to cover a chuckle. Bess had hit the bull's-eye, allowing no defense. Only a few months before retirement, the cop was spending more time riding his desk chair than riding the state roads investigating.

Their interview with Walter Bates had yielded little but grief, more grief at having to talk about his son again. Bates seemed shocked and horrified at an attack on Miriam Littlefield.

Bates had hauled himself upright in his sagging seat. "Who'd want to do a thing like that? She hurt bad?"

"Critical condition. That's all I can tell you." Justin asked where he was that night.

He glared, and his hands fisted on his knees. "You think *I* hurt Miriam? That nice old lady? I put new shingles on her gazebo last summer after another guy'd put on a new roof. She sent me home ever night with cash and supper."

Neither Justin nor Bess, playing good cop, could get a verifiable alibi out of him. He'd said he was home alone. Drinking, they guessed. Bates was yet another suspect with motive but no alibi. Damn case.

When Bess joined him, he said, "Spear's lawyer any more cooperative this time, Bess?"

"Give me a minute." She unfastened the waist pack with her equipment and deposited it on the adjacent desk. "Last parking spot in the last row. Puddles a foot deep, I swear. I feel like one of those TV reporters standing in a horizontal torrent while covering a hurricane."

"Nothing like an April shower."

She sank onto her chair. Moisture dripped from her hair onto her face. She mopped herself with tissues. "If you say anything about May flowers, I'll deck you."

"Never crossed my mind. I'll update you while you warm up." He punched keys. "Lab reports on Adam Spear. The coat we took from the Spear house. Lab found strands of Angela's hair. Not her brother's. He's bald. No blood, skin, hair, or saliva from the deceased. On Spear's clothing, blood, hairs, tissue are his."

"In other words, nothing."

Dammit, he wanted a break. "Maybe. Angela Spear's hiding something." He flipped to another page in his notebook. "Gil MacRae says he was out early the morning of Spear's murder, on the road to a job site. Same thing for the vandalism to Deb Delano's van — on the road."

"If he made calls, you might find out from the records," Bess suggested.

He lifted a shoulder. "Down the road if I have enough for a warrant. The night of the attack on Miriam Littlefield, MacRae was at the Wheelhouse. Bartender says he's a regular, often stumbles out at closing time, but that night he left after a few brews, no hard stuff. Nobody saw him after that. Wife was asleep when he got home, so nada there."

She pulled her long braid around and daubed here and there with more tissues. She gazed at the ceiling. "Big man as I recall."

"Big enough to toss a smaller man over a cliff. Hasn't wielded a hammer in a few years, but his grip's that of a working man. Might hate Spear enough, but why wait four years?"

Justin looked at his computer screen and typed another sentence in the report. The date of the crime struck him, same day as the Spear murder, over a week ago. Asswipe who hurt little Toby and killed his mom had lawyered up, but been denied bail. So he sat cooling his jets in jail. Where he belonged.

"Okay, I'm reasonably dry and warm." She took out her tablet. "Quentin Frost deigned to spare me a few minutes. I didn't ask, but he repeated his search warrant dare."

Beside his desk, rain peppered the window like BBs. "As much chance of that as seeing a rainbow today."

She scrolled down. "Seems he had no standing to allow a search. Attorneys don't do a buy-sell agreement. It's not a true partnership. The deceased's share is liquidated—and is part of the estate."

Justin swiveled toward her. "He told you that?"

"Not him. Frost lives up to his name." On a shrug, she tossed her braid over her shoulder, leaving a damp spot on her shirt. "Had lunch with Owen afterward. He clued me in." A slight smile lifted her lips.

Owen, her latest squeeze. Even ticked off at Frost,

Justin couldn't stop a grin. "All riiiight. Business lunch. Good to have the inside track with an attorney." When she didn't comment, he added, "A delaying tactic from Frost about a buy-sell agreement."

"Maybe, but I can't figure out why. Unclear whether they had any arrangement other than a shared office since Spear gave up practicing."

He frowned. "So you got nowhere with him."

She wagged her head. "Not completely. He did give me the names of six people the vic pissed off or got the better of in court." She grinned. "Including some of his legal colleagues."

"A shame the judge denied our request to get into the home safe and files. But if the grieving widow hasn't seen the will, she may be willing to let us bring in a locksmith." Then he could question her some more.

"Worth a try."

Justin took out his official phone to call Angela Spear, but it rang before he could punch in her number. Sheri Harte's number appeared on the screen.

"Hi, Sheri, everything okay?"

"Okay… I think. Justin, I've found a connection between Adam Spear's murder and the attack on Miriam. But I have to show you."

Chapter Nineteen

JUSTIN MADE IT to Dragon Harbor in record time. He'd left Bess at the office, calling Angela Spear and Adam's enemies. As soon as he pulled into the driveway, Sheri dashed from the mudroom door and toward him. He climbed from the state SUV. He thought she might run into his arms, but she stopped at the path to the gazebo. Her gaze solemn, she was worrying her lower lip. Whatever she'd discovered had her stressed.

He reached for her hands. Icy. He turned them over to check her palms. Small bandages only. "How do your war wounds feel?"

"Better now." She smiled, not a nervous one, but a genuine stunner that lit up her face. "Warmer too."

"Happy to oblige, but you could've stayed inside."

She tugged from his grasp, and he zipped up his rain jacket.

"First show and tell is in the gazebo." She led the way through some shallow puddles.

Once inside, she held out an arm to halt his progress. "Let's not go any farther."

Justin chuckled. "Afraid we'll get the floor wet?"

"You're joking, but that's it." She snugged her jacket around her. Back to nervous. "Do you see any water on the floor?"

He peered at the wide boards. "Not a drop except where we're standing."

"Exactly. The roof is tight. No leaks."

He scratched his chin. "New roof."

"Of course you noticed. You're trained to notice small and large details. Or else you already knew Miriam had a new roof done."

He had doubts. Maybe she was seeing clues where there were none because she cared about Miriam. But he didn't want her to hold back. "New shingles. This dry floor is significant because?"

"That first day, Deb met me at the car and dragged me in here — like I did you — to tell me about seeing Spear and his attacker on the cliff path. It was raining that day too, mostly a misty drizzle, remember?"

He nodded, remembering only too well.

"Once inside I skirted puddles." She pointed to locations on the floor. "Small ones here where we're standing, larger ones there in the middle and on that side. Other damp spots between them. Deb and I sat on the left, facing the house." She turned toward him. "Someone was in here before us."

"Not Deb waiting for you?"

"She came from inside the house. She'd been watching from the living room window. She barely had time to put on a slicker before she met me." She shook her head and huffed. "Do I have to spell it out?"

"Please do."

She closed her eyes a moment. Fascinating how she could recall and visualize what she'd seen.

"Damp spots from footsteps here where we are and to the middle. A bigger puddle, where someone stood. He then moved to a better vantage point for watching the road. Another big puddle there. From that spot you can see both directions on Cliff Point Road." She jammed her hands in her coat pockets. "I believe this is where Adam Spear's attacker waited and watched for him." She hunched her shoulders, watching for his reaction.

He mentally tracked the trail she'd just made. Her wet boots made it easy to follow. Then he walked to the middle and looked around before returning to her.

"Clear view of the road. Doubtful we'd find anything here this long after the fact to confirm your conclusion, Sheri, but it could be a lead to where the killer *might*'ve hidden. I'll send for an evidence team."

She blew out a breath. "You trust my memory? And it makes sense to you?"

"I have no doubt you saw those puddles the way you described them. And yes, it makes sense. But sense isn't proof or evidence." He swiped a hand over his hair. "That it for out here?"

"The rest is inside."

They hung up their coats and entered the kitchen, where Comet dashed happy circles around Justin.

"I brewed coffee." Sheri indicated the coffeemaker and two mugs.

"A life saver after that damp cold." He tilted his head and inhaled the aroma. "Smells like a special brew."

"Miriam's personal blend from a local organic roaster. I'll have to replenish the supply soon. When I return home, I'll take my own supply."

He bent to greet the dog. "Deb Delano told me earlier that her grandmother's still in a medically induced coma but stable."

"I hate to think of her connected by tubes to all those monitors—cardiac, oxygen, intracranial pressure, and more." Her shoulders moved in a small shudder, but then she smiled. "I talked to Deb too. Family members are taking turns sitting with her. The nurses say that the monitors indicate a change whenever someone she knows is in the room."

"Even that little bit of awareness has to be a good thing."

"I agree." She handed him a tall mug decorated with the words *Dragon Harbor* and the town's dragon logo. She added milk to her mug and led the way to the library.

"The dog must miss Miriam," he said.

"Definitely. I wish I could explain it to her." She turned on the gas flame in the fireplace. Comet followed and curled up on the hearth rug. "While she was with me in Weymouth, she acted nervous and uncertain. But here she seems more at ease and has accepted me as, um…"

"Pack leader?" He wandered the room, browsing artwork and books as he sipped coffee.

"Spoken like a man who knows dogs."

"My family always had at least one dog, sometimes as many as four. Hunting breeds usually, retriever or setter." His gaze turned inward. The words had conjured childhood memories. Some happy, some not.

"Leader? Let's say I'm part of her pack. She stays nearby except for time curled on her mistress's bed. I wasn't sure Miriam would approve so I covered the spread with a fleece blanket."

"The room where Miriam's scent would be strongest." He gestured at the laptop on the sofa. "I see you've set up shop here."

She strode to the computer and closed the lid. She turned to him with a bright smile. "And that's a perfect segue to the next topic. Someone searched the house. Whoever it was, they weren't too careful. Perhaps they were in a hurry."

He accompanied her to the desk. Desk items were pushed aside and crooked. "This it?"

"Part of it, yes. These desk items aren't arranged the way Miriam keeps them. When I was working with her, I moved them to the left to make room for my laptop. When I'm working in someone's house, it's my habit to leave things as I found them."

"Your amazing memory works for you there. So maybe you didn't this time?"

She shook her head. "When I arrived yesterday, I thought I'd forgotten to put them back. "But then I remembered doing so. Deb and her mom came to the house on Wednesday to straighten up after your evidence techs. I asked Deb about the desk, but she said everything looked okay."

"So you think whoever moved things did so between then and your arrival yesterday?"

"That's it. Sorry, but I touched several things here. There's more." She pulled out the desk's two drawers. The shallow one displayed a jumble of small lined pads, a box of paper clips, and other desk items.

"While we worked, Miriam took out a pad so she could take her own notes. Everything was neatly arranged. Both drawers have been messed up."

Justin scowled. "If you took the shallow one out and set it on the desk, it might fit the space made by shoving the other items aside."

"Exactly my thought."

"Could Deb or other family members have come in? Or the cleaning people?"

Nope. I asked Deb yesterday. No one. But the house was unlocked when I arrived. The locksmith's coming this afternoon."

"Good." Finally he'd feel a little better about her safety here. He took a photo with his phone and wrote in his notebook. "Is there still more?"

"Definitely," Sheri said. Great he was taking all this seriously. "On Monday, Miriam sent me home with three heavy cardboard boxes. She said they would help me organize the memoir in sequence. We were interrupted, and I didn't get to ask what she meant by that. In the short time we worked together, she amazed me with her clear recollection of past events and her emotions and impressions of them." She gestured to the boxes on the floor behind the couch. "Those cartons contain journals, one for every year since she turned thirteen."

She sipped from her mug and waited for Justin to analyze and reach the same conclusion she had. This was not the guy who'd hit on her and kissed her silly. He was in total cop mode, even dressed for it in a Mario Brothers tie. As he paced the room, the way his jeans traced the flex of thigh muscles drew her gaze. Not the time.

He scrubbed a hand through his short dark hair. "She was consulting her journals."

"I believe so. The entries are very detailed and personal. Even her writing conveys her distinctive voice."

"And personality?"

"In spades."

Justin chose one of the club chairs and set his mug on the side table. "Do you enjoy writing people's memoirs?"

"Oh, yes. People who want to create memoirs usually have great stories. I've always loved reading biographies, so I guess this is an extension. I've ghosted a couple of autobiographies as well. A way to participate vicariously in a life much more interesting than my humdrum one."

"Not humdrum recently." His eyes crinkled with his smile.

She heaved a sigh. "Sadly, no."

"But then we wouldn't have met. You've made my life more exciting too. I never know what you'll come up with."

No one had ever said she added excitement to their life. His words and the masculine glint in his eyes kindled a glow inside her.

"You've made my day, Justin. But the journals are the next part of the connection to Spear's murder. At least one of them is." She picked up a journal from the side table, where she'd set it earlier. "This is last year's addition. But nowhere can I find the journal for this year."

"The family says nothing is missing." He leaned forward, propping his elbows on his knees.

"But they don't know Miriam kept a journal." He started to speak, but she rushed on. "Yes, it seems inconceivable she kept this secret for so many years, let alone decades. Before I even opened these boxes, I asked Deb if her grandmother kept a diary or journal. She's never seen Miriam writing in one and she's never seen a journal-type notebook anywhere in the house."

"Wouldn't they have seen these boxes?"

"They're labeled *Décor* and kept in the upstairs hall closet below the linens."

"What about the journals?" He looked down as he made more notes.

"The last six are part of a set from a London

stationer. All bound in red leather. There are five more blank ones in the same box. The journal for this year would make an even dozen. I've looked everywhere in the house, even in the kitchen cupboards and in the cellar. No red leather journal."

"Could be important." He scribbled in his notebook. "More?"

She set aside her empty mug and headed to the hallway. "Let's go upstairs."

His eyes crinkling with amusement, he set down his mug and stood. "I thought you'd never ask."

Chapter Twenty

HER CHEEKS FLAMED. "I *meant* what I need to show you is in Miriam's bedroom. Upstairs."

Justin grasped her fluttering hands. "Sheri, it's okay. I get what you meant, and I for one can use a little humor."

When he tugged her forward, she went willingly into his arms. "What I am is frightened."

"Because of yesterday and because somebody was in the house." He tipped up her chin and pressed his mouth to hers. "Remember, the house was *un*locked."

She nodded, her lips tingling from the firmness of his mouth. But somehow the kiss settled her. She inhaled deeply and sighed out the breath. "What about that Ram pickup? Or can't you tell me?"

"I can. The plates were switched, as I thought. The red Ram pickup belongs to an administrator at Maine Med. The police contacted her, but she hadn't even noticed the switch. The officer told me they found the black pickup abandoned in a parking lot, minus the plates. It was reported stolen this morning."

"Prints?"

"Portland's working on that. Wish I had more. Wish I could tell you it was a one-shot thing."

"Me too, but thanks for telling me."

"And for the record—" he jerked a nod toward the stairs leading to the bedrooms "—I want like hell to take you to bed, but now's not the time."

It had been a long while since she'd been in a relationship, and that one, although brief, had ended badly. But oh my, she wanted Justin as much as the heat in his gaze said he wanted her. Some writer. She had no clever rejoinder for his weighted line.

"And I want us to have that time," was all she could come up with. "For now, come look at Miriam's room." She backed out of his arms and strode away.

Close behind, he chuckled, a sound both rough and smooth that did nothing to cool her face. Or the rest of her.

By the time she reached the top of the stairs, she'd recovered her poise. "The attacks on my friends are personal. Worry is—"

"Stressing you out? Keeping you up?"

"You've hit it. I'm not sleeping. I need to jog more to tire myself out. You face tragic and gruesome situations all the time. Humor must be necessary."

Comet trotted ahead into Miriam's room and leaped up onto the four-poster and curled up. The room's feminine elegance and blue and gold colors fit Miriam perfectly.

"Part of the culture. Humor helps to deal with it, but cop humor can get pretty dark. And inappropriate. Some cases are tougher to handle than others."

"Like that abused little boy? I read about the man's arrest for that and the mom's murder in the Bangor paper." Although the article had omitted the boy's name, she knew.

His expression darkened. "Yeah, the part I didn't tell you was the homicide. I hope the guy will slip up or plead guilty, so the kid won't have to testify."

Her throat tightened. Poor child. "I'm thinking humor's not enough to help you deal with that one."

He shook his head. "Some cops drink, hazard of the profession. For me, it's a sweaty workout with weights or a few rounds with a punching bag. When I have time, I go fishing with my brother."

"He must need humor too."

"Yup, being a game warden often amounts to the same thing as a cop, except he spends more time in the woods." He scratched his nose. "We seem to have gotten off track."

Her turn to laugh. "Hazard of my profession. Once I start asking questions, one thing leads to another." And to imagining his biceps bulging as he lifted weights.

"So what's significant in this room?"

She crossed to the dressing table beside the bathroom door. The top drawer gaped open. "More uncharacteristic disarray here. This drawer for one. The cosmetics inside are messed up. And the calendar on the side is open and crooked. One page is torn. As if—"

"Somebody did a hasty search and wanted or needed to get out of here in a hurry." He joined her and peered at the furniture in question.

"Exactly." Three steps took her to the window. "I started my search for the journal here. It makes sense that she'd keep it in her bedside stand, to write in before sleep, or on the dressing table. When I found nothing, I wondered if I could see the water from this window. Well, you take a look." She twitched aside the embroidered sheer. "What do you see?"

Wagging his shoulders—he was indulging her—he joined her at the window. "I can't see the bay. Only the road. The driveway. The gazebo."

"Specifically?"

"The screen door in and out of the gazebo." His wide shoulders moved as if he were thinking about it. His eyebrows climbed. "You think she saw Spear's killer."

"And recognized him." She tried to stifle emotion, but a teeny bit of triumph leaked into her voice. "She'd have been in here, dressing. Maybe she heard a noise. Maybe she was brushing her hair and saw him when he walked out into the mist, she saw his face or recognized the way he held himself."

She stood by, nearly holding her breath, as Justin paced around the bed and back. A hand to his chin rasped on shadowed stubble.

He halted in front of the desk and folded his arms. "For the sake of argument, let's suppose it happened as you say. Why did Miriam say nothing?"

At her mistress's name, Comet's ears perked. She crawled to the edge of the bed and whined. Sheri sat beside her and scratched behind her ears. The dog snuffled and laid her head on Sheri's lap.

"I've been wondering that too. I noticed no hint she knew anything. At first she might not have connected the person she saw with the attack on Spear. Maybe she couldn't imagine him committing such a crime. Or maybe she hoped he'd step forward." She looked to Justin for reaction, but he wore that give-away-nothing cop face. "Suppose the journal contains her suspicions and later her expectation she could urge the person to go to the police."

"The reason for a chat over tea and cake." He stared at his shoes as he mulled that over. "Spear's death had been confirmed as homicide. Seems damned trusting and naïve of such a worldly woman."

190

"Something I considered too. But in the short time I worked with her and examined her journals, I've seen other qualities. Miriam is confident, supremely so, in her ability to manage people, to turn others to her way of thinking." Or to run roughshod over their plans.

"If you're correct, in this case, her powers of persuasion failed."

"Yes, badly." The image of Miriam helpless on the floor punched her in the stomach and she had to collect herself.

Gruff throat clearing brought her back.

"What you suggest is possible. If it's her evening tea date, he might've wondered if she'd written it down. Maybe he saw the red journal when he shut Comet in the bathroom. The evidence techs found no reference to an appointment that night on any of the house calendars. Or on her phone. And no journal. I've been through her phone records. Nothing."

"So why would he worry if no one had already questioned him?"

"Too many questions with no answers. I have another. If he took the journal the night he shoved Miriam down the stairs, why this search?" He tucked his notebook into his shirt pocket. "I need solid evidence, a lead. Proving her assailant was the same person who killed Spear would winnow the cast of suspects to people who know her. Make my job a hell of a lot easier."

"It would be someone she knew well enough that she felt she could intervene. Not Steve Spear. But this morning he was doing something I should tell you about." She described his furtive behavior with the boxes.

"Something going on with that guy for sure." He

made no notes, but eyed her critically. "How'd last night's dinner go?"

Was the man a mind reader? Sheri's loyalties were to Deb and Miriam, not the extended Littlefield family, and not in this situation. She described her conversation with Gil MacRae and his angry reaction. "Not out of control, but taut as twisted steel, violence seeming to be just beneath the surface."

"More dangerous than an outburst. I'll keep this in mind when I interview him again."

Again. So he had suspicions about Gil too. "He worries me, but I can't see him hurting Miriam."

"No telling what somebody will do when their back's against the wall."

A sad aspect of human nature she'd learned years ago. She'd have never guessed Noah would take his own life. Her fault he'd seen no other way out. Before she sank into a maudlin funk, she shut the door on further musing.

She looked up into Justin's questioning gaze. "Just more speculating."

"A lot of that going around. Maybe the evidence techs will find something in the gazebo to back up your theory and in the places you've shown me. Whatever the reason for that attack, by now the perpetrator knows she's alive and could identify him."

"She was safe in the I.C.U. It's a pod with a nursing station in the middle. But Miriam's now been moved to a private room in a secure corridor beside I.C.U." She bit her lower lip.

His brows snapped together and out came the notebook again. "I'll arrange with the hospital administration to require visitors—family only—to sign in at the nursing station. Don't tell anybody, even Deb, about the journals. If the missing one *is* connected to the murder and Miriam's attack, our killer must *not* know we've learned about it."

A conclusion she'd already reached. On this peninsula, if one person knew, everyone would know. Deb and her mom and other family were in and out of the house all the time.

"Since you had these boxes at the time of the attempt on Miriam's life, they're not evidence. For now." He helped her return the boxes to obscurity in the hall closet.

As they walked downstairs, it hit her that she'd gotten what she wanted. She pumped a mental fist. Justin actually accepted her theory as plausible. Not evidence, not even close, but she'd given him a new direction. Or complicated the case even more. She couldn't be sorry about that. The two attacks had to be related, and so did the missing journal.

At the mudroom door, he gestured to the deadbolt. "Glad to see better locks. But this house should have a security system."

"It would've made no difference for Miriam. She invited her attacker in," she said, "but no worries. I'll lock up." As she did both day and night.

"I hope that'll be enough. I appreciate you keeping me apprised of anything you learn, but don't put yourself in the middle of this. Leave the investigating to the police."

"Investigating? I'm not. You mean Gil? I was only—"

"Asking probing questions."

She couldn't refute that. He was right. Exactly why she'd promised herself the same thing.

He touched the side of her face, and his earthy scent and masculine aura made her pulse quicken. He kissed her again, a lingering kiss. His tongue teased the seam of her lips and she opened to him, joining the dance of her tongue with his. The kiss went on, tender and thrilling and arousing. He pulled her closer. His hand on her derrière pressed her against his erection. The heat they ignited was enough to melt her shoes to the floor.

A furry body nudging its way between them broke the spell.

Justin leaned his forehead against hers. "Be careful, Sheri. I don't want anything to happen to you."

When he'd gone, she turned the knob lock. Soon the locksmith would add a deadbolt. She leaned back against the wood and savored Justin' kiss. He was a man worthy of respect. Of love.

She deserved neither.

Chapter Twenty-One

"I HAVE A right to be in my mother-in-law's house," Gil MacRae said on Monday morning. He leaned forward in his office chair, planted wide palms on his battered wooden desk. His belligerent eyebrows dared Justin to contradict him. A neck vein jumped.

"Of course," Justin said equably from the chair opposite the desk. "But why did you search her house, including inside the drawers in her desk and in her bedroom?" He'd sent a tech to dust for prints. Due to an O.U.I. two years ago, MacRae's fingerprints were on record. They popped up as a match.

The other man shifted in his seat, looked away out the side window. When he again met Justin's steady gaze, his temper was banked, or rather concealed behind a congenial good ol' boy demeanor, the attitude he must don with customers.

"I was looking out for Miriam's interests while she's laid up. Figured whoever attacked her was a burglar or home invader looking for drugs or valuables. I wanted to make sure nothing was missing." He lowered his voice. "And I hoped I'd find a clue to the fucker's identity."

Minutes later, Justin drove away from MacRae Construction, equidistant between Bayport and Dragon Harbor. Gil had lied about why he searched Miriam's house. Made up that excuse on the spot. Looking out for her interests? More likely his own. He was a big man, tall and burly, strong enough to have tossed Adam Spear off Echo Cliff. He seemed to be able to control his temper with some concentration, but resentments festered inside him, as Sheri had said. But MacRae didn't waver from his story, and Justin hadn't been able to shake loose the truth. Yet.

He bought lunch in the general store and unwrapped his ham sandwich as he passed Buddy's Garage and Bait Shop. None of this morning's interviews had added to what he and Bess already knew, although some had verified information. Like Buddy Gamage.

Many Maine people eked out a living with several jobs. In that spirit, it appeared Buddy diversified the gas station business. Next to the building was a bait tank, a "convenience" for fishermen gassing up their trucks. A small fleet of rental cars occupied the back lot. Somehow the place retained the motor-oil ambiance of a traditional small-town gas station. It had been Justin's first stop since he needed gas anyway.

Sure enough, after he'd filled up, Buddy had ambled over to join him, clearly hoping to glean gossip about the "crime wave," as some were calling it. Instead, Justin was the benefit of Buddy's finger on the pulse. The garage man was a wiry-strong forty something with a shrewd gaze and a thin mouth. He wore grease-spotted coveralls and work boots. He knew the detectives had interviewed Walter Bates, but shrugged off the notion he'd killed Spear. "Man's too far into the bottle," he said.

Buddy's daughter Paula, who ran housekeeping at the Fireside Inn, saw Angela Spear and Quentin Frost leave early one morning a few months ago. Angela and her husband's law partner. That was a head slapper. The Fireside was off Route One in a secluded grove. Justin could think of no explanation other than the obvious. And a possible motive for murder.

Another bombshell was Buddy's report of overhearing Adam Spear's intimate phone call with a woman he addressed as Liz. "Phone sex, they call it," Buddy had whispered.

Justin would ask Bess to have another chat with Quentin Frost. He'd call Sheri later and ask her to search through last year's journal for Miriam's thoughts about Bates. He'd rather do it in person, but he had another interview on his schedule.

A few minutes later, his SUV bumped down the dirt lane leading to the working docks, a mile or so away from Dragon Harbor village's public landing. A low-slung white lobster boat was tied at one of the several piers. Stacks of barnacle-encrusted traps lined another. More moored boats rocked on the incoming tide. Other than a woman in waders who was hosing down a boat deck, he saw no one. Crack of dawn, not a Monday afternoon, these docks would buzz with activity.

The sign on a neat white clapboard building announced it as the Dragon Harbor Fishing Cooperative. When Justin hopped out, his boots crunched on the gravel. A fish processing business should smell like fish, but he detected only salt air on the breeze. A single vehicle occupied the lot, a GMC with the co-op's dancing-fish bumper sticker. License plate belonged to his guy.

A chill greeted him as he entered the building. A sample of logo T-shirts and sweatshirts hung beside the small lobby's sales counter. The chalkboard on the wall listed today's wares—hard-shelled lobsters, frozen crabmeat, and hake. No wonder the place's temp felt like

February. He zipped up his jacket.

"Be right out," a husky voice called. From the back came a metallic clank and then the splash of water running in a sink.

A large man wearing a shiny yellow apron strode toward him, peeling off rubber gloves. "We're closed for the day."

A T-shirt many sizes larger than the one displayed on the wall spread the dancing fish and the wording *Wicked Fresh* across a broad chest. Shrewd hazel eyes above a heavy beard assessed him as if he knew why Justin was there.

Boyd Rankin's driver license photo showed him as clean shaven but this had to be the right man. Justin introduced himself and showed his creds. "Boyd Rankin?"

"That's me. I figured you'd get to me soon. No secret me and Adam Spear clashed more'n once. Had no love for the man but I didn't kill him." The tattoos on Rankin's forearms jumped as he flexed his wide hands into fists.

"Not making any accusations." Justin took out his notepad. "Just gathering information. Like to ask you some questions."

"Finest kind," the other man said, "if you don't mind us talking while I work."

Justin agreed and followed him into the back. Long stainless-steel tray tables and washing equipment filled the work room. Two huge metal doors with heavy latches took up one wall.

"Bunch of us processed and packaged fish this morning but nobody took time to organize proper. Have to finish up in the cooler." Donning gloves but no coat,

Rankin propped open the right-hand door and walked inside. His rubber boots squeaked on the wet floor. "Hope it won't be too cold for you."

"I'll be fine." Justin took a position at the entrance. He'd grown up fishing and hunting in Maine's north woods, no matter the weather. But this open walk-in's fan drilled the cold right into his bones. He'd like to carry this off without his teeth chattering and finish before he froze to death. He set his jaw. "I understand the source of your disagreement with Spear rose from his interest in the co-op's property."

"Weren't just *me* he pissed off." Rankin peered at three plastic packages on a metal rack before slapping them onto another lower down. "Only, as manager, I was the one mostly faced off against him."

Continuing to organize, he explained. Spear and a group of investors made several offers for the land, which boasted prime shore frontage and deep-water dockage, perfect—"in their greedy fuckin' minds"—for a condominium resort. They had plans drawn up, financing developed, hired lawyers to dig up deeds, hoping to find some loophole.

"Spear and his buddies figured we'd jump at the chance for a wad of cash instead o' working outside haulin' traps and nets." He left the cooler and latched the massive door, closing inside the frigid air.

At last. "But you didn't jump," Justin said.

Rankin slapped his wet gloves onto the sink rim. "No way. This property's belonged to local fishing families since 1934. Nothing against tourists and summer people, you understand, but this working harbor's the heart of the peninsula. Us fishermen banding together's the best thing we could've done. We do the processing, packaging, and distribution. Makes us independent business owners — men and women."

Brows scrunched, he paced and gestured at the gleaming facility. "Entrepreneurs, not the ignorant hicks those damn rich types from away think we are. We do this work 'cause we like working for ourselves, workin' outside, providin' for our families in time-honored fashion. Besides, we're trendy. Fresh from the Gulf o' Maine, fish and seafood have always been organic." He drew in a great gulp of air, then grinned. "Guess I went on a bit."

Passionate, definitely. Angry, maybe. "No problem. You're proud of what your group is doing here. Nice facility."

Rankin's grin widened. He rubbed the back of his hand over his bushy chin. "We do all right. Started small but then got lucky with the cooler and this big freezer." He pointed to the second metal door. "Supermarket in Bayport renovated, so we got their freezer. Then a restaurant burned, sparing the toilet, the freezer, and the cooler. Steals."

"But Spear didn't see this as an important contribution to the community."

"Not even close. Kept badgering us, especially me. I guess he figured if I caved, the rest would go along. He'd stop me on the street and yell something about me being the man to hold back economic development in Dragon Harbor. I came close to punching him a couple times. After the last go-round, about two months ago, he took the case to the select board in hopes of getting the zoning changed."

"And?"

"Planning board scheduled a hearing for next

month. Don't know now if they'll go ahead."

Justin made a note to check with the town office. "I'd like to know your whereabouts the morning Adam Spear was killed."

****

"THANK YOU SO much for sharing your anecdotes and insights." Sheri hooked her tote strap on her shoulder and shook the hands of Miriam's friends. Isabel and Hope had known her client since she arrived in Dragon Harbor as a bride. The sisters insisted she use their first names, a practice they might've borrowed from Miriam.

From them she'd gleaned insights into Miriam during the years when she was her husband's office nurse. A skilled medical practitioner, she also knew to soothe when patients were hurting and to cheer with hugs and smiles when children were frightened, but when straight talk was needed, she could be as no-nonsense as a corporate CEO. Sheri easily pictured her in all those roles and couldn't wait to transcribe the recordings.

"You're so welcome, dear. I pray she gets well so she can read what you're writing about her." Hope dabbed a tissue at the tears glistening in her eyes.

Isabel showed Sheri to the door, and she waved goodbye as she climbed into her car. Yesterday's interview with the retired minister's wife had been equally fascinating and helpful, rounding out further the story of Miriam's life and personality.

She drove away from Isabel's tidy ranch house and past Hope's small Cape to where the lane led onto the East Road. On her right was the original wooden farmhouse where Hope said her son and his family now lived. Not uncommon in rural areas to have family members build on ancestral property like this saltwater farm. An alien concept for Sheri. Live in such close proximity with her mother? She shuddered. Her brother and his family, maybe.

A few minutes later, she pulled into Miriam's driveway. Comet greeted her at the door, bouncing as if on springs. She reciprocated with caresses and happy talk, then hurried to change from her work outfit of black pants and silk blouse. The weather was sunny but cool, so she chose skinny jeans, a cotton pullover, and slouchy low boots. A half hour throwing a ball and a stick for the pup in the backyard made both happy. After a sandwich of multigrain bread and turkey breast left from last night's supper, she left Comet napping in the library and grabbed her canvas bag on the way out the door.

Sheri was looking forward to reading to Miriam from the novel she'd plucked from her shelf. The woman had pointed out *A Tree Grows in Brooklyn* as one of her favorites, one she reread periodically. Maybe she would hear Sheri reading and take comfort from the familiar story. Because of work schedules, most of the family members came during the evening. With no one else scheduled this afternoon, the time should be peaceful for them both.

As promised, only the family and Sheri knew Miriam remained in the local hospital. Justin had worked out confidentiality with hospital personnel. If anyone asked, those who knew were to say she'd been transported to Maine Medical Center. Inquiries at Bayport Hospital received the reply that they had no patient by that name.

She drove to the Seaside Resort's fitness center. After a quick workout, she took a cab to the hospital. No one watching her — the very thought the attacker might be doing so gave her the willies — would learn she was visiting Miriam, or anyone, there.

Inside the secure corridor beside the I.C.U., the clatter of bottles and the ever-present antiseptic smell greeted her. At the desk, two nurses bent over computers, and a third stopped her to sign the visitor record. A knot untied in her chest. Miriam was well taken care of and safe.

At the end of the corridor, she found the door ajar. Detecting only the hum of equipment inside, she pushed the door open wider. Miriam lay propped up on pillows, her eyes closed, face pale and devoid of makeup, a look she'd hate. Tubes and wires snaked to her, around her, and to monitors on the wall behind her and on stands.

A tall figure stood at her bedside, clad in scrubs, green skullcap, and paper mask. Probably her surgeon checking on her. Why didn't the nurse say something?

"Oh, Doctor, I'm sorry to intrude. I'll come back when you're finished." She started to back out of the room.

His hands lifted from something on the bed. A monitor began beeping, softly at first, then louder and louder. He yanked at wires, and more beeping joined the alarm. Sheri's ears rang and adrenaline flooded her system.

She dropped her bag and flung the door open wide. "No! Help!"

He rushed at her and shoved her aside.

She grabbed at his shirt with one hand and caught the mask's elastic edge with the other. Maybe she couldn't stop him before help could arrive, but she'd know his identity, dammit.

He knocked her away.

The force slammed her against the wall. Pain flashed, a hot sunburst. Her breath exploded from her lungs as she dropped to the floor like a bag of wet laundry. She wanted to scream, but couldn't draw in enough air.

On all fours, she grabbed at his pants leg.

He tripped on the spilled contents of her bag. But he regained his footing and dashed from the room.

Amid the cacophony of beeping monitors, Sheri fought dizziness, but couldn't make it to her feet before an army of nurses raced into the room. She lurched against the wall and sank downward. She stayed there on her butt, propping her head on her hands.

Oh God, please let her be all right.

Chapter Twenty-Two

"THANKS FOR WALKING me through all this, Doctor." In Justin's experience, surgeons of all types were arrogant, self-important pricks, but so far Miriam Littlefield's neurosurgeon had been affable and cooperative. And well dressed, no surgical scrubs. Escorsio's shirt, pants, and leather wingtips probably cost more than Justin's rent. They stood by in what had been Miriam's room while the evidence team dusted and photographed the medical devices.

"Happy to do it. I can't imagine how that impostor got in here. I'll be conducting my own investigation. As will hospital administration. You can be certain of it."

"Please let me know your results." The surgeon's investigating from a medical angle might lead to different information, helpful in one way or another. "We should be able to release this room and the equipment by tomorrow afternoon. As soon as I make sure the evidence response techs have all they need."

The other man's high brow crimped. He gestured toward the three machines beside the bed. "Sooner rather than later, detective. Some of those devices may be damaged and will need repairs. *Expensive* repairs." One thick black eyebrow rose, as if he blamed the police.

So much for affable.

"I understand. I'll do what I can. May I get back to you if I need more information?"

"Anytime, detective. If you'll excuse me, I need to check on my patient." Escorsio glanced at his watch. "You'll find Ms. Harte in Emergency. The physician on duty should have finished examining her by now."

"Appreciate it."

After the surgeon left, Justin snapped pictures of the medical equipment. What he really wanted to do was go to Sheri, assure himself she was okay. But he had to add to his notes on these devices and their uses before all the technical stuff fled his brain. The evidence team would send him their images but maybe not before he started writing his report.

This attack supported Sheri's idea that Spear's killer wanted to make sure Miriam couldn't ID him. Not good methodology for a detective to fall in love with a theory, but Justin hadn't been able to discern any other motive for two attacks on the old lady. Well liked in the community except for Spear, who'd liked nobody. Unless the dead man could reach out from the grave, Justin could cross him off the suspect list.

If only he could cross off live suspects as fast. This case was in a ditch. Unless Sheri had something for him.

Leaving the techs to complete their work, he headed to Emergency.

He easily found her room, open except for a curtain partway across the front. She was on her cell phone but waved him in.

"I'm fine, Deb," she said in a voice edged with strain. "Bumps and bruises but no concussion, the doctor said. What did Dr. Escorsio say about Miriam?" She listened, murmuring occasionally.

Justin took the chair by her bed. After traipsing all over the hospital questioning people, he welcomed plunking his butt in a seat. Sheri didn't look *fine*. Hell yes, she looked more than fine. Streaky, dark blond hair and a trim body with real curves hidden in an ugly hospital johnny. But the bonk against the wall had left her fine features pale. The brown depths in her eyes— eyes that missed nothing—held pain.

A slow boil flared in his chest. He'd get the asshole who'd done this to her and nearly killed Miriam.

"I'll be heading to the Point soon. Bye," Sheri said after a few moments. A pensive look on her face, she dropped the phone beside her on the bed.

"You're in the thick of it again." He smiled as he took out his digital recorder.

"You'd think someone is alerting the cosmos. If this keeps up, I'll need to refresh my self-defense lessons. I'm glad I stopped whatever that attacker had intended, but I could do without the aches and pains. Thank God Miriam's unharmed."

"You feel up to telling me what happened?"

"You have your fingers crossed I got a good look at him, don't you?"

"Guilty." He grinned. "And?"

"Not much of a look, sorry. But I'll tell you what I can." She patted the bed. "Please sit over here. I won't bite."

"So you are inviting me into your bed."

"Onto it anyway." She laughed, then winced.

So as not to jar her, he lowered himself carefully. He set the recorder close to her. With her permission, he pushed the Record button. As she described in detail what she'd done and seen, he listened without interrupting. The impostor wore surgical gloves, so no fingerprints, dammit.

"Size, shape? How tall? Any impression there?"

She closed her eyes and lay back on the pillows. A moment later she blinked and straightened. "Tall, yes, maybe as tall as you. Wide shoulders. Neither slim nor heavy. Height similar to Dr. Escorsio's."

The reason the nurses didn't pay attention when he walked by their station. Justin pressed on. "Are you certain you're not mixing up the impostor with the surgeon?"

"Possibly, but I hope not. I met Dr. Escorsio the morning after Miriam was brought in. He came to the family room to see Deb and her mom. I remember thinking when I entered Miriam's room that it was him." She held out her hands, palms up, in the universal gesture of futility.

No bandages there. Her palms looked better. He hoped the new injuries healed as fast.

"Could be coincidence." Or the attacker knew Escorsio. Or it was the surgical get-up. Justin jotted a reminder to check on whether physicians were searchable on the Internet.

"One last thing, he wore Nike sneakers, gray and dark red, the only clothing that wasn't scrubs. But I lost him, dammit." Tears sheened her eyes. "His surgical garb let him blend in with the staff rushing to the room. They blocked me from seeing where he went. I was too disoriented to get off the floor. Gone, he was gone." Her fingers curled into fists.

"Don't beat yourself up about it." He leaned forward and smoothed the deep crease in her forehead with his index finger. "You saved Miriam from further injury. Maybe death. Again."

"Pure luck. How did he know she was here? Only

family and I were supposed to know." Her eyes widened and a hand flew to her throat. "You don't think?"

"I think a lot of things, but mostly I'm just rattling knobs until a door opens up. Wouldn't surprise me if somebody slipped up and shared that information." That was to reassure her, but at least two family members were on his list. He flipped a notebook page. "You described the suspect as *him,* similar in build to the surgeon. Are you certain it was a man?"

"Yes. Broad gestures, taking up space like a man does. And he *moved* like a man."

"Or an athletic woman?"

"Angela Spear? She's a swimmer. A tall woman with muscular shoulders. Perhaps." She looked downward, placing a finger to her chin.

"Or Gil MacRae?"

"Seeing him from the back, and then only through my tumble, I suppose it's possible."

"Enough speculation." She was too tired and sore for more. He hit the Off button on his recorder.

"I feel better now. I'll get dressed and head home. To Miriam's, I mean. Comet will need to go out."

"I'll wait in the hall until you're ready. I'm driving you." He tucked away his recorder and notebook.

"What do you mean? I'm okay."

If okay meant exhausted and bruised. Maybe what he was doing wasn't professional but neither was what he felt for her. Which didn't bear examining.

"You've been shaken up. I'm driving you."

****

THE SUN WAS setting as Sheri unlocked the door to the mudroom. She pushed, but the old door, swollen in the wet spring weather, resisted. She pushed again and winced at the pain the effort stabbed through her back and shoulders. After being slammed into a wall, a few hours lying around in the ER had stiffened her joints.

And what was she going to do about Justin? The damn man had taken over. He'd insisted on driving her home, arranged to have Deb drive her car here. She couldn't risk letting herself depend on someone. It wouldn't be fair to him. How could she deal with this?

Justin, his phone at his ear, came up behind, reached around her, and shoved the door harder. "Got it. Make it for two. I'll tell her."

The door creaked open, and she gathered herself to step inside. She'd thought her knee scrapes had healed, but this tumble had awakened that sting too.

"Thanks, Justin." Wincing, she hung up her jacket. "You're right. I'm too achy and too wiped out to have driven. I'll be fine now."

His eyebrows bunched together. "You pushing me away? Think again. You're in danger, maybe more now. That creep is probably worried you could ID him. It's not safe for you to stay in this house alone." He turned and double locked the door.

She'd shake her head if it wouldn't hurt her neck. "Look, I appreciate you driving me home. But the house has better locks now—deadlocks and bolts. I'll be fine. I'll take a few ibuprofen and climb into bed. New woman tomorrow."

"I believe you, and as a rule I do appreciate an independent woman." He brushed a lock of hair back from her face, and dammit, she wanted to lean into his warm hand. "But I'll sleep better if I know you're safe. Stay here while I check the house." He undid the strap on his belt holster and checked his pistol. He eased open the inner door and entered the kitchen.

Hell, now she *was* scared. What if she'd dashed into the house and run into the same guy who'd tried to kill Miriam? Except how would he get in? She'd locked up when she left.

A yip from the kitchen told her who she'd run into now. She opened the inner door and walked into a brightly lit kitchen. Justin had probably turned on lights as he went.

Tail waving madly, the little dog wriggled up to her. She whined, Comet speak for "Let me out."

"Oh, sweetie, I'm sorry you've been stuck inside so long." Sheri petted her and then opened the doggy door into the backyard.

While she fixed the dog's supper, she could hear footsteps above her and floorboards creak. Justin checking all the rooms. Probably the attic too. Then she would be safe and he could leave. He *should* leave. Her breath caught and her stomach tightened—and not with hunger, although her stomach disagreed.

She stared at the scoop full of kibble.

Dammit, did she want Justin to go or not? She suspected what could, would happen if he stayed. He was a man who sought justice and was so forceful about everything. When they were together, his intense focus on her made her scalp tingle—and other body parts. Whatever was happening between them was so new she couldn't call it a relationship. How did he make her feel such conflict, anticipation and alarm at the same time? She did know one thing. She wanted him and he wanted her. She was no naïve virgin. So why should that scare her?

Happy panting and the clatter of doggy nails on the

floor interrupted her meandering thoughts.

"Here you go, sweetie." She dumped the kibble into the bowl and set it down.

Comet didn't hesitate to dig in.

Sheri pressed a hand to her lower back. Bending hurt and inching upright hurt more.

"House is all clear," Justin said as he joined her, pistol tucked away. "One window in the living room was unlocked. All tight now."

She sighed. Dammit, so maybe someone could've gotten in. "Thank you."

"I turned up the heat and brought you something I found in the medicine cabinet." He held out a medicine bottle.

Ibuprofen. "My hero." Damn, she hadn't meant to say that. "But don't let it go to your head."

"Too late, but you're the heroine." When she opened her mouth to object, he held up a hand. "And before you order me out again, I'm not leaving. When your friend Deb brings your Rav, she's also bringing shrimp scampi from the Italian restaurant in the village. For *two*, complete with garlic knots and salad. Neither of us has eaten and it's getting late."

Finished with her supper, Comet came to Sheri and sat. Once she received her biscuit, she trotted off.

"Dessert," Sheri said. "I'm following house rules."

"My family's dogs always got dessert too."

When tires crunching on the driveway announced Deb's arrival, Sheri let Justin go meet her. Well, not exactly *let* him, but she didn't object because frankly she wasn't up to her friend's mothering.

For some reason, his hovering was growing on her. Besides, having a sexy, armed detective here with her was reassuring. And more. As long as he didn't try to tell her what to do.

Chapter Twenty-Three

JUSTIN TWISTED AROUND on the couch and rolled his shoulders. Stared at the report he'd written on his department laptop. But this late at night, his mind was wandering.

Tonight he'd thought Sheri might be too bushed to eat much, but she devoured most of her pasta and salad. No wine, he suggested, or she'd probably fall over. She laughed, agreeing water was a better choice. He cleaned up the dishes while she gathered a pillow and blanket from upstairs for him. Then he shooed her to bed and took Comet out for a last pee.

"Let's check the shrubbery for bad guys," he told the dog.

They sniffed around, Comet literally, in the front yard and by the gazebo. Nothing.

The dog chose her spot, squatted, and grinned at him. Angling for another biscuit, he figured. Once securely locked inside, she made short work of the tiny one he gave her and headed upstairs to bed. On Miriam's bed? Or on Sheri's? He imagined Sheri with her hair spread across the pillow and knew which one he'd choose.

He read through his report on today's attempt on Miriam Littlefield one more time, saved it, and closed out. He'd file it in the morning and hurry the techs on what they found in that room.

He walked through the downstairs again. All buttoned down. Outside all was dark except for the soft glow of a streetlight where the road turned past the cliff. From the foot of the stairs, he listened for Sheri's breathing. A sigh. The rustle and slide of covers. At least one of them was getting a good night's sleep.

A jaw-cracking yawn had him returning to the library couch and kicking off his shoes. He laid his pistol within easy reach. Not likely the killer would try anything tonight, not with a state SUV in the driveway, but Justin would be a fool not to be prepared. He turned off the light and stretched out with the blanket over him.

Sleep eluded him. He stared at the pendant lamp above him. He'd count the damn tin ceiling tiles if it was light enough. He stacked his hands beneath his head.

Not every case kept him awake at night. But this one had him grinding his teeth and wanting to punch more than his pillow. He could distance himself from the murder of Adam Spear, a man nobody liked. Less so from the attack on Miriam Littlefield, a woman everybody liked. But then the asshole had made it personal, going after Sheri on Thursday. That could have nothing to do with IDing him. But it made it urgent.

Justin wanted this fucking guy bad. Preferably before he killed again.

Creaking floorboards sent him reaching for his 9mm. He eased upright and listened. Soft footfalls. He pivoted to his feet and crossed to the doorway.

"Oh!" Sheri spun toward him. Her hands went to her throat.

"It's just me." He clicked on the safety and tucked the pistol in his pocket.

He waited for his heart to settle. It didn't. Her hair

lay in loose waves on her shoulders, and static electricity plastered the thin pajamas to her curves. His blood supply detoured to his crotch. He couldn't remember ever wanting a woman this damned much. He had to force his gaze up from where her nipples poked against the silk.

"Sorry I woke you. I couldn't sleep and came down to heat some milk." She came two steps closer to him.

He made a face. "I like milk, but hot with chocolate. Plain warm milk is foul stuff."

"But it's supposed to work. I've never tried it." A small smile lifted the corners of her mouth. "Apparently you have."

"Mom's remedy. I pretended sleep so she wouldn't dose me. But you didn't wake me. I can't sleep either."

He closed the distance and gave in to the urge to touch, but limited it to only the silk molding her upper arm in case he was misinterpreting the smile and the look in her eyes.

"Well, then." She tilted up her chin, looked him up and down. Settled on his chest, where he'd undone three shirt buttons. "What do you suggest as a sleep remedy?"

"A massage can be very relaxing. Except you have too many bruises for that." He grazed the back of his hand along the fine bones of her jaw and chin, and she leaned into the caress.

"Not everywhere. I can think of a few places that might benefit from massage. Even enjoy it. And you?"

"If you're the one with hands on my body, I'm up for a massage… or something."

"Or something." Her lashes lowered as her gaze dropped to his jeans zipper. "It's pretty clear you're *up*. But are you prepared?"

"Honey, I've been prepared since our first kiss." Protection waited in the library, in his jacket pocket.

She took his hand and placed it on her left breast. Her breasts weren't large, but firm and a nice handful. A nipple that had poked at the pj silk now poked at his palm. Sweet.

"My favorite place to massage." His blood began to simmer. "I don't want to hurt you."

"Not painful, but sweet torture." She leaned into his hand and closed her eyes.

He bent and replaced his hand with his mouth, licking and suckling on the tight bud until the silk was wet and molded to her skin and she was panting. Then he looped his arms around her, careful not to hurt her, and kissed her. When she kissed him back and pressed herself to him, cupping his ass, he wanted to take her on the damn floor. The taste of her sang in his head, and heat poured through his body. Somewhere he found the strength to set her away a step and lowered his forehead to hers so he could breathe.

"Upstairs," Sheri whispered, all she could manage for words after the sensation of his mouth on her, hot and firm and devastating. His dark eyes burned with the same heat blazing through her veins. She thrummed with desire, her skin tingling and her thigh muscles so loose, the stairs would be a challenge. Sex might be a mistake, but she'd risk it. He was funny and possessed that edge of danger and incongruously an air of calm steadiness. Stopping was not an option.

"I'll be right behind you." Justin hustled into the library, but a moment later followed her upstairs and into the bedroom. He glanced around. "No dog?"

"She takes turns sleeping in here and on Miriam's

bed. I thrashed around too much for her and she left earlier. I closed the door on my way by Miriam's."

"Excellent. Now where were we?"

He drew her close and his kiss claimed her, his tongue hot and insistent, his hands lightly caressing her back, her hips. The light touches trailing sparks through her entire body ignited tingling low in her belly. As she clung to him, fire coursed through her, and she was all heat and need. Her heart pounded.

Their mouths still sealed, she tugged him to the bed and unbuttoned his shirt the rest of the way. She'd imagined touching him like this and reality was better. She uncovered a powerful body, leanly muscled, sleek and rock hard.

His heart throbbed against her fingers. She slid her hands over the lean bands of muscle on his shoulders, threaded her fingers through the dusting of brown hair on his chest, lighter than on his head. Muscles contracted with her touch. Down her hands went, over the rigidly banded sinew of his abs. Her fingers felt singed.

"Your skin is so hot." She lifted her gaze to his blazing blue eyes.

"My turn." He made short work of her pajama shirt buttons and when he'd slid the garment away, hummed his admiration. His gaze still locked on her body, he stepped back and removed his gun from his pocket and placed it on the nightstand.

She resisted making excuses and covering herself in favor of enjoying him. She slid the shirt from his shoulders. As they undressed each other, they explored, touched, tasted. They climbed into the bed together. She sighed as his kisses covered her neck, her breasts, her belly. He returned to her mouth, and she opened to him, eager to taste him again. Damn, this man could kiss. She burned for more, aching with arousal.

His fingers found the hot, wet warmth between her legs and rubbed the sensitive bundle of nerves, scorching a high-voltage flash through her. Her skin felt tight and hot, achy, and she couldn't get close enough to him. When she closed her hand around his heated length and stroked him, he arched above her and moaned.

He rolled away, and she heard the crinkle of a foil packet. A too-long moment later, he returned to her. She watched him watching her, as he slid into her, one millimeter at a time. At the combination of their gazes joining them as their bodies did, her heart went wild. The strain of restraint on his face must be mirrored on hers. She clenched and unclenched her muscles, drawing him in completely. She loved the feel of his body on hers, the texture of his chest hair on her breasts, the roughness of his skin, his heat and earthy scent.

His blue eyes went to smoke and he propped himself on his elbows. His kisses tangled all her circuits as he began to move within her, in long, luxuriant strokes. She tensed and he increased the pace. Her breath was speeding and shallow and silky threads of excitement wound and wound inside her. She was close, so close…

"Come for me, Sheri honey, come for me."

That liquid baritone plea and one more stroke and she went utterly still for a heartbeat before shock waves rolled through her, and breathing his name, she splintered at the seams. Sensation after sensation rocketed through her body.

He thrust in deeper, arching and groaning as he found his release, and then lay on top of her and gasped for breath. His heavy weight should've been too much on her, but instead she savored his salty male scent, the fevered perspiration slicking their bodies, his ragged breath on her neck. She stored the way he made her feel into her memory, so she could take it out and relive it when whatever this ended. Because it would end, had to end. She didn't deserve this man who was becoming too special to her.

****

AN ODD SOUND opened his eyes. Justin blinked away the grogginess of sleep. He scooted to the bed's edge and wrapped his fingers around his pistol. Not footsteps, a voice. The dog whining?

Small moans, almost cries. Sheri thrashed beneath the covers.

It was Sheri's voice he heard. No sound in the hallway, nothing outside this room.

"No... no... Noah, no!" She moaned, her hands clutching at the covers.

Should he wake her or would that be worse than letting the dream play out? Today's attack on Miriam and her probably caused this flashback.

"Sorry... so sorry... never... forgive."

She rocked back and forth as her words drifted into murmurs, fainter and fainter. And then she lay quietly, again sound asleep. Or exhausted.

Justin returned his service weapon to the nightstand and rolled to face Sheri. Did she believe Noah's suicide was her fault? She'd been, what, fifteen, sixteen when he died? Teenagers sometimes placed heavy blame on themselves for things they didn't cause or couldn't control. Could she still blame herself all these years later? She was sensitive and caring and loyal, so maybe she did.

They'd known each other less than a month. It didn't seem right for him to ask her about the dream, about her feeling of guilt. Despite tonight's incredible sex, it wasn't like they had an actual relationship. Neither of them did relationships. He did want her big time, wanted her again right now. If anybody asked, he'd never admit it, but he cared for her more than any woman in a long time.

But he had the suspicion she was holding back or keeping something from him. Maybe about Noah. And then there was her computer. Before she'd showed him the disarray in the desk, she rushed to close her laptop lid in a hurry. That could be about her work, keeping clients' privacy, but still…

****

TWO NIGHTS LATER, Sheri pulled into Miriam's driveway. Nine o'clock on the dashboard clock. Later than she'd meant to be. Comet slept beside her on the passenger seat. She'd had a romp and a run in the Bayport dog park before Sheri met her friend for dinner.

She hadn't seen Rhonda since high school and catching up took a long time over several courses of Thai cuisine. Their lives had diverged wildly. Rhonda was twice divorced, with four children, two from each marriage. Her mom was on sitter duty, so she wanted to make the evening out last as long as possible. What was that kind of life like? Chaotic, yes. A struggle, clearly. But full, a full life with some heartache, but love and family.

She couldn't let herself even imagine what life with Justin might be like, no matter how tempted she was after that amazing night with him. She hadn't been able to stop reliving it. But—

She pushed away the maudlin reaction threatening to ambush her. When she shut off the engine, Comet sat up and yawned. The motion sensor turned on the outside light that illuminated the mudroom entrance. All was quiet. She had no reason to be nervous.

House keys in one hand and the strap of her knockoff Hermès handbag on her shoulder, she climbed out.

The little dog hopped across the console and out the driver side with her. She trotted beside Sheri. As they approached the door, the dog whined and hung back.

"What is it, Com—"

The outside light shattered. Darkness crashed down with the broken glass.

A heavy weight rammed into her, nearly knocking her over. Her purse fell away. A hand clamped over her mouth. It pulled her back against a hard body. The stench of heavy sweat assaulted her nostrils.

Her heart pounded with painful thumps, and she dragged in air. *Why? Who?*

Comet launched into fierce barking. It was too dark to see her, but the dog was close. Would he hurt her too?

Adrenaline jolted her into action. She flailed her arms, reached behind, but could get no purchase. She twisted and kicked backward. Her boot heel connected with bone, a shin or a knee.

The attacker uttered only a muffled grunt. The grip tightened on her mouth. Her lips stung, and she tasted blood.

His free arm wrestled with something. He draped the thing over her shoulder. Looped it around her neck. Its movement scratched her throat. *A rope.*

White noise roared in her ears. *No!* She wrapped the

fingers of her left hand around the rough weave, kept it from tightening around her neck. With her right, she maneuvered the house keys between her knuckles.

As he fought one-handed with the rope, the grip on her loosened a fraction.

Sheri wrenched around and jabbed the keys toward where his head must be.

She hit only air.

But his hand pulled free from her mouth.

"Help! Help me!" Was there anyone nearby? A car passing? Someone. *Please, someone be there...* She dug in her jacket pocket.

He grabbed at her arm. Caught hold of her sleeve and reeled her in. Comet growled. She set up a fierce snarling near Sheri's feet. The attacker wrestled the rope around her neck and yanked her against him.

He leaned, off balance. More growls. The sound of cloth ripping. He leaned again, maybe standing on one foot. A big jerking move as he seemed to kick out. *Comet, run!*

A thump and a yelp. Silence. *No!*

"Help! Help me! He's trying to kill me. Hel—"

His free hand clamped down on her mouth. He yanked the rope tighter.

Sheri gagged, fought for breath. Bright spots wavered before her eyes. One-handed, she clawed at the rope. Her fingers closed on the device in her pocket. Her only chance. She pushed the button.

An ungodly shriek blasted her ears. A siren, a ringing peal into the darkness.

Lights blazed, as if the sun had cranked on. Blinded, she blinked, squinted against the glare. She couldn't breathe. Her knees gave way.

Susan Vaughan

"Who is that? What's the hell's going on there?" a man's furious voice called.

Arms shoved her forward and the rope's tension collapsed. The pounding of feet scrabbled on the driveway stones and then faded away.

She fell to her knees. She panted, struggling for enough breath to answer. "Call 911… attack."

Chapter Twenty-Four

THANKFUL FOR THE rescue, Sheri massaged the abrasions on her neck and settled back in the parlor armchair. She sipped water through the tightness in her throat while Detective Peters questioned the next-door neighbors, seated on the sofa. Comet, apparently unhurt, lay at her feet.

"We were watching TV in bed," Edwin Maxcy said, "and I thought Sheri's cry for help was part of the movie, but Peg here knew better." The white-haired man curved an arm around his wife's shoulders. Both were dressed for bed in pajamas and fuzzy bathrobes.

Peg Maxcy explained she'd insisted her husband go see what the racket was outside. Edwin then heard Sheri's SOS alarm and ran out with a baseball bat and his phone. Neither saw the assault nor anyone running away afterward.

Once Edwin called the police, Sheri had invited the couple in and called Justin.

Police spotlights and light bars lit up the outside. Justin was out there somewhere directing state evidence techs and other officers. State and local D Harbor officials swarmed the neighborhood searching for her attacker.

Detective Peters thanked the Maxcys as she finished. She hustled to the door, saying she had a call. Yawning, the couple pushed to their feet, and Sheri walked them to the mudroom door.

"You were just in time. You saved my life." She managed a teary smile as she hugged the two of them. "I can't thank you enough. But it's late, and you need your rest."

"You too, I expect," Peg said. "We'll talk again tomorrow. Well, it's actually today, isn't it?"

"Unfortunately." Sheri tightened her jaw against a yawn.

She bid them goodnight as Justin entered. He tipped up his ball cap emblazoned with the state police logo. He looked like every police recruiting poster with his strong jaw and steady gaze, and the anxiety and relief in his eyes made her heart skip a beat. Or more than one.

"You okay, honey?"

Her neck was bruised, and her throat felt as if she'd swallowed sand, but she was okay. She nodded and stepped into his open arms, grateful for the support and comfort. He was warm and strong and *here*.

He made her sit by the library fire and refilled her glass with water. She'd be floating soon with all the water people had offered her. First the EMTs, then Detective Peters, and now Justin. "Tell me the details, not just the summary."

She'd gone over everything in her mind since she sketched it for him when he first arrived. She described it step by step, finishing with the rescue. "My little SOS alarm brought out Edwin and his baseball bat, thank God."

"I've heard of these personal alarm things. Show me."

She lifted the red heart-shaped device from her jacket pocket. "I usually have it clipped to my handbag.

If I hadn't put it in my pocket for jogging earlier…" Her breath caught and she shook her head.

Justin took it from her and turned it over in his hands. "*This* is an alarm?"

"It's deceptively small and cute, so potential attackers don't suspect or grab for it. You push the button and it goes off like an air raid siren. Ear-splitting. Hundred and twenty decibels."

"I'll take your word for it. We don't want to scare the neighborhood a second time tonight." He handed it back and took out his pocket notebook. "You said you didn't see the attacker, but you must have some impression. Size? Man or woman? Any idea what they wore?"

She made herself go back to her struggle. "No idea of clothing, but Comet must've chomped down on the pants leg. I heard a rip."

He hiked a shoulder. "Good for Comet. What else?"

"Tall, close to your height, but I don't know exactly since I didn't see him. Yes, I said *him*, but I'm not certain of the sex, only that *he* was stronger than I am." She looked away, wishing she'd been able to pay closer attention. "I was so worried about the dog, afraid he'd injured her. Comet's my hero. If she hadn't attacked him, I wouldn't have gotten loose enough to call out or use the SOS alarm."

He smoothed her hair back from her forehead. "Hey, you were fighting for your life. We'll get this guy. How's the pup doing?"

"She's worn out mostly." Comet was heading up the stairs to bed. "She might be bruised, but seems basically okay. I'll call the veterinarian in the morning."

"Who knew you were going out this evening and

might return home in the dark?"

"Deb. She gave Rhonda my number. I can't think of anyone else." Having learned a bit how he thought, she held up a hand. "Before you ask, I saw no one around when I drove away. Which was in broad daylight so I could take Comet to the dog park."

He took her empty glass from her and pulled her to her feet.

She walked him to the back door. He held her close, and covered with his tender kisses, the pain in her bruised lips and neck melted away. Her hurt and fear dissipated. She wanted his embrace to last all night, but soon she felt him gather himself and pull away.

"You sure you don't want to move back to Weymouth after that?" he said.

"I can't run away now. And wouldn't the danger just follow me home? Here, at least, I have friends, and you're on the peninsula nearly daily."

"Maybe, but I see there's no arguing with you." He sighed. "I don't like to leave you alone after all that, but I have more to do outside and a report to write. Lock up tight and keep your phone close just in case."

"I'll be okay." And she would. She felt stronger because she'd taken action to save herself. "But I probably need a new battery in my SOS alarm."

****

JUSTIN AND BESS Peters left the Spear house Thursday afternoon after two hours in the always charming company of Angela Spear. They watched as the truck from Jimmy's Locks & Safes headed back to Bayport.

In Adam's three-drawer filing cabinet they'd found a rubber-banded stack of old client files and Adam's will, dated four years ago. Justin had already learned its contents. Everything was left to his wife. Zip to Stephen. The locksmith said he knew that safe and getting inside would take a while. He manipulated the dial in an effort to suss out the combination one number at a time. When after an hour, he was able to come up with only one number, Angela gave the go-ahead to drill into the safe. They had found a felt-lined cavity. Empty.

"All that for nothing," Bess said, leaning back against her unit.

"Do you suppose Angela found the file key and the safe combo behind that picture and cleaned out everything?"

"Possible, but she seemed to want to see what was locked in there as much as we did. For all the good it did." She nodded toward the other end of the Point. "Any useful evidence last night?"

"Not much. Sheri's attacker used—" he checked his notes "—twisted polyester/Dacron rope, mostly used for hauling lobster traps. This was old and worn, maybe discarded and handy on some dock. Not traceable. It's been dry lately, no clear prints, and the woods path has the same crushed shells as the cliff path. She said nobody saw her leave, and only Deb Delano knew she was going out. All I got is maybe our guy saw her headed out for the evening and lay in wait for her. When we find the scumsucker, I'll charge his ass with attempted murder."

"Damn right." Bess tilted her head as if she wanted to say more, maybe ask about him and Sheri, which was off limits. But she said only, "I hope Sheri's okay."

"She seemed normal on the phone this morning." He blew out a breath. "I keep thinking about the rope. Fishing gear because he's a fisherman or he wants the crime to point that way, or a rope because of how Sheri's boyfriend died?"

"Just keep at it, Justin. I didn't have time to tell you earlier. Spear's cell phone records came through. Multiple calls back and forth between Adam and a Liz R. That's it, no real last name. Calls started in October and petered out in March, mostly calls from her to him. What if Adam was planning to leave his wife, and he's the one who cleaned out the file cabinet and the safe?"

"Or he broke things off with Liz. Or he had her ease up on the calls so he didn't get caught."

They batted that around a bit and then spent a few minutes reviewing what they had.

Bess's info from Buddy Gamage's daughter verified she had seen Angela Spear and Quentin Frost at that inn too early for anything but the morning after. And a couple of people in committees with Angela said she spent at least one weekend a month away, supposedly with an old school friend in Massachusetts. Maybe with Frost, maybe legit.

"Bank colleagues and employees find Angela competent and smart but abrasive and overbearing," Bess said. "We already know she has a temper. More than a few folks said she's prone to outbursts, takes time to cool off. Took her time finding ways to fire people who crossed her."

"Plotted their work demise, so to speak."

She grinned. "But here's a surprise. I found out she's a supporter of the Bayport Community Theater, and the manager told me she also helps with costumes and played parts in a few plays. One was a hospital fundraiser with actors dressed in surgical gowns."

"And masks?" Justin's mind raced. Killing her

husband and trying to silence Miriam fit, but why go after Sheri? By now Miriam's attacker in the hospital would know they were in the clear.

"The whole deal. A bit faded or patched and donated by the hospital laundry."

"So Angela had motive and opportunity to kill her husband. She could have pilfered scrubs from the theater. Nobody there would've paid attention. She's tall enough, maybe strong enough. And why attack Sheri a second time?"

"That sure as hell doesn't seem to fit, but I'll see if she has an alibi for last night. I'm guessing it'll be home alone unless she was with Frost. Could be interesting." Bess made notes on her tablet. "I'll see if I can find out if anybody in the ICU could've leaked Miriam's location. Or could be a family member got chatty."

Residents on the Point had returned from warmer climates, so Justin had checked if they found anything suspicious. One thing—broken lock on one house's free-standing garage. Techs found oil drippings on the cement floor that looked recent. Typical synthetic oil used in newer car models. Justin speculated that Spear's killer might've parked his car there. He explained what he'd gotten from Sheri. She found references to Walter Bates in the journals. He did do odd jobs for Miriam Littlefield. Did good work, didn't drink on the job, and she did feed him.

When they discussed Steve Spear carrying out boxes, she said, "Unless they contained school trophies or clothes, it could be important. Maybe files from his dad's office."

"We need more than suspicion to obtain a warrant for Steve's apartment," Justin said. "Didn't the techs dust for prints around the safe and the pictures?"

Bess tapped keys on her tablet. "They found Steve's prints in the room, but I'll check on exactly where. What did the tech team find in Miriam Littlefield's hospital room?"

"I already knew the attacker pulled wires and tubes loose. But that seems to have been an improvised move when Sheri caught him. In his haste to escape, he dropped a syringe full of fentanyl."

She shuddered, rocked her shoulders like she was ready to jump the asshole. "Who'd do something like that to a sweet old lady?"

"I don't know about sweet, but Miriam's a feisty old gal. I like her."

"That everything we got?"

He caught Bess up on Boyd Rankin. "He has no alibis for anything. Either on his boat or at home alone. Might be too beefy to have masqueraded as the surgeon."

"One point for him." Her brow crimped in thought, Bess adjusted the jacket of her blue suit. "Is it possible we have two suspects?"

He tilted his head back and stared at the clouds. "Bite your tongue. No more complications, please."

She left, and he climbed into his vehicle. Hell, while he was on Echo Cliff Point, why not call Sheri? Or stop by? He rubbed his eyes, massaged his sternum.

Although she had friends here, she was alone. No family. Her dad was in Florida and she and her mom didn't get along. Sheri needed him. What was it about her? What made him keep thinking about her? Wanting her? Calling for no real reason other than wanting to hear her voice, warm like heated maple syrup?

Monday night they'd practically set fire to the bed.

She enjoyed sex as much as he did, had fun in bed, knew what would please her, and him. Beyond that, he lost himself in her. That had never happened. After the next morning's session of lovemaking, he had to resist calling in sick so he could stay with her. He'd never before felt that temptation.

Women always disappointed in the long run. Lied, kept secrets, cheated. Like Vicki. He'd been about to ask her to move in with him. He found out she was married only when she told him she couldn't see him anymore because her husband was coming home from Iraq. Fucking bitch cheated on them both. He heard later the guy divorced her ass.

So he was a short-term guy. A relationship was out of the question.

Still, he was worried about Sheri. She was taking precautions—better locks, alarms—and insisted on staying in Dragon Harbor. Said interviewing Miriam's family and friends would be unmanageable if she had to drive back and forth. Not that he wouldn't worry about her in Weymouth too. But since last night, fear for her clawed his chest and would until this dickwad was stopped.

Chapter Twenty-Five

ENOUGH FOR TODAY. Sheri couldn't concentrate anyway. She closed her laptop and stowed the journal she'd been consulting in a desk drawer.

When Miriam's attacker took this year's journal, he could've guessed there were more from previous years and that one might contain something about him. The reason the house was searched. After finding what Miriam thought about Walter Bates, Sheri read not just for the memoir but to look for clues. Nothing so far.

She rose and paced the length of the library. Her mouth wasn't sore today, but her hand went to her throat, where the rope burns had left welts. Did the attacker know the significance of strangling her with a rope? Or was it coincidence?

She kept replaying last night's attack in her mind. Wondering what she could've done to prevent it or stop it. Ten times she asked herself if she'd been reckless.

"Enough!" Since she prided herself on being a rational person who didn't give in to what her nana used to call whim-whams, she concluded she couldn't change anything now and should let it go. She might have another nightmare or two. She'd be fine.

She preferred to turn her thoughts to a certain detective. Smart, strong, an aura of tough competence that only enhanced his sex appeal. Justin seemed to respect her and didn't resent her particular memory talent, unlike some men she'd known.

How long could she let this go on? And what could she call what was between her and Justin? An affair? A romantic relationship? To use an old-fashioned term, a liaison? Hookup or friends with benefits didn't work. She enjoyed his company immensely, and the sex was amazing. Thinking about seeing him sparked a thrill inside her. He made her feel… She had no words.

Whether it ended in a month or tomorrow she couldn't be with Justin again intimately unless she dealt with her past. If she couldn't make peace with her guilt, she could at least face it.

The click of doggy claws on the oak floor followed her down the hall.

In the kitchen, she knelt and caressed Comet's silky ears. "Sweetie, you can't come with me this time. I won't be long. When I return, I promise to throw sticks and the ball for you."

The pup's tail swished back and forth on the floor, and her head tilted as if she understood. But when Sheri stood and opened the mudroom door, Comet dropped to the floor and laid her head between her paws.

She had to go alone, no matter how much she might want the comfort of Comet's presence.

She closed the door behind her, double locked both inner and outer doors, and dumped the keys, the alarm, and her phone in her jacket pockets. The day was cloudy but not cold, so she went on foot. She kept looking behind her, but told herself the attacker wouldn't strike in full daylight. Cars passed, people waved, and she waved back, a friendly small-town gesture.

She was safe enough. But what should be an easy walk to the Tardiff house, point six miles—she'd measured it—bowed her back and twisted her stomach.

As the old farmhouse and what was left of the garage came into view, she nearly turned around. Dread prickled her skin and hitched her breath. She had to force her legs to keep moving her forward.

Finally at the house, she kept the garage in her peripheral vision. Not yet. Tears threatened, but she blinked them away and straightened her shoulders. She made her way to the front porch through overgrown shrubs and across weeds mashed flat by winter's snow and ice.

Weather and age had leached away most of the paint on the house. Few windowpanes remained intact, maybe from kids throwing rocks. Noah's parents had moved away after his death. She'd heard they couldn't bear to stay. No one understood that better than she did.

She turned away and plodded toward the open garage. The rope was gone, but the beam remained. Someone had dragged her away before they cut him down.

She'd tried to build inner walls but had no defense against the gauzy shroud of grief and guilt that clung to her here. Noah had had everything to live for, a full-boat scholarship to Johns Hopkins. And… she ruined everything. Everything. The autopsy said a toxic brew of drugs and alcohol fueled his courage. Courage or cowardice? For a long time since, she'd denied feeling anger because his despair was her fault, but it hovered beneath the guilt.

Staring at that ruin of a garage, Sheri gave in to the stew of emotion that churned inside her. She sank to her knees and wept. "Noah, oh, Noah, I'm so sorry." She released her grief in great hot tears, her guilt in low, keening cries until she had no more tears, no more voice.

When a car door slammed, she looked up to see Justin striding toward her. She struggled to get to her feet, but stumbled. He caught her and wrapped his arms around her and held on even when she tried to break free.

"Take it easy, honey," he said, his warm breath against her temple. "I can't imagine how tough this was for you."

She nodded against his shoulder and stuffed her wad of sodden tissues in a pocket. She let him hold her for a few minutes, then drew in a shaky breath. "I'm okay now."

His gaze steady and comforting, he studied her for a moment before he released her.

"Here, this is what I use for a handkerchief. This one's clean." He handed it over.

"A paper towel? You and my brother. Thanks." She wiped her nose. "How did you know I was here?"

"I didn't. I stopped at the house to see you. Your ride was there. You weren't. I called. No answer."

She pulled her phone from a pocket. She'd wanted only silence while she was here. "On vibrate. Sorry."

His shrug was an eloquent shoulder hike that said "no problem," but there clearly was more. He'd been worried. As he should've been. She'd gone off alone without telling anyone. "It's broad daylight and I have my alarm. New battery."

She expected a smug smile at her defensiveness, but his expression remained sympathetic. "Thought you might be jogging. When I didn't see you the other direction, I was trying this way and found you here. Do you want to tell me about it?"

Maybe that would help. Nodding, she turned toward

the house, him by her side. "A Friday night. Middle of April. Noah went with a bunch of kids to a game in Bayport."

"You didn't go?"

"I didn't feel well. A cold or something, I don't remember now." A cold was what she'd told everyone. "I rode my bike to his house the next morning. All was quiet, blinds closed. Noah's parents were visiting friends somewhere Down East, so I thought at first he'd slept in. And then I heard a creaking noise—" Her throat closed, and she lowered her gaze to the dead grass.

Justin said nothing, just stood quietly beside her.

"It was the wind moving... him... the rope... on the wooden beam. I looked up. At first I didn't understand what I saw." The image was burned into her brain. He'd been hanging there, an overturned crate below him. She ran to him, tried to get his feet onto the crate, and saw his face. Gray and... no longer Noah. "And then I screamed." And screamed. And screamed. For how long she didn't know. She hugged herself and shook her head.

Justin curved an arm around her shoulders and turned her away from the garage. They crossed the yard, Sheri stumbling a bit, the weeds' dampness leaching into her running shoes. The knees of her jeans were already soaked.

"I read the report," he said. "A jogger stopped when they heard your screams. A truck driver called the police."

"I haven't been back here since." She waved to encompass the Tardiff property. "I decided it was time to face it."

"And now?"

"I feel better." Amazingly, she did. If he asked if she

238

still loved Noah, she could say no, not for a long time. The guilt would always haunt her, but perhaps the grief and anger would fade away.

"What are the outbuildings there behind the house?"

"Barn and some sheds and pens. The Tardiffs kept chickens and goats. In the summer, they always had a big garden and a vegetable stand at the roadside."

They headed into the backyard. The sheds had rotted like the rest of the structures. But Justin was staring at the ground. When she started forward, he stretched out his arm as a barrier.

"What is it?"

"Tire tracks. Looks like a truck of some kind, probably a pickup." He asked her to stay there while he fetched something from his SUV.

Someone had tossed three beer cans near the tire tracks. Not particularly dirty, colors bright.

He returned with small paper bags. Sitting on his haunches, he stuck his pen in the first can and dropped it in a bag. He repeated this with the others. Liquid drizzled from one of them. Rainwater or beer?

She swallowed. "Could this have been the murderer? Did he park here and then go to the gazebo to wait for Adam Spear?"

"A possibility." Justin stood. "I'll have these tested and get a tech team out here to get casts of the tire tracks." He grinned. "You have my thanks for leading me to this."

"Unless it was just kids hiding beers from the parents."

"Also a possibility. No matter what I find out, I'm glad I stopped." He kissed her and curved his free arm around her shoulders as they headed back to his SUV.

He placed the bags in a plastic bin in the SUV's cargo space.

"You must've been at the Spear house," she said. "I saw Detective Peters and a locksmith's van go by. Are you close to a breakthrough?"

"You do like to push the boundary, don't you, honey?" He scraped fingers through his hair. "No breakthrough. And nothing I can tell you. Or maybe one thing. I don't see Walter Bates being organized enough to have plotted or carried out the crimes."

"Thank you for that. One down and too many to go."

****

JUSTIN BARELY STOPPED himself from slamming the phone on the dashboard. One of the techs just reported wet weather had degraded the tire tracks at the Tardiff house too much for a decent cast. Still working on the beer cans, she'd added.

He drove past the Littlefield house, but Sheri's SUV wasn't there. Yesterday she'd been damned torn up about her old boyfriend. Had to be traumatic discovering his lifeless body suspended from the beam. Happened years ago, but she hadn't really dealt with it. Strange for such an intelligent and level-headed woman. But he had the feeling she'd confided more to him than she'd told others. Except maybe her friend Deb.

Soon emergency vehicles beside the East Road came into view, and he pulled in behind Chief Galt's unit. Yesterday's gray skies had cleared, but the cool air had him reaching for his windbreaker. All the windows and doors of Reed Keniston's Cape stood open to the breeze.

The chief met him in the driveway behind a Bayport Energy Company truck. "Wylde, come on in. I wouldn't have counted this as anything but an accident, but, well, you'll see. EMTs are finished with Keniston—checked his vitals and provided oxygen. I've talked to him."

"All I got was he was unconscious and unresponsive," Justin said as they trooped up the gravel drive. What do you know so far?"

"My daughter cleans house for Keniston on Fridays." Galt lifted his cap and resettled it. "She arrived about nine and smelled gas. Found him on the hallway floor. When she couldn't wake him, she opened windows and doors and called 911. EMTs are waiting. Told them you might want a word. The house is clear now, and the gas company technician's waiting for us in the kitchen. He wore his work gloves when he moved the stove. Neither of us touched the rest."

The porch led into a small mudroom, and then into the kitchen. Typical of older Capes, it was small with a low ceiling, but with new, high-end appliances as well as new cupboards and counters. A look Justin's mother would've considered odd in an antique house.

The gas range was pulled out from the wall at an angle. Behind it, a work light and an open tool kit sat on the floor. A slim gray-haired man stood up from a high-backed wooden chair at the kitchen table as they entered. His green work shirt bore the Bayport Energy logo on the pocket and the name Larry above.

"Tell the detective here what you found."

Galt had said on the phone he figured this to be part of the overall case, so Justin had called for an evidence team, but they were still en route from Augusta.

He introduced himself to the technician and took his information, asking permission to record their conversation. "I appreciate any help you can give us."

"Glad to," Larry said. "No gas lines out here. Folks have propane tanks outside with lines leadin' in to their gas cook stoves and heaters."

"Sure. Most of the state's like that," Justin said. "Was there a leak?" Although a simple leak wouldn't be why the police were called.

"No leak." At the stove, Larry clicked on his work light and pointed out the copper gas line from outside and the flexible tube snaking into the stove. The copper fitting that should've connected the two had detached from the line, and the tube hung loose.

"Could that fitting fall off by accident, or could vibration cause it?" Justin asked.

"Nope." He bristled, squared his shoulders. "Company takes pride in our expertise. We make sure that compression nut's fitted proper. No vibration's gonna shake it loose. Somebody wrenched 'er off on purpose."

Obvious scratches on the fitting. "One more question, Larry. If gas was pouring out, like that open pipe suggests, should Mr. Keniston have smelled it?"

"Surprised he didn't. LP gas has no odor, so Bayport Energy and every other company I know of adds something with a distinctive odor, like ethyl mercaptan."

"Thanks, Larry. You've been a big help. This is a crime scene, so we'll have to leave the stove as is until the evidence techs finish."

The technician packed up his tools and left.

Justin took photos with his phone, and the chief headed out, saying he had reports to write. Justin wandered down the hallway in search of Reed Keniston. Water running and a feminine voice singing a Springsteen classic located Genie Galt upstairs. He'd talk to her later.

He found Keniston stretched out on the living room sofa. Contemporary furnishings crowded the small room. A glass of water and a box of tissues sat on the side table where the man's cane was propped.

He levered himself to a sitting position with effort when Justin entered. He wore a big Irish-knit sweater and baggy corduroys. Worn boat shoes, maybe his usual house shoes. Heavier, waterproof shoes had been in the mudroom.

"Come in, Detective, and have a seat." His voice was nasal, scratchy. He grabbed a tissue and blew his nose. "Sorry. Bit of a cold. Stupid reason, but maybe why I didn't smell the gas. I'll tell you what I told the chief, but I don't see this as a state case."

"Might not be, but it doesn't hurt to cover all the bases." Justin chose a side chair and followed protocol before recording their conversation. "What happened this morning?"

"I went to the Wheelhouse for breakfast." Keniston scratched the bridge of his prominent nose and grinned. "A dive, but their cook does a great breakfast. Best pancakes on the coast."

"Have to try it sometime. When you went out, did you lock your door?"

"No, I don't generally lock up unless I'm going out of town. I get occasional deliveries from a couple of the fishermen. If I'm not here, they can come put the fish or shellfish in my fridge. And today Genie might've arrived before I returned."

Damn, another Mainer who didn't lock up. Even this man who'd lived in the San Francisco Bay area for years. God save him from careless citizens.

"The attack on Miriam Littlefield in her house didn't change your habit?" he said.

Keniston's chin dipped and his shoulders drooped. "I should've locked up, I know, and will now, but I didn't think we had a crime wave."

Neither had Justin. Until now, crimes on this sleepy peninsula involved domestic abuse, driving while intoxicated, or vandalism. Galt had said their few home invasions were one half of a family feuding with the other half.

"What happened when you returned this morning?"

His forehead crimped as he thought about it. "I put away dishes, got chicken out of the freezer." He shook his head, ran a hand over his hair. "I had trouble breathing, but chalked it up to the cold. Anything after that is fuzzy. I remember feeling nauseous and heading to the bathroom. Then nothing until EMTs were bending over me."

His statement jibed with what Galt had said. Justin would know more after talking to Genie and the EMT crew.

"You probably want to get some rest, but I'm talking to everybody on the visitor list for Mrs. Littlefield. You up to a few more questions?"

"Shoot." Keniston reached for another tissue and dabbed at his nose.

"Tell me about your visits to her in the hospital."

"Let's see." His gaze rose to the ceiling. "I went twice to sit with her, last Wednesday and Thursday about two o'clock. I signed in at the nurses' desk and went to her room. Took something to read. My aunt's so full of life. Terrible thing, sad to see her just lying there."

Justin questioned him further about who else he'd

244

seen there, anybody who didn't belong, but Keniston only shrugged and said he saw little except the patient and the pages of his professional journal.

"If you don't mind, I have other questions relating to the Spear murder."

"I know nothing about that except what I've seen in the news. But go ahead." He leaned forward. The hint of derision in his expression suggested he was humoring Justin.

"Did you hold a grudge against Adam Spear for your dad's lawn-care business failing?"

He stared at the crumpled tissue, then looked up. "People think I ought to blame Spear. A lot of folks back then said it was his fault Dad's business failed. But it was Dad's drinking that ruined it. He lost more contracts than that one. He'd been drinking heavily when he drove the truck into that oak tree. I miss them very much." He blinked a few times.

"A tough loss. I'm sorry, Mr. Keniston," Justin said.

"Thanks." He brightened. "Hey, I was lucky today. I don't like law suits, but something like that on a new gas range… a valve or something just loosening up. I might have to talk to Sydney about Bayport Energy's liability."

Justin kept the recorder running. Keniston seemed to have recovered enough to deal with the facts. Now rather than later worked.

"The connector between the two lines at the back of the range didn't loosen on its own. Somebody opened it."

Keniston stared for a long moment, a puzzled frown on his face "Deliberate you say?"

"Yes, on purpose. And if Genie hadn't arrived when she did or if she or you had turned on a light or lit a match, we wouldn't be having this conversation."

He collapsed against the cushion, his eyes wide. "Holy shit! Why? Who would do that?"

"Exactly what I'd like to know," Justin said. "Who might want to kill you?"

Chapter Twenty-Six

SHERI STIRRED THE chicken and vegetables before covering the cast-iron pot and closing the oven door. Standing shoulder to shoulder with Justin at the range turned her on like one of the stovetop burners, glowing and sizzling her juices. It was also a little intimidating. She'd never cooked with a man before, and it seemed too domestic. More *involved* than she'd ever permitted herself. Not that she was going to do anything to change that tonight.

Since she was already deep in the case, or cases, he'd shared with her tonight that Miriam's attacker had intended to inject her with fentanyl, enough to cause death within minutes, and Sheri's intervention had scared him off. None of the drug got in Miriam.

Thank God. Sheri shuddered. After the emotional return to the Tardiff place the other day, she wanted to relax and enjoy the evening—and the night—with Justin. Without her baggage and without talk of murder. Or attempted murder.

"Damn, that chicken smells great," he said as he mashed cream and butter into the potatoes. Aromas of poultry and wine sauce filled the kitchen.

"True chefs would scream French curses at the shortcuts in this coq au vin recipe, but Mom didn't have four hours to create the authentic dish. She was a full-time teacher when Mike and I were growing up."

"Thought you and your mom didn't get along that well." He added parsley and stirred.

"We butted heads a lot, and still do, but working together in the kitchen was okay. Mike cooks too." She poked him with the spoon handle and winked. "Hey, you know all about my issues with my mom, but you never talk about yours. Some deep, dark secret there?"

He lowered his head, not looking at her, and stirred the potatoes harder. Her stomach tightened. Had she crossed a line? He covered the potato pot and turned to her.

"Yes, a secret I've kept to myself since I was a senior in high school." His face blanked, but not to his cop look but a deliberately unemotional, flat expression.

This might be the family secret he alluded to once before. She didn't want to trap him into sharing. "You don't have to tell me. I was teasing."

"I know. But I want to. You're the only person I've wanted to tell." He swallowed. "We got out early that day for a teacher meeting or something. I went to the medical office where Mom was the office nurse. Nobody was in the waiting room, so I went on back to the doctor's office. I walked in on him and my mom having sex on his office chair."

"Oh, Justin, how awful for you." She gripped his forearm. The muscles were as hard as steel girders.

"I turned and ran out, ran all the way home. I couldn't blot from my mind what I'd seen. Dad was still at his office, but Mom showed up five minutes after me. Begged me not to tell Dad and swore it would never happen again. I agreed and kept quiet because I had no idea how else to deal with what I'd seen or the anger raging through me." He pressed a fist to his chest as if struggling to contain that fury. "She quit that job and went to work for a female pediatrician."

"And you kept this secret all this time. No wonder you hate secrets." And the reason he didn't have long-term relationships. He didn't trust women. His relationship with his mother was more strained than Sheri experienced.

"And lies." His blue gaze was sharp enough to cut glass, and his lips were tight against his teeth. "I've… known other women I trusted but shouldn't have."

If she were the woman he thought she was, a woman he could trust, she'd divulge her own dirty secret. But she wasn't. And now her stomach churned as his must have back then.

"Sometimes we have to let go the things that damage our lives and move on." As if she'd followed that advice. "Didn't you tell me something like that a few days ago?"

Justin's expression brightened. "I have moved on. I have a job I love and busy life. Enough of that downer. I feel better now I've told you, so let's enjoy tonight." He brushed a kiss on her lips. "I'm drooling like Comet, and my stomach's begging. How much longer?"

Sheri checked out the dog on her blanket in the corner. Not lying, sitting at attention and yes, drooling. "She had her supper, and I recall you scarfing down crackers and cheese a while ago."

"Snacks are no substitute for coq au vin. I repeat, how long?"

"Almost done. How are the mashers coming?"

He peered in the pot. "You can't hurry a real chef." When she slanted him a skeptical look, he added, "You got me. No chef. Mashed potatoes are in my repertoire, my *short* repertoire."

"A man of many talents."

"Some of which I'll demonstrate later. I hope. Here's a sample." He turned off the burner. Pulling her close, he kissed her thoroughly, tasting of red wine, as their tongues tangled and teeth grazed. A curl of need burned through her all the way to her toes.

The timer dinged.

His head came up and he hauled in a breath. "Saved by the bell sure as shit doesn't fit here."

"But it does save supper." She kissed him lightly and pulled away. "And now I can hardly wait for dessert."

"Then we have two desserts, cheesecake and another later." He curved a hand over her hair and brushed a lock from her shoulder.

"Cheesecake? My favorite!" She removed the chicken onto a hot pad and ditched her hot mitts. She slapped the sides of her thighs. "I'll have to run twice as far tomorrow."

He grabbed her again, holding her to him with both hands on her derriere. She murmured and her pulse quickened, her blood fizzing as if she'd touched a live electric wire. She clung to him and reveled in his hardness and earthy scent.

Heat raced down Justin's spine when she kissed him back, her tongue against his, sweet and insistent. The need to make love with her now on the kitchen table warred with other instincts, emotions he refused to name.

Stepping away was almost painful. He kissed his way upward and then leaned his forehead against hers. She matched him breath for breath. They panted as if they'd swum across the bay.

"Sheri, we've talked about this. Running on the

peninsula could be dangerous."

"Then you'll have to run with me."

"I'll do just that tomorrow morning." He almost growled. He stepped back before he obeyed his inner cave man and ordered her to stay locked in the house. As if that would work. It might get him kicked to the curb. "With my service pistol on my hip."

Putting dinner on the table meant a cease fire in their safety discussion, but no truce.

Sharing the food and wine, a nice Zinfandel she'd also used in the chicken dish, they talked about everything but the danger. He grinned when she proved to know as much about the new Red Sox players as he did. She asked about his police work in general, which he took as an opening for after the meal.

After the cheesecake and over coffee, they both declared the meal a ten.

"I know you're aware of the danger, so why do you insist on these solo runs?" He watched her as she took a sip of coffee. A stalling tactic.

"I have to exercise. My work involves mostly sitting, either doing research or writing on my laptop. I need to move or I get fidgety. Besides, as you may have noticed, I also enjoy food. I wasn't kidding about my thighs."

"Your thighs are perfect." He arched an eyebrow and affected a leer.

Her response was a clear, happy laugh that reassured him and heated his blood.

"Well played, sir."

Justin watched Sheri's mouth as she tasted the cheesecake. He couldn't think of the last time he'd felt this way, the need to touch her in every way possible.

She fascinated him and turned him on, and somehow she'd torn down some of his walls and tempted him to trust her. He took risks all the time, but a real relationship? He needed to protect himself, but a few weeks longer wouldn't be reckless. And Weymouth was only forty minutes from his rental in Gardiner.

He lifted her free hand and kissed the palm. "You said you were coming close to all you can do on the memoir alone. Won't you be moving back to Weymouth soon?"

"I will. And taking Comet with me." Her fingers squeezed his hand and tugged free. "She can ride back and forth with me when I need to be here. I'm hoping Miriam will be able to work with me before long. The neurosurgeon told the family he'll bring Miriam out of the drug-induced coma soon. She'll need a lot of care, but she'll recover."

"That's great news." He cleared his throat. "I've never been good at relationships. Some of it's the job, and some is me. But even after this case ends, I'd like us to keep seeing each other."

She was silent, her brown eyes studying him, her mouth serious, and then she smiled, and his heart started again. "I'd like that too."

"I can't be here to run with you every day. So I want you to be careful."

"I *am* careful. I carry the pepper spray and my SOS alarm. And my phone. I keep my eyes open." She lowered her gaze and lifted a bite of dessert. "Maybe I need a gun, a pistol, smaller than yours though. What about a Beretta?"

Mischief lighted her eyes, so maybe she wasn't serious, but still… "In general, a gun's not great for self-defense." For females, but he'd omit that. "Unless you want to get training, enough for comfort with the gun. Or else you could fumble it or fire wildly or shoot yourself. And likely lose the gun to your attacker."

"So much for that idea." She looked away and sighed. "I keep thinking there's something I've missed, something I should know or have seen. That maybe a morning jog will *jog* something in my brain."

The state police had issued a statement today, so she was bound to hear soon. Better coming from him. She knew the man, so maybe she'd have a take on things.

"There's been another attack that may be part of the Spear case. Or may not. You heard about Reed Keniston and the gas?"

Eyes wide, she leaned forward, flattened a palm on the table. "But I heard a loose valve or a leak on the gas range."

"No loose valve. Somebody deliberately opened the fitting connecting the two gas lines, the one from outside to the one feeding into the stove."

"How can you be certain it was deliberate?"

"The gas company repairman insisted it wouldn't loosen on its own."

He couldn't tell her the rest. Scratches on the fitting indicated a tool worked the nut loose. Justin bagged it, and if it turned out the two cases were connected, maybe finding the tool would nail the guy. Or the fingerprints would. He had his doubts about the scratches, but Galt seemed to think they had a chance for a bluff to work, that is *if* they had a suspect. He'd struck out with Keniston providing names of enemies. The man said he didn't know of any. And lots of folks knew he often went to breakfast at the Wheelhouse.

She stared, thinking, at her plate. "I can't imagine there's no connection to the rest of what's going on. Too much of a coincidence."

"Genie said when she cleaned, nothing looked out of place." He drank the last of his coffee. "She confided that she didn't know why 'Mr. K' wanted his house cleaned every week. It hardly had time to get dirty, and she has to be sure to leave everything in its proper place."

"That sounds like the Reed I remember from school. He tutored me in algebra. All the books and papers and his pencils were lined up just so."

"You needed help with math? I'm shocked."

She shook her head. "Not a math whiz. I'm a writer. I take after Mom."

"What can you tell me about Reed Keniston?"

"Not much. He worked in Silicon Valley for years and returned home a few years ago. He retired after a ski accident, the reason for the cane. He seems nice enough but strikes me as trying too hard in social settings, maybe a nerd out of his element. I learned after returning to Dragon Harbor he was Miriam's great-nephew."

Another sad subject. He picked up the plates and headed for the kitchen.

After they cleaned up, they both took Comet out. He wasn't about to let her step out into the dark without an escort. When they returned, the little dog trotted off with her bedtime biscuit.

"You going to send me home tonight?"

"I couldn't possibly send away a man who makes such great mashers and brings cheesecake."

Chapter Twenty-Seven

SHERI WAITED IN her car while Deb talked to Buddy Gamage. Tuesday afternoon was her turn to sub at the fish co-op sales counter, so Sheri'd brought lunch to share.

She'd spent the last two days interviewing the Littlefield siblings for stories about their mother. More fascinating background on Miriam, but Sheri struggled to concentrate while transcribing stories into anecdotes that could fit between Miriam's reminiscences. Her mind — and body — kept replaying her Saturday and Sunday morning with Justin.

Just remembering heated her skin and loosened her thigh muscles. He was tender and smart and sexy as hell. In a flash he could turn so protective, the intensity in his eyes mesmerized her and made her heart go wild. What she felt for him was simply lust. And respect. She liked him. A lot. That was all. All it could be.

But something about him made her want, want more than she could have.

His confiding in her humbled her but also made her want to hide her face and curl up in a ball. She couldn't bear to return his trust with her truth. He would look at her with loathing, and she'd lose what little time she had left with him. She'd have to end their relationship — yes, she was thinking of it as that — but not yet.

"I told Buddy only a tune-up, no tire rotation," Deb

said as she climbed in. "I heard sirens earlier. You know where they went?"

Sheri shook away her thoughts, drew a deep breath against her longings and whatever else churned in her chest.

"No idea. I didn't see anything on the way here."

Deb sniffed the air. "So what'd you pack for lunch? Something from Donna's?"

"One dish is Donna's. I can't make coleslaw as delish as hers. But the caprese sandwiches on ciabatta bread and the lemon cookies are mine. It'll be chilly at the co-op, so my beverage of choice is coffee." She drove out of the village proper and toward the fishing docks.

"Yum. My mouth is watering already." Deb looked longingly at the basket in the backseat. "Dad said he didn't know how you coaxed out his youthful misadventures."

Sheri had interviewed him that morning. "He was eager to share. When he got into some trouble as a teen, Miriam made certain he learned from his mistakes." What Noble had said was more specific. *"Mom made me admit to the neighbors I was the one who'd peppered their mailbox with shotgun pellets. Had to earn money and buy them a new one."* She glanced at her friend. No, she'd read it eventually.

"So is Miriam's memoir now a tell-all?"

"Hard to say. She might not want to share page space with her children and grandchildren."

Deb stuck out her lower lip. "When we were kids, you weren't this mean." Her giggle spoiled her pretend pout. "I know most of Dad's stories anyway. He confessed long ago. But I'll bet Aunt Sydney, Attorney at Law, wasn't a cooperative witness."

"You got that right." Sydney hadn't volunteered any details about her youth, leaving Sheri to pose question after question. After a painful forty-five minutes and few notes to show for it, she gave up and asked Sydney to write out something when she came up with a memory to share. At some point, Sheri would telephone the youngest Littlefield, Craig. Gawd, she hoped he'd be more forthcoming than his sister.

"How was the weekend with the lover-boy detective?" Deb turned toward Sheri and made herself comfortable, settling in for a gabfest.

"That's not a tell-all either." Deb didn't know the deep reasons for her reluctance to get involved. Maybe someday, but not yet. "We had a great evening over dinner."

"And *after* dinner?"

"And after dinner. We have some things in common, and yes, he's fun and sexy and strong, etcetera. That's it."

"I know that tone of voice. It means The End." She flounced in her seat and faced forward. Deb knew when to stop probing.

"Thanks. You do know me."

Sheri would leave Dragon Harbor soon. The dining room furniture would be moved into the library and the dining room transformed into Miriam's bedroom. Deb and Vera had hired a contractor to enlarge the first-floor powder room.

Sheri drove down the rutted dirt road leading to the working docks. At the co-op's dancing-fish sign, she started to turn toward the parking lot. Beside a DHPD cruiser, its light bar flashing, an officer holding up a hand froze her hands on the steering wheel and her breath in her lungs. *Oh, God, what now?*

"This is where the sirens were headed," Deb said, her voice pitched higher. She clutched Sheri's elbow.

Ahead, all was flashing lights and emergency personnel. The Dragon Harbor ambulance blocked the building entrance, and a police SUV sat beside pickup trucks, one also with flashing lights.

As the officer marched up to the driver side, Sheri managed to peel her fingers off the wheel. She shifted into Park and lowered the window.

His gaze swept them and the car's interior, assessing, before he returned his attention to her. "Ma'am, you'll have to move your vehicle off to the side."

The reason for his order was heading toward her. The siren blared *bruup-bruup* warnings in short bursts as the ambulance neared. She threw the gearshift into Drive. As soon as she'd pulled over onto the grass, the siren ramped up and the vehicle raced away.

The officer strode toward them with swagger, thumbs tucked in his utility belt. He looked to be in his mid-twenties. His appearance, the angular body and slot-like mouth, seemed familiar.

"What's going on—" she checked the brass tag beside his badge "—Officer Gamage?" Her voice sounded hoarse, and swallowing took effort. She couldn't get words out to ask who was in the ambulance.

Leaning over the console, Deb fluttered a hand at him. "Hi, I heard you were working for the town."

His lean cheeks colored. "Hey, Mrs. Delano. Chief's sending me to the academy next month. How you doin'?"

"Okay so far. Tell your mom hi from me. This is my

friend Sheri Harte." To Sheri, she said "Joe is Buddy's son."

No wonder he looked familiar. He tipped the brim of his cap and eyed her with curiosity.

"Who's hurt?" Deb asked.

He worked his jaw. "Boyd Rankin. Can't tell you no more."

The chill of frost ran up Sheri's spine. *Not Boyd...*

"C'mon, Joe," Deb said in her most persuasive mom tone. "Len's part time on the force, and everyone'll know soon enough anyway. We both know Boyd. Maybe we could help."

Joe looked back at the cluster of people at the co-op. He adjusted his duty belt.

"Some fishermen arrived a while ago with their catches. Saw Rankin's truck was here." He hooked a thumb back toward the direction of the pickups. "But when they went inside, they couldn't find him. They looked all around, finally checked in the big walk-in freezer."

Sheri gasped, guessing what was coming. Beside her, Deb seemed to hold her breath.

"Rankin was inside. They said he was unconscious, near frozen. Called 911 right away. I was just down the road on patrol, so I come first."

"Poor Boyd." Sheri spoke because Deb seemed unable to.

A muscle in Joe Gamage's jaw jumped, and his mouth tightened to a thin line. "Yup." He shook himself into an official stance, shoulders back, chin up. "You folks'll have to leave. This is a crime scene." Behind him, officers were stringing familiar yellow tape at the building.

****

JUSTIN CARRIED IN a big box and set it on his desk. The MCU office was nearly empty. Most detectives were at a meeting in the lieutenant's office.

The fingerprints on the beer cans found behind the Tardiff farmhouse belonged to Steve Spear. That had given them cause for a search warrant of his Portland apartment, so Justin and Bess had spent that morning interviewing him.

Steve swore he'd hidden from sight only to wait until his father went to work before visiting his mother. Or he could've been sitting there, drinking courage to murder his father. But how did that connect to the other attacks? Steve had no alibi for any of them. In his apartment, he said, where techs found only his fingerprints and one other. Those of the cleaner, according to Steve. Hired by Angela, she'd worked yesterday. Too thorough or they might have had the girlfriend's prints.

But the search had yielded the two boxes Sheri saw him carry from the Spear house, this one and a second. They contained the files from his father's home office.

"Any word yet on Boyd Rankin?" Bess Peters said as she entered with the other box.

"He made it through the night," Justin said. "They have him on re-warming treatments, inside and out, and a heart monitor. Doctor said if anybody could survive that cold, it's a big tough guy like Rankin. Part of the problem is nobody knows how long he was in that freezer."

Both he and Bess had spent yesterday afternoon in Dragon Harbor, at the fish co-op and on the docks interviewing boat captains and crew. And dodging reporters. He parroted "no comment" and "you'll have to wait for an official statement" so many times he felt like the feathered critter. On TV, the local news broadcasts broadcast daily updates— whether or not there was any change—over the murders and attacks in Dragon Harbor. Justin winced when one anchor called it a crime wave. And again when a so-called expert suggested the crimes could be the work of a serial killer.

Connected, yes, but a serial killer? Didn't feel right to him.

Too many tire tracks in the co-op parking area to sort out who was there when. Boats were out during the morning's high tide, so nobody saw what went on anywhere near the building. Too many fingerprints in the public part, and the back room was kept sanitized, so he had little hope of a set of prints leading to the perpetrator.

Bess set her box beside the other on a long table near their adjoining cubicles. "This missing girlfriend is a puzzle. She gets Steve to look for valuables at his folks' and then vanishes."

"A sketchy character, Ellie Stone. And cautious, not letting him take her picture." Steve had said she was superstitious about having her picture taken.

Sure. Justin opened one box and both donned latex gloves. They sat and leafed through stacks of files, taking notes and adding a new label to each folder.

When Bess's phone rang, she stepped away and took the call. A few minutes later, she returned and waved her tablet at him. Yesterday, I put in a call to the Bayport Hospital security chief. Just fishing, but he just got back to me. Some lapses two weeks ago in the laundry department where they were having renovations done. I asked about surgical scrubs, but he said they had trouble keeping an accurate count. But here's the kicker. Gil MacRae's company was doing the finish work. He was there nearly every day checking on the work.

"So another suspect with access to scrubs." Justin looked away, analyzing. "He fits the body type to impersonate Miriam's surgeon. Could've gotten the fentanyl on the street."

They discussed previous interviews with MacRae before going back to Spear's files.

A few contained old client files, cases that appeared closed. Most folders held printouts of reports on investments, offshore at places like the Cayman Islands. Dates started from when Adam Spear won the big paper-company case. Built his fancy house and invested the rest of his windfall wisely, it seemed. Justin emitted a low whistle at the amounts.

"You seeing what I'm seeing?" Bess said. "Millions. Spear was stinkin' rich."

"Yeah, but look closely at the reports. No account numbers on them."

"And no inserts in the folders for cashing out or investing more. You think the girlfriend saw there was no payoff in young Steve and that's why she split?"

"Makes sense. She may have done this before. You don't suppose she has a record?"

Justin grinned. "Wouldn't hurt to find out if her fingerprints are on any of these printouts."

He phoned for evidence techs to pick up the boxes. While they waited, they closed up the first box and tackled the other. More of the same, with more recent dates. By the time they finished, the hour was late.

Justin stood and stretched. "That's it for me. Tomorrow I need to go back to Dragon Harbor and finish up at the crime scene. The most recent one. One more walk-through to release the co-op for opening. It's sooner than I'd like, but the fishermen need to open."

"And to see Sheri?" Bess set down her coffee and cocked her head.

"To check on her."

Her smirk said she wasn't buying it. "You denying the hot romance between you two?"

"Bess." He folded his arms. "You do recall somebody tried to kill her?"

"Of course, and you ought to *check on* Sheri." Her expression softened, and she leaned toward him. "But you phone her two, three times a day, spend nights in Dragon Harbor—and not just weekends. Yes, I've seen your overnight duffel in your unit. You're spending more time there than in your place in Gardiner. You haven't moved on yet, like usual. So all I'm saying is she must be something special, and it's about time."

Justin's phone chimed, and he pulled it from his pocket. He didn't recognize the number. "Major Crimes Unit, Detective Wylde speaking."

He listened for a moment, thanked the caller, and disconnected.

"That was the Bayport Hospital. Boyd Rankin just died."

Chapter Twenty-Eight

"I CAN'T BELIEVE it." Sheri held onto the back of a kitchen chair and drew a shaky breath. She pictured Boyd outside the general store, a bear of a man hugging the breath from her. "When they took him off in the ambulance, I thought he'd recover, be okay."

"If it's any comfort," Justin said, "his mother and sisters were there when he passed."

"That's good." She blew her nose. "Maybe he knew somehow they were with him. His dad died a few years ago. Boyd is—*was* so robust, such a force. Can you tell me anything more?"

Justin hooked his windbreaker from another chair and sat to tie his running shoes. "I can. You know nearly as much as the police about this case anyway. Rankin had been in the freezer too long to survive is the short answer. His body temperature dipped so low his organs couldn't function. The hospital did everything they could, but his heart gave out. The co-op's no longer a crime scene, and they can open up."

So he'd come this Friday afternoon to run with her, saying this case had kept him out of the gym and on the road, but on wheels. She suspected his cases were often like that, and this was a sneaky way to protect her. She wouldn't complain or admit, even to herself, how that melted her insides. And made her yearn.

Comet nudged her leg, looked up with soulful eyes.

Sheri knelt and buried her face in soft fur and warmth. "I'm okay, sweetie."

They'd agreed at the start to keep their relationship casual, but this felt nothing like casual. Especially since he'd shared the moment that defined his life. For years, she'd kept her heart whole, never allowing a man too close. Not that there'd been that many, and none who'd tempted her to yield, to break her promise. Justin was different, but whatever he felt for her, he hadn't said. Nor had she. And she wouldn't.

But whatever either of them felt, she couldn't let it change things.

"Hey, I'm sorry about your friend," he said, pulling her up and into his arms. "If you don't feel like running, we can hang out here."

She'd been so deep in thought she didn't notice he'd donned his jacket, ready to go. "No, I'm ready. I need the exercise as much as you."

"Good." He eyed her warm-up pants. "I just wish it was warmer. I'd like to watch those legs while we run."

"Dangerous. I can picture you tripping over your own feet."

He laughed and delivered a quick kiss.

After telling Comet to stay, she slipped on her jacket and locked up.

They started at a slow pace toward the Point. April's rains and soggy ground had dried, and May began with a predicted stretch of sunny days coaxing green shoots to sprout in lawns. Few vehicles passed them, and they could admire the scenery—a sailboat coming about beyond the cliffs, daffodils exploding in a yard, painters refreshing the exterior of an old Cape. She let the warmer weather and sunshine cheer her.

"About poor Boyd," she said as they turned toward the East Road, "Deb told me the co-op bought the second-hand freezer cheap because the inside safety release was broken. They kept a five-gallon bucket of cement beside the door for propping it open whenever someone went inside. Could the bucket have fallen over so the door closed? Are you certain someone shut him up in there on purpose?"

"Dammit, Sheri, I don't want this to be another murder anymore than you do, but yes, I'm certain." He reached for her hand and slowed their pace. "The ME will make this official, but somebody whacked Rankin over the head with twenty pounds of frozen haddock and dragged the doorstop away to a far corner. Somebody who knew about the broken safety release."

"That's the other thing Deb told me. Everyone in town knows about the freezer lock and the bucket of cement. At least everyone who's ever worked at the co-op or bought fish."

"Hell of a thing. But it points to the attacker being somebody local." He kissed her hand and released it.

They picked up the pace and followed Sheri's usual five-mile route past the Devil's Elbow and then back. Afterward, Sheri retrieved Comet for the cool-down. The dog bounced her joy when she clicked on the leash.

Justin had to leave early the next morning, so they had an early dinner at the Eastward Inn, which opened mid-week that month. Both ordered the seafood paella, loaded with scallops, mussels, lobster, and haddock.

After they returned to the house, they settled with glasses of wine before the library fire.

The black-bound book on the side table caught her

eye. She picked it up. "I meant to show you this morning, but losing Boyd erased it from my mind. I ran across something in here that might be related to your investigation. Read the right-hand page where her ribbon bookmark is." She leaned back and sipped her wine. "She wrote this not long after Reed's parents died."

Eyebrows raised, he opened the diary and read. He rubbed his chin. "After the gas incident, I asked him about their deaths. He said back then people suggested it was Spear's fault his father started drinking, but the drinking began before the business went downhill. He said he didn't blame Adam Spear for firing his dad." Justin tapped his index finger on the journal page. "According to what Miriam wrote here, he believed the opposite. Reed did blame Spear. Was angry and resentful."

"I thought you should see this because Miriam seemed very concerned something wasn't right with Reed." She set down her goblet and threaded her fingers together. "Then after he went to live with the MacRaes, she noted that things evened out for him. He continued at MIT, where he had a scholarship. Maybe his initial grief colored his perspective and later he understood his father's drinking was what caused his business to fail."

"Possible." Justin's drawn brow said skepticism.

"At least Reed lived. The gas didn't kill him. It tore all that class apart when Noah died." Her pulse leaped and she shot to her feet. She held her hands out to the flames' warmth as her mind raced. The next words rasped in her throat. "That would've meant... three in that high school class."

As he jerked up straight, wine splashed onto his hand. "What did you say?"

"They were in the same class—Noah, Boyd, and Reed. Along with my brother. Oh." Her hands shook, and she twisted them together.

"And Stephen Spear, if I'm remembering correctly."

"Steve, yes. Oh my God, all of them." The tension of it hurt her head as she searched her memory. "Mike, Noah, and Boyd, Deb's husband Len's older brother, and one or two others were a tight bunch."

He came to his feet and placed his big hands on her shoulders. The warmth and strength in them calmed her.

"A clique, the BMOCs?" he said.

"I was two years younger. Although I was Noah's girlfriend, I was such a nerd, I didn't grasp the social dynamics, but the Big Men on Campus moniker makes sense. Reed hung out with them sometimes, and I saw Steve with them only in a big group. That high school's closed now. Even then it was small. The class couldn't have been more than twenty, twenty-five kids."

"Apparently Steve was often in trouble. He dropped out junior year." He jotted a few lines in his notebook. "I might as well tell you that we executed a search warrant at his apartment yesterday. Only thing of interest was those boxes you saw him lug to his pickup. They contained printouts of his dad's investments. He said his girlfriend, the one nobody can find including him, suggested he deserved some of what his dad had. Young Spear found the keys to the file cabinet and the safe combination in the home office and helped himself."

"This mysterious girlfriend sounds like a winner, urging him to steal from his father's estate. And from his mother." Brows drawn together, she shook her head.

"The twist of fate is that the printouts won't do him any good. No passwords, no account numbers. Adam was just saving back-ups it seems. We haven't found his real records yet. Although I'm not certain it matters, I wish we could find this Ellie Stone. She split soon after he brought those boxes home."

When he pulled her into his embrace, she leaned into his strength. He always knew. "It's terrifying. Someone seems to be stalking all those guys." *And me.* She shuddered.

"I'll talk to Steve about taking precautions. Since your brother's part of the group, you should alert him to watch for trouble."

"I'll call him now. Sometimes he stays up late working." She didn't want to wait. She pulled away with reluctance and picked up her phone from the side table.

When Mike answered, she explained about possible danger, and he said he read about the deaths online, saw the TV news coverage. Then she asked him a few questions and listened carefully. "Thanks, Mike. I'll let you know. Be careful. Love you. Bye."

"Well?"

"He'll be careful." She heaved a sigh and blinked away tears. "He added something you'll want to hear. Two weeks ago, his car went off the interstate and into a ditch. He wasn't hurt, thank God, but the car's in the body shop. Here's the significant part. The cause of the accident was loosened lug nuts."

"Shit."

"Could he be in danger again? Or Steve? Or might the killer try again to kill Reed?"

"Possible." His mouth worked. "By now you must hate that word. So far anything's possible. I have more questions. Why is somebody killing members of that high-school class? How do you and Adam Spear fit this pattern? I have no answers to those."

"Is it possible there are two killers?"

"Hush, woman. Enough for tonight. I know an excellent way to take our minds off all this."

A rush of heat coursed through her. All evening he'd been finding ways to touch her, to hold her. She felt his gaze as palpable as a flame. It ignited tingling head to toe. She would relish this and every moment they had together. Because before long this would end.

*****

AFTER COMET WAS tucked away in Miriam's room and Justin had checked all the locks, he approached Sheri by the bed as she started to undo the buttons on her blouse cuffs.

That small bit of undressing released the hot flood of want that had been building all day. Beneath their teasing, their serious conversations, a current of awareness always hummed between them. Wanting her was complicated, indefinable, ramped up because of the danger around them. Always there. He felt turned inside out, something new, and committed the nameless feeling to memory. He shouldn't examine it further.

"Don't." He plucked her hand away from the button and turned her to face him. "Let me. I want to peel off the layers one at a time, starting with this sexy blouse. I want to kiss every inch of you, delicious bit by bit."

She leaned closer and, languid and sexy, planted a kiss on him, and he barely hung onto his plan to take this slow. When she pulled away, her brown eyes had darkened to almost black and burned with sensual heat.

"Justin Wylde, romantic?" she said in a husky whisper, lightly dragging a nail across his collar bone.

"It's you, honey. And this soft blouse that clings to

your body." His fingers were having trouble with the damn tiny buttons at the cuffs. He shook with need.

"It's silk. My favorite blouse."

Soft and warm like her skin and he wanted it off. Now. "You do the buttons. Please, or I'll probably rip something." His belly crawled with desire. He'd have to resort to reciting MLB stats if he intended to hold out.

"There." She held up her arms, which lifted her pretty breasts against the silk. "Peel away."

Thankfully, the garment went off over her head. He tossed it onto a nearby chair, too small and frou-frou for much else. He kissed down one arm to lavish attention on each pulse point, and back up again to the warm, salty cleft between her breasts and then her throat. Low murmurs rose from her, and her eyes closed. Her skin felt warmer to the touch than when he began.

"You may have to hold me up," she whispered as her head fell backward and her hair drifted across her shoulders.

He let his mouth explore her neck, around to her back, where he kissed down her spine. One flick of his fingers released her bra, and she let it fall. He turned her in his arms. "Ah, there." He sucked on one turgid tip and then the other until she cried out and he was so hard he ached.

He kicked off his shoes. His shirt went next, and his jeans. He tipped her back onto the bed. She'd turned back the covers, ready.

"Skinny jeans?" he complained. "How do you get these on? I mean *off*?"

Her laugh sounded more like a groan. She began rolling them, along with her panties, down her hips. "Stretchy."

He took over and finished the job. "Like peeling a banana."

She snorted. "Bad analogy. You're the one with the banana. Peeled and ready."

"Hey, you're the writer, not me." He rolled her over and licked his way up her long, gorgeous runner's legs and to her fine ass before turning her to face him.

Her tongue brushed across his nipple, making him twitch while his fingertips found sensitive places and left her breathless. Then he nuzzled lower, breathing in the very essence of her, memorizing the scent, flicking her with his tongue until she arched her back and moaned. He added a finger to his ministrations until her orgasm tightened her body around it.

She gasped and reached for him. "Justin. I want you... want you inside me... now."

He covered himself and scrambled up the bed to her. Propped himself up so he could look into her beautiful brown eyes as he pushed into her warmth. She wrapped those long legs around him and rocked her hips, urging him deeper, clenching and unclenching her muscles around him. Every cell in his being pulsed and he couldn't breathe, couldn't think, could only thrust again and again until she came in molten spasms that sent him spiraling over the edge into his own release, rushing through him with a throbbing pleasure that left him gulping for breath.

Chapter Twenty-Nine

TAKING SHALLOW BREATHS so she didn't make noise or bounce the bed, Sheri crept from the bed. She grabbed her robe and slippers and left the room. She avoided the noise of closing the door, leaving it open a fraction. Hearing nothing from Comet as she passed Miriam's room, she padded downstairs.

In the library, she collected her laptop from the desk, turned on the gas fire, and pulled a chair around to face its warmth. The terry robe wasn't enough to dispel the chill that had overcome her as Justin fell asleep beside her. He'd made love to her with such tenderness, lavishing attention on every part of her body, taking care to arouse her and then to bring her to climax, more than once. The second time they made love he called out her name, not seeming aware of it.

So many emotions welled up. An expansive feeling in her chest, joy, a longing for that connection with him. And then afterward? A crash into the abyss, a searing recognition that she wasn't falling for him — she'd fallen. And it was impossible.

She'd come downstairs to sort out what she must do the only way she knew. She opened the file labeled "D.D." and began to write where she'd left off.

Too many things have happened keeping me from writing you. When I last...

Her fingers flew as she explained about the loss of

her friend Boyd, and the danger she faced. She talked about Justin, about how protective and honorable and smart and funny he was. She wrote about her promises, that she meant to adhere to every one, but this time doing so was harder than ever before. She thought for a moment, then continued a few minutes before her usual closing…

I need you to know that no matter what, my darling, I love you. I loved you from the first moment I saw you, the moment I held you in my arms. I'll always love you—

"What are you doing?"

Sheri's heart punched against her ribs. Chills again skittered along her arms. She slammed the lid down.

Justin rounded the chair and faced her. He'd pulled on his jeans and nothing else. His lean-muscled chest and taut belly rose and fell with harsh breaths. His mouth was set on grim, his eyes stormy. "Are you all right? Why did you leave the bed?"

"I… I couldn't sleep." Which was true. For the rest, now was not the time. "I'm all right. I didn't mean to wake you." She worked up a wobbly smile.

"Too late to hide that." The long muscles of his forearm jumped as he jabbed a stiff-fingered hand toward the laptop. "I saw the screen. You're writing to some guy you call 'my darling.' You're in love with *him* while you've been with me? While you're having sex with me?"

White noise filled her head, and she struggled to make her brain work. She could let him believe that, believe what he chose based on what he'd read. She wouldn't have to end it between them. He would take that decision out of her hands. She didn't care what he thought of her, but she did care that he'd believe he made a poor choice in pursuing her. Or worse, he might believe himself not worthy. She'd seen that scenario in too many memoirs.

She'd have to tell him the truth. The result for her would be the same.

"Well?" His shoulders were hunched, his features stiff.

She opened the lid, woke the screen, and turned it toward him. "Scroll up to the beginning of the letter, the greeting." She clamped her jaw against the trembling.

He bent and tapped the up arrow a few times. Stared at the screen as if he couldn't decipher the words. His brows snapped together. Confusion in his gaze, he straightened.

"'Darling *Daughter*'?"

She set the laptop on the side table, scooted to the edge of the chair. She began to rise but stopped herself and remained seated. She feared her legs wouldn't hold her.

"Yes, a letter to my daughter. She's sixteen."

She knew that look, his forehead crimped, his mouth twisting. He was working it out.

"Noah's baby."

"Yes."

"Where is she?"

She could no longer bear the anguish in his gaze and bowed her head. "I don't know. I gave her up for adoption. I don't even… know her name." This last she choked out on a sob.

"You kept this from me? Even *after* I shared my family secret?"

"I… wanted to tell you then, but I knew doing so would chase you away." As it was doing now. "Yes, I

275

kept it from you. From the world, even from my best friend. Only my parents know. And now you." Somehow she found the strength to rise so she was closer to eye level with him. "I told Noah that day. It —*I*— killed his dreams... his future. It was my fault he killed himself. I must bear this alone. It's my albatross."

She knew what he would do now. She lifted her chin, propped a hand on the chair arm. Ever since making her promise on Noah's grave to bear her guilt alone, she'd kept busy with family and friends and work, alone but most of the time not lonely. When she ended relationships, or when they fizzled out, she felt the loss only briefly and then moved on. This time would be... different... harder. Impossible.

"You know how I feel about secrets." His features blank, still, he barked a bitter laugh. "I thought I could trust you, but now...."

He shook his head and strode from the room.

Sheri made herself remain standing before the fire as he hit the stairs. After some rustles and thumps, he returned and headed to the back of the house.

Over his shoulder, he called, "Lock the door."

The corners of her mouth lifted in spite of the tears that choked her throat. The protector, even as he was leaving her. The warmth that sparked in her chest at his admonition fizzled out like a dying star, leaving in its place a heavy, jagged boulder.

The mudroom door shut firmly, then the back door. She'd have preferred he slammed them. Better anger than hurt. A moment later, the SUV peeled out of the driveway.

Justin was gone. Out of her life. She was alone. As she had to be. She let the tears flow.

****

JUSTIN SLUGGED DOWN the last of his coffee and pondered another cup. He shouldn't. He'd had too many today.

Work was what he needed. Given the situation in Dragon Harbor, the lieutenant had set up Bess and him in an interview room. Not in the conference room, as they'd had for a larger, statewide case. Only a couple of support staff were allotted since the incidents were confined to one peninsula. Big table in the middle, laptop computers. On a white board, he and Bess had created a timeline and to it taped photos of the victims of homicide and attempted homicide and other shots of the crime scenes. They'd noted connections among the players and suspects. And dammit, kept having to add to the list.

He hadn't slept the whole weekend, so who fucking cared. He kept seeing Sheri wrapped in her bathrobe, her face drained of color, her beautiful brown eyes haunted, bleak. Or Sheri, her lips parted in passion as he entered her slick tightness. Or Sheri, cheeks pink with happiness as she teased him about his mashers.

Enough. It was over and he wasn't going back. She'd hidden her past from him, kept it secret, not something he could get beyond.

He left the room, aware Bess was watching him like a mama panther, as she'd done all day. When he returned with a new cup of coffee, she pounced.

She hiked a hip on the table beside him. Expression fierce, she looked over her reading glasses at him, throwing him back in time to his teenage screw-ups.

"Justin, I love you like a brother, and I thought you'd finally found a woman who made you look beyond the short term. I hate to see you this way. You've been moping around ever since the weekend."

Every muscle in his body knotted. Bess had always made light of his serial dating. She cared about him. He respected that so he sat still and took it.

"If you broke up with Sheri, you're an idiot. She's smart and independent and loyal. God help her if she's fallen for you too. Don't be a dickhead. You're too stuck in your *I-don't-do* relationships mindset to see it. Or to accept your own emotions."

He set his features to wooden. "I have a call to make. Are you finished, Bess?"

"I am, for now. But I hope *you* are not." She stalked back to her computer on the other side of the conference table.

Whatever he felt for Sheri didn't change things. Moping? He had no time for anything but the job.

He rolled the kinks from his shoulders and found the number for the FBI profiler who'd previously aided the MCU He might have some ideas on this case even though it wasn't an official request.

The profiler answered right away. They spent a few minutes catching up. When Justin explained why he'd phoned, the man's curiosity was piqued and he agreed to listen. Justin crossed to the white board and jabbed a finger at the timeline as he described each case. When he finished, he returned to the laptop. The other man offered ideas while Justin typed notes.

"Thanks, man. I owe you one," he said after the profiler had answered some questions.

"That's what they all say, but no one ever delivers."

Justin dredged up a laugh at the quip.

No sooner had he hung up the phone than Bess wheeled her desk chair around to his side. "If you hadn't called him, I would've. We need a shit load of expertise on this case. Give."

His shoulders lowered in relief her harangue seemed to be over.

"He agreed with us it's unlikely our guy is a serial killer. He thinks it's more of a revenge issue. Maybe a paranoid personality, somebody who perceives small slights as major insults or offenses requiring retribution."

"Attacks punishable by death?"

"Even that." Justin checked his notes. "They want to belong, but on the inside are tortured and unforgiving. These could be revenge killings, the anger and hatred festering over time, and possibly triggered by a traumatic event."

"Or opportunity? Circumstances changed, for example."

He peered at the computer screen. "Yes, that's there. Bess, you holding out on me, taking profiling classes?"

"I kept thinking these were revenge attacks, stemming from when those guys were in high school, so I consulted the psychiatrist who was stalked last year. He pretty much agreed with your guy. The revenge motive fits Gil MacRae for Spear. And then maybe he covered up by going for Miriam and thought Sheri might ID him. But what about Keniston, why him? Gil and his wife took him in after his parents' deaths. And how does Boyd Rankin fit into all this?"

"Hard to see how the high-school revenge thing fits MacRae. Sheri's thought on that could be wrong. Or our killer's trying to throw us off the track."

"You may be giving them too much credit." She flipped her braid over her shoulder. "What about Reed Keniston?"

"You thinking that failed attempt on him was too pat? Too much coincidence there?" When she raised her eyebrows, as if urging him to run with it, he leaned back in his chair and loosened his tie. Damn thing was strangling him anyway. "He left the Wheelhouse at eight-thirty, so he had plenty of time to remove the gas coupling and wait to inhale the gas until five minutes before Genie arrived. She always arrives at nine. No fingerprints except his on the range, and only on the controls and the oven door. Did he really have a cold preventing him from smelling the gas?"

"Could've faked that. His job in Silicon Valley was something in computers, right? So he'd know how to find out about gas lines and brass knuckles disabling people." She frowned, shook her head. "With that gimpy leg, would he really have been able to toss Adam Spear over the cliff? Or have enough balance to control a strong, struggling woman?"

An image of Sheri with that rope around her neck and panic on her face made his stomach flip over like a landed trout. Working his tight jaw, he erased the image.

"I don't know, but something about him is off. Sheri mentioned it too, that Keniston tries too hard in social situations. Whether that makes him a murderer and not just a nerd or on the spectrum is something worth looking at. I've put in a call to his old employer."

"The profile could fit if he resented not being part of the cool group."

"I don't know that he wasn't." He could ask Sheri. Better he talk to her brother Mike, who was one of the leaders. "I'll call somebody who'll know."

Bess pushed up from her chair. She crossed to the white board and pointed to the list of possible motives.

"Maybe he still hated Spear because of his parents' deaths. The high-school revenge thing fits Steve Spear. He probably hated his father, and Sheri ran with the cool group."

"Steve was always on the fringes. Didn't really belong to the cool group. I can see him resenting all those kids. The only way they partied at his house was if his mom threw the party." Picturing Steve, Justin shook his head. "Hard to see him smart enough or savvy enough to have pulled off these attacks."

"But his mother is. Remember the surgical costume, her height, her strong upper body? Same goes for her as for Keniston. She's computer savvy. She has no alibi for any of the attacks. She could've snatched an old fishing rope from a dock anytime. She might resent the kids who had to be bribed to hang with her son back when. Adam's infidelity might've been the trigger."

"And her lover, Spear's partner, is nowhere to be found. Not at his office or his house. Doesn't answer his phone. Maybe he and Angela were in on it together, and he got cold feet and split."

"Maybe Quentin Frost is with the mysterious Liz or Ellie." Bess brightened. "Hey, like my name, Liz and Ellie are both nicknames for Elizabeth."

"Damn, what if father and son were seeing the same woman?" Justin smacked the tabletop. Another devious, lying woman. The secret Sheri kept from him wasn't like that. Nothing like that, but still, keeping secrets ruined lives. He should know.

"I have an idea, something Owen said to me the other night we were out to dinner. I'll give him a call and see if it pans out." Bess made more notes.

"And another thing," Justin said. "Whatever we do

next, it better be fast." He joined her at the white board. "Look at the dates. A week after Spear's killed, Miriam Littlefield is attacked, and then three days later, Sheri. The next week, Miriam, Sheri, and Keniston are attacked. Only four days later, Rankin is killed."

"Serial killer or revenge killer, he or she is escalating."

"Our helpful profiler suggested the UNSUB, to use his term, is becoming unglued, unraveling, maybe because events aren't going to plan. Things could get uglier." He gripped Bess's forearm. "Sheri's in that big house alone. The locks are secure, but... Would you see about protective custody?"

Chapter Thirty

SHERI TUCKED TWO more reference books beside the rest in her file box. Her folders of printouts would go in her big tote. She had a couple of interviews tomorrow morning, but should be out of Miriam's house by late afternoon at the latest. The bathroom renovations were scheduled to begin the next day, Thursday. Carpenters first, Deb said. When Sheri returned, she'd spend no more nights, only days working with Miriam at the hospital or the rehab facility.

Detective Peters had tried to talk her into protective custody, but she'd refused. She'd be safe in Weymouth, where she had an alarm system and a tenant in the other half of the duplex.

Remaining in this house longer would only keep fresh memories she was strong-arming out of her consciousness. Justin's impossibly blue eyes, soft as he was about to kiss her ghosted in front of her. His voice, rumbling as he held her tight, echoed inside her.

Darkness swamping her heart, she sank onto the desk chair and pressed a hand to her stomach. If only she could pack up her emotions as easily as she packed her belongings. The pain that had tightened Justin's features meant that his mother's terrible betrayal, reinforced by girlfriends' lies, still evoked strong emotions and resentments. Telling her had made no difference. His reaction changed nothing. She'd been right to have kept her secret from everyone. What she'd done, what she'd caused could not be forgiven.

Comet jumped onto her lap and placed a paw on her arm. She whined, looking up as if asking what was wrong.

"Too many things, girl. Comfort I gladly accept, but my trouble is nothing you can fix." She hugged the little dog. "Let's go. It's time for your supper."

She lugged the box out and stowed it in the back of the car beside her weights. Miriam's handyman had come Monday to clear away fallen twigs from the yard and mulch from the gardens. Usually she loved May. Daffodils and tulips were starting to bloom, and grass was greening. But this year she couldn't work up much enthusiasm for spring.

After locking the car, she hurried inside and prepared the mix of kibble and canned food. She set the bowl in the dog's food stand. Her dining table, as Miriam called it. Gawd, she hoped the woman would recover. This Friday they planned to bring her out of the coma.

Finished, Comet came and sat, gaze bright with expectation.

"Here you are, sweetie." Sheri handed over the dessert biscuit. Another thing that reminded her of Justin. His family dogs always got dessert.

Enough. What was done was done. She refused to cry any more. She strode to the library, determined to force her mind to focus on anything else.

Comet trotted in with her and lay down on the hearth rug. No fire there on this warm day.

Her gaze fell on the journal she'd been consulting, a recent one bound in the red leather. Something about the attacks kept niggling at her brain, something she'd missed or misunderstood or… Something more about Reed in that journal passage? But there was nothing she and Justin hadn't already discussed.

She paced the room, touching the tables. She looked out at the gazebo, scene of the killer's telltale puddles.

Turning her back to the window, she folded her arms and stared at the orderly ranks of the bookshelves. Her first day here, Miriam had gone unerringly to the photo album, had known where on the shelf to pluck it up. These shelves were organized almost like in a library.

Unlike the ones in Reed's living room. A haphazard mess.

Her scalp prickled, and she ran fingers through her hair as her pulse skipped. She gripped the back of the sofa and closed her eyes, calling up the image of those bookshelves. A variety of titles and genres and sizes, colorful covers, books lying flat, books upright with spines out, some face out.

And standing among other books with spines out, one with no writing on its red leather binding.

Holy shit.

Her eyes flew open. Her throat constricted and light-headedness rocked her. She leaned over the couch and gathered herself, drawing in a few deep breaths. Marginally calmer, she picked up the journal from the side table and crossed to the shelves. After sliding it in among other upright books, she stood back and considered.

Yes, it was similar, but could she be certain the spine she saw belonged to one of Miriam's journals? The missing journal? Would it be safe to go look? She could jog past Reed's house and stop for a visit, as he kept suggesting. If it *was* that journal, doing so would be beyond foolhardy. But how could a man with a bum leg toss another man off a cliff? Too puzzling to answer.

Comet's solemn eyes followed her from the hearth, watching the crazy lady pacing to and from the couch. Rousing herself, she padded to Sheri's side and nudged her leg.

Scooting down to sit in front of the couch, Sheri patted the rug. Once Comet was cuddled up beside her, she said, "You can help me make it through what I need to do now."

She withdrew her phone from her tunic pocket and selected Favorites. He was still there. Both numbers. She held a finger over his personal number, trembled, pulled it back. Deep breath. She threaded the fingers of her other hand in Comet's soft fur. This time she placed the call.

It rang and rang and rang. When she heard Justin's smooth baritone on voice mail, her throat filled and she had to swallow. "Justin here. Leave a message." Terse and to the point. Okay then.

"Hi, it's Sheri." How inane. He'd know. What if he deleted her message without listening? Nothing she could do about that. She reached down deep for a controlled, even voice. "About the case, I remembered what it was that bugged me. When I was at Reed's that one time, I saw what might be Miriam's missing journal on his bookshelves. It was only spine out, so I'm not certain. I wanted you to know."

She tapped End before the temptation to say more made her stupid. Comet crawled into her lap and licked her cheek. She buried her face in soft fur.

****

JUSTIN DROVE AWAY from Mike Harte's graphic design office, located above the garage attached to his nice two-story in the Rosemont neighborhood of Portland. He stopped at a little park down the street and looked at his notes.

Tall and lean, Mike bore a family resemblance to his

sister. He'd been forthcoming in answering questions after saying, "Some asshole has attacked my sister twice and killed my buddy Boyd. I'll tell you anything if it helps catch this guy."

Although he'd acknowledged the police report that the lug nuts on his car were loosened deliberately, he put it down to vandals or a kids' prank. His answers to Justin's questions about the group of guys and their girlfriends in high school verified that Reed and Steve were on the fringes, but ran with them sometimes. Reed was stiff, awkward. Steve was easygoing, but didn't get their jokes. Noah, outgoing and dynamic, was the leader of the inner circle. The night of his suicide, only four guys went into town for beer—Mike, Noah, Boyd, a couple of girls but not Sheri, and another guy who now lived out of state. That night, Noah was in a strange mood but hadn't drunk as much as the others. Then Mike grew pensive, saying nobody knew why Noah did it. Justin left that alone.

As he was leaving, Mike confronted him, fists clenched at his side, about Sheri. "Are you banging my sister?"

Justin had kept his expression even and calmed his voice. "I'll say this once, and nicely because you're her brother. We went out a few times and now we're not." He'd turned and walked down the stairs and to the SUV.

He underlined in his notes Mike Harte's statement that Noah hadn't drunk much. So where did he get the drugs and alcohol that fueled his suicide?

He slipped the notebook into his pocket and took out his personal phone. Looked once again at yesterday's voice mail alert. He'd silenced the alert tone in case she tried again. If it was an emergency, she'd have called the official number.

Once again the temptation to hear her voice had his thumb inching toward the icon. Once again he set aside the phone. Chalked up the urge to just having talked to her brother. Worked the tightness out of his jaw. It was over. *Let it be.*

He opened the lunch cooler in the passenger seat and took out the sandwich he'd bought earlier, his favorite corned beef and coleslaw from a Portland deli. He looked at it. Could smell the Russian dressing on the rye bread. Tossed it back in the cooler and drove away.

****

ON WEDNESDAY AFTERNOON, Sheri cast a glance at the kitchen clock. Five-forty. Comet was outside harassing squirrels before it was time to go. She'd loaded her suitcases in the car and given the dog a short walk. A peaceful stroll with the late-afternoon sun glinting on the bay's dark water, and no killer jumping out of the bushes.

Her stomach tightened and a shudder worked through her shoulders. She placed her hands on both sides of her neck. Still sore and abraded from the rope. After that attempt on her life, she'd purchased a second personal alarm, which she kept on her at all times.

Her work tote and handbag sat by the mudroom door, ready for her...what? Getaway? Escape? Desertion? She shook her head. No, none of those. Simply moving on, as they'd both said, even if the thought of the main reason made her feel like a hollowed-out husk. She couldn't muster much enthusiasm for seeing her house with its new coat. Maybe she'd tackle the flower and scroll wallpaper in the living room, a job that should tire her enough that she'd sleep.

She dried her coffee mug and stowed it in the cupboard. She'd pick up a takeout supper on her way through Bayport. Her bed sheets and towels were in the washing machine. Deb had said she'd handle the rest.

Time to go. She'd go out and collect Comet. Sheri tossed down the dishtowel and headed outside. As she stepped onto the grass, Comet barked and growled, leaping toward her. A rope fastened to the little dog's collar jerked her back toward the fencepost.

"Comet, what—"

An arm clamped around her neck.

A gush of adrenaline rabbited her heartbeat. Struggling, she gasped in a shallow breath, struggled for more. She couldn't make a sound. She couldn't scream. She clawed at the arm, but couldn't get a grip. Another strong arm wrapped her head. A hand pushed her head forward. *No!*

Frantic barking, howling.

Don't the neighbors hear this? Help!

Sheri fought to wrest free, but was rapidly losing strength. She couldn't breathe. A storm of fury buzzed in her head. *You fucker, I won't let you win.*

Justin… She groped at the small device fastened to her jeans waistband. The trees and a leaping dog swam and spun in front of her. Her vision blurred.

Where was the damn ring pull? Clumsy… fingers… *Got it… can't…*

"Lights out."

That voice… I know…

Chapter Thirty-One

"THANKS. I APPRECIATE the information." Justin said goodbye and ended the call. He leaned back in his chair in their small command post. Support techs were working on Adam Spear's financial records. The remnants of lunch—crumpled sandwich wrappers smelling of mustard and pickles—littered the table between him and Bess.

As Bess had pointed out, the perpetrator was escalating. And the profiler had said maybe unraveling. Who was the next target? Sheri had been attacked twice. The saying *third time's a charm* echoed in Justin's head. Fear tightened his chest and filled his veins with ice. Shoving his chair back, he shot to his feet.

Eyes wide, Bess closed her laptop lid. "You sure as hell asked a lot of questions."

"And got answers." He grabbed his windbreaker and checked his service pistol. "Based on what his former boss says, I figure Reed Keniston's our man. Hearsay and suspicion, not enough for a search warrant, but plenty of ammunition to fire at him. Bring your sidearm. I'll fill you in on the way. You don't know how bad I want this asshole."

"I do know," she said, collecting her jacket and weapon, "which is why I'll drive. You can seethe while riding shotgun. Grab your vest."

After alerting the lieutenant they might need backup, Justin joined Bess in her unit, and they hit the road.

"Okay, spill," she said, once they headed south on I-95. "What did this hotshot tech exec have to say about Keniston?"

"He was a highly paid software engineer and developer, whatever that means, and bounced around a few different firms over the past ten years or so. Talented and brilliant, but didn't get along with colleagues. Lorded it over people, claiming to know more than they did. Poached data so he could take credit for some breakthrough that rightly belonged to somebody else."

"So they fired him?"

"Yeah, but not for that," he said. "After he developed a new program or software, something to do with security for finances, he sold the software to this company's rival for mucho dollars. That income is where he got the money that let him retire to Dragon Harbor."

They took the exit toward Bayport and Dragon Harbor. Bess pulled onto the secondary road behind an old Volvo motoring ten miles under the speed limit. Massachusetts tourist. Usually they were speeders. Vehicles began stacking up behind them, and a longer line behind a semi filled the oncoming lane.

Damn two-lane highway. Justin couldn't justify using the siren. They were just going to talk to Keniston. That was all. Bess would advise him to take deep breaths.

They were a solid hour away from Dragon Harbor, but Sheri was probably safe in Weymouth. He gripped the armrest and willed the SUV to hit warp speed. His mouth went dry. Why the hell had she refused protection?

He shook himself to alertness. "His boss said Reed used to work out in the company gym, weight training. Pushed his pictures of hiking and biking trips all over the West in everybody's face."

Behind the parade of oncoming traffic, the highway finally cleared. Bess overtook the Volvo and sped ahead.

Damn straight. But the delay tied square knots in his gut.

"Hiking, biking, weight training," she said. "Hard to do all that athletic shit if you need a cane for support. Not a lawsuit payout. Then what about the skiing accident?"

"No accident of any kind. And according to his old boss, Reed doesn't ski."

****

SHERI'S HEAD ACHED. Inhaling drew an oddly sweet chemical odor into her nostrils.

She lifted her head and opened her eyes, blinked a few times at the overhead light. When she turned her head, the room spun.

Dizzy? She remembered feeling the dizziness coming on. Then nothing.

Where was she?

A kitchen, not Miriam's. Smaller. She twisted to look around, but something held her tight.

That woke her up. And woke her memory.

The grip around her neck. Getting lightheaded. And the alarm. Did she trigger her alarm button? How long ago was that? She could tell through the window in the door ahead that it was almost dark outside. So she must've been out for at least a couple hours.

Justin. Oh God, did he get her message? She looked down. The device was still pinned to her waistband. Would he come? What if—

Her pulse rioted and her breath caught, but she made herself focus and inhale deeply. *Think, think.* She sat in a high-backed wooden chair. Nothing covered her mouth, but a wide strip of something soft like felt secured her against the chair back. The same kind of fabric tied her wrists to the chair arms, her ankles to the legs. Why felt?

She rotated her hips against the chair back. Nothing clanked against the wood, so no phone in her back pocket. She pictured it on the kitchen table where she'd left it when Comet started barking. Damn.

She drew in a deep breath and opened her mouth to yell for help.

"Ah, you're awake! Perfect." The exuberant voice came from behind her.

Reed! Conflicting emotions warred within her. Satisfaction that her instincts and memory were correct and horror that she was correct. Her shoulders slumped. His house was located far from any others. No one would hear her if she called out. No one but *him.*

He strode around the chair and stood at attention, hands propped on his hips, in front of her. Gone were the ill-fitting sweaters and slumped posture. His stride was confident and even. No cane. Arm and chest muscles bulged beneath a skin-tight knit shirt. Both shirt and cargo pants were black. He stared at her with haughty approval.

Who was *this* Reed Keniston?

"Reed, is this some kind of joke?" She was no actress, but maybe he'd take her tight voice for fury rather than fear.

"No joke, Sheri. Surely you must see that."

"Untie me." At his quirked eyebrow, she added, "Please."

"Can't. It's too soon." His mouth turned down, the gaze above his prominent nose rife with what? Contempt? Scorn?

Her stomach quivered. She clenched the chair arms to prevent her hands from trembling. Dots of blood seeped through the gauze bandage wrapping Reed's left hand. *Good dog, Comet.*

Time, she needed time. If she got him talking...

"It was you, wasn't it, Reed?" She kept her voice low, calm, her tone reasonable. "You killed Adam Spear."

"He deserved to die. My family died because of him." He scowled, biting off each word as if it were chunks of Spear.

"That made you very angry."

His forehead smoothed. "So you understand."

"I do." He must've kept the hatred and resentment buried for years. Until he returned to Dragon Harbor. "It must've been hard coming back here, driving past his big new house."

"I saw him at the post office one day talking to some guy I didn't know. When I went out the door, he made a comment to the man about my father, 'a drunk and a loser.' I couldn't let him live." His eyes were two dark pits of hatred.

So on that foggy morning last month, he'd waited for Spear and tossed him over the cliff. Deb and Miriam could've died because of his sick craving for revenge. When Miriam came home, she would again be in danger. Her heart pounded. She couldn't dwell on that now. She had to keep him talking, delaying whatever he had in mind for her.

"And Boyd? He had nothing to do with your dad's business or the car accident."

His upper lip curled in a nasty sneer. "Boyd and the rest, swaggering around, acting like they were fucking hotshots. Nothing but small-town punks. I was smarter than any of them—Noah, Boyd, Mike. I was their buddy only when they needed help in calculus or chemistry."

His words pounded in her head. Good God, he was talking about high school. He kept this grudge inside him for seventeen years? Her stomach rolled.

"They're all losers. I've made more money than anyone in that class. Boyd smelled of fish all day. Mike works over his garage. And Noah." He snorted a harsh laugh. "Dickhead thought he had it all going for him, thought he was going to be a doctor. But I put a stop to that."

His words rocked her brain. A whimper started in her throat, but she swallowed it. "Noah?"

"He crowed about how you were going to be a family and how he'd make college work no matter what. He was already half drunk when I showed up that night. We shared some of my dad's whiskey. His cup had a little something extra. Made him pliable."

Heat exploded in her veins, white hot rage displacing the years of sorrow and self-reproach. This man she no longer knew had no idea, no concept of others' emotions, others' lives. Only his. She writhed and yanked at the cloths that bound her to the chair. Her struggles rocked the legs but didn't free her.

Her mouth was a cotton wad, but she managed to croak, "Noah didn't kill himself."

"Of course not. As soon as he got the fucking scholarship, nearly as good as mine, he had to die. It was only a matter of time." He bent over her, placing his big hands on her arms. Her skin crawled, and she flinched. He smiled. "I was too impulsive going after you with that pickup and even the rope. But it gave me time to develop a truly brilliant plan. The poor, grieving girlfriend will hang herself where her lover died."

She tongued enough saliva to spit in his face. "Damn

you!"

He recoiled, stepping away as he wiped away her spittle. "You're as much a loser as the rest. That night at Aunt Miriam's, as soon as I saw those long legs and tight ass, I wanted to bury my dick in you. I even considered letting you live. But then I caught you kissing that detective, and I knew my first plan was the right one."

He was mad. Paranoid. Warped by his own delusions of brilliance. And hatred.

He picked up a water bottle from the counter and unscrewed the cap. "Thirsty?"

A toxic brew churned inside her like a tornado, but she had to bide her time. What had he said? He would hang her where Noah died? She'd look for an escape when he took her there. Were there other houses nearby? She couldn't remember.

"I want nothing from you."

"I guessed you would say that."

He approached her with the water bottle, holding it in his left hand. The strong fingers of his right hand clamped her jaw like pincers.

****

"JUST SHUT UP and let me drive, Wylde." Bess took the right turn for the side road that skirted the main part of Bayport. "It won't help anybody if we don't get there in one piece."

Justin shut up, still grumbling inside. Whenever Bess used his last name, she meant business. She was right.

His MCU phone jangled. The screen ID'd Debra Delano. "Hey, Deb."

"Oh, thank God." Her voice was tight and breathless. "It's Sheri. She's gone. I—"

Justin's pulse took off like a moonshot. He jerked upright. The time on his phone was seven-thirty. He put her on speaker and got out his notebook. "Take it easy, Deb. Where are you?"

A half sob. "At Miriam's. I just got here. Sheri was supposed to leave for Weymouth with Comet before this. The dog's here alone."

Maybe she'd jumped to conclusions. Sheri could've gone for a walk or a jog before the drive. "What makes you think there's a problem?"

"Her car's here, and the house is unlocked. Her overnighter and her favorite Gucci canvas bag are by the door. She'd never leave that behind. Or her phone. It's on the kitchen table."

Bess jerked a grim glance his way, then accelerated.

"Any sign of violence? Chair overturned or something broken?"

"No, nothing. Where is she? Could *he* have her?" Her voice broke on another sob.

Dammit, did he screw up by not listening to Sheri's voice mail? "We don't know yet. Here's what I want you to do. Take Comet with you and go home. Detective Peters and I are headed your way. Let us handle this."

"But…"

"Go. Leave. I don't want to worry about you too. You'll hear from me."

She agreed, reluctantly, and he disconnected. Took out his personal phone and brought up Sheri's voice mail.

A short, awkward greeting and a pause before she said, *"About the case, I remembered what it was that bugged me. When I was at Reed's that one time, I saw what might be Miriam's missing journal on his bookshelves…"*

After hearing the rest, he related the gist to Bess. Swearing viciously, he dropped the phone onto his lap. Hell, he'd been right to suspect Keniston. If he'd listened to this yesterday, she'd be safe today. He wiped his slick palms on his jeans. The phone's message icon blinked. How long had that been there? He'd silenced that alert too, so no telling. He opened the text. *Sheri.*

I'm in trouble. Come now.

A time stamp that read 5:50 p.m. and a GPS link followed the text.

"Justin? Hey, tell me."

He barked out the message, punctuated with more than one *fuck*. "She must have a new alert device. I'm trying the GPS link now." He kept hitting wrong letters or numbers. The damn keypad was too fucking tiny. Sweat dripped down his back inside the body armor. Finally he got a map—Dragon Harbor peninsula. "Looks like she's at Keniston's house."

"Stay with the tracking." Bess turned down the country road leading to the peninsula. "I'm calling for backup." She hit the dispatch icon on her phone.

So focused on the phone screen, Justin barely listened. His nerves snapped like a live wire, and a dark ball of tension tightened in his gut.

When Bess said his name, he looked up, ready.

"Backup's too far away," she said. "Tractor trailer accident on Route 1. Chief Galt's waiting in the village. He and his officers will follow us. I told him no sirens."

The green blip on the phone screen showed Sheri on the move.

Chapter Thirty-Two

FUZZINESS FADED LIKE a receding tide. Cool air lifted goose bumps on Sheri's arms. She squinted, forcing her eyes to focus. Darkness. A shake of her head thickened the blur, and she had to reach for support, grabbing the nearest object, a wooden post. Outside, but how did she get here? Where? She didn't remember. She could call up only impressions.

A voice. Someone, a man, was talking. To her? "You'll be so much happier, I promise. You won't suffer the loss. No more pain, only peace."

Reed's voice.

She looked down at the felt strips binding her wrists together. Now she remembered, some. Being tied up, realizing he was the attacker, learning he'd murdered Noah. Then he'd forced water in her, laced with some kind of drug. That was all, not how she got here.

Where was he? Where was *this?*

Still sluggish, but more clearheaded, she looked around. A lantern inside an old open garage shed its light on Reed. Standing on a wooden crate, he was tossing a rope over a beam.

His words tolled in her head. *"...grieving girlfriend will hang herself where her lover died."*

It was *that* beam, the same beam… Her heartbeat kicked up, slamming against her sternum. *Run!* She took off toward the road.

Not running. More like forcing one foot in front of the other. She still felt logy, as if deep mud sucked at her shoes, not dew-wet grass. *Away.* She had to get away or she'd die. She glimpsed the pavement ahead.

Something slammed her to the ground.

"Bitch! You woke up too soon. What the fuck happened?"

He hauled her to her feet, but she was still sucking in the breath he'd knocked from her. With one arm around her shoulders and the other hand locked around her other arm, he marched her back across the yard and into the garage. His movements were stiff and impatient, rife with fury. He reeked of the sweat pouring off him. Muttering to himself, something about not making her drink enough, he began manhandling her up onto the crate.

A rush of adrenaline jolted her into action. She elbowed him in the jaw, but the effort dropped her to her knees. The crate creaked and dipped but held.

He swore and yanked her upright. Turned her around to face him.

She kicked one knee. Raked her nails down his face. "Help! Help! He's going to kill me."

He flinched but uttered no sound of pain. "No one to hear you, so don't bother." He clapped his hand over her mouth anyway. Blood dripped from his cheek. He paid no attention.

Someone has to hear. She had to keep trying. She wrenched loose. She opened her mouth and bit down. Damned if she wouldn't cause him enough pain to give her another chance.

He backed away but kept his steel grip on her arm. "Bitch! Don't make me hurt you. You're not supposed to have any bruises."

She yelled again and fumbled for her alarm button. Yanked on the ring and prayed.

"What the hell is that?" he bellowed. "Some kind of signal?" He ripped it away and stomped it into bits on the garage's gravel floor.

She jumped down from the crate and went after him. She balled her fists and jabbed at his throat.

He dodged. Now he was panting and straining as much as she was. Still he held onto her.

She kicked at him, but couldn't keep her balance and fell to the ground. She scrambled to her knees.

Before she could drag herself to her feet, he grabbed her.

****

JUSTIN WATCHED THE map while Bess stayed on the radio with Chief Galt. He and another DHPD unit would hang back until they got the word.

"Signal's stationary," he said. "Has been for a while." Good or bad. A tossup.

"Have the ambulance on hand," Bess said to Galt as they passed through Dragon Harbor village. "Our vic may need patching up. Keniston too."

"Fuck, the signal dropped." Justin refreshed and willed the evil device to work again. Nothing, only the map. But he recognized that part of the East Road, where it curved a little before the turn onto Echo Cliff Point. What was he doing? Few houses along there, mostly summer people according to locals. And the— He went cold and hot at the same time. He knew what Keniston intended.

"It's the Tardiff place."

They quickly coordinated with Galt and proceeded.

Luckily they were close. Before reaching the property, Bess doused the headlights and the ceiling light. She pulled off the road behind a clump of overgrown bushes..

"Justin," Bess stopped setting up her comm unit and reached past the equipment on the console. She gripped his forearm. Steel was in her words and in her eyes. "You're personally and emotionally involved. No way you should even be here, but at this point we have no choice. If you can't handle this, tell me now and you stay put. Norman Galt's a good cop. I can assess the situation and he'll back me up."

Bess was right. Again. Ending things with Sheri didn't wipe out how he felt. Didn't wipe out the fact that it was him she'd called for help. But he had to get his head straight. He breathed in and out deeply three times, taming the roiling in his chest. He locked himself down.

"I can do my job. Let's do this."

"Okay then."

They conferred while he organized his comm—radio on his belt, collar mic, Bluetooth earbuds. Checked his 9mm, racked the slide. "I'm good to go."

They climbed out and edged close enough to see around the bushes. A lamp cast faint light on the tumbledown garage's interior. Keniston had a tight grip on Sheri. He swore as he was forcing her toward a low crate. He looked bigger, stronger in tight clothing. The baggy clothes had hidden the real Reed.

Sheri's wrists were tied, but she swung balled fists at him. He dodged. She backed away and aimed a kick at his crotch. But the blow struck Keniston's thigh. He grabbed her again. Shook her like a rag doll.

Justin's gut clenched.

Bess whispered, "I don't see a weapon. Maybe he

thought he wouldn't need one."

He headed toward the house. Keeping low, he loped across the yard and continued around behind, and on past Keniston's car. Shit-head had parked in the same spot as Steve Spear. Once around the house, Justin had a good view inside the old garage.

Keniston had maneuvered Sheri up onto the crate. He was trying to loop a noose over her head. She continued to fight him, but having her wrists bound knocked her off balance.

Oh, hell yeah. That's it, honey.

He relayed the scene to Bess. "He's too busy to notice us. Get in position."

"Roger that."

He held his weapon at his side as he crept closer, keeping to the side out of the light. He could now see the source was a battery-powered lantern.

"Police! Reed Keniston, step away from the woman and put up your hands."

"Justin." Sheri sounded game.

Keniston swung toward the sound of Justin's voice, but didn't release her. He pulled a pistol from behind him. Pointed it Justin's direction.

As he fired, Justin hit the dirt.

Keniston shot more rounds into the dark.

Wood chips flew from the oak to Justin's left. No cries from beyond, where cops waited.

"You can't stop me. She has to die. They all have to die." Keniston waved his weapon at the unseen enemy.

He forced the noose down to her chin. She lifted her bound hands to the rope, but he slapped them away. The noose hung loosely around her neck. He tightened it. She again clawed at the rope but didn't seem to have a firm grip.

Keniston let go of her. Contempt on his long face, he looked up at the struggling woman. He placed a foot on the edge of the crate. If he shoved it from under her, her feet would dangle just above the ground.

She would choke in a matter of minutes. Or the sudden fall would break her neck.

"Give it up, Sheri." His lip curled in a vicious sneer. "You'll be with that fool Noah again."

Fuck, Justin couldn't fire. He might hit Sheri. "Enough dicking around. I'm going in," he said into his mic.

He raced forward, gun in a two-handed grip. "Let her go, you bastard. You can't get away."

Before Keniston could shove the crate away, Sheri chinned herself on the noose and kicked out. Her boot nailed him in the crotch.

He toppled to the ground, clutching his nuts with one hand and groaning.

"Drop your weapon," Justin ordered.

Keniston swung the pistol toward him. Fired.

Justin feinted to the left. He fired twice as the bullet whizzed past him.

The rounds struck Keniston center mass. Crimson bloomed on his chest. He fell on his back, not moving, his weapon by his side in the dirt.

While Justin held his weapon trained on the fallen man, light bars flashed on, and headlights lit up the lawn and garage. Uniforms and Bess Peters, weapons drawn, ran forward.

Bess kicked away the pistol and checked for a pulse. "Gone."

"Damn right." Justin holstered his weapon and

worked the noose off Sheri's head. He wrapped his arms around her and held her as she stepped down. Buried his nose in her hair, breathed in the familiar fragrance of her shampoo. Her warm breath on his neck reassured him. He let her go only so he could untie the cloth binding her wrists.

She looked up, tears in her beautiful eyes. "You came... you came."

He couldn't speak, could only nod. When Genie Galt and another emergency tech hustled up to tend her, he forced himself to release her. He turned away.

"Bess," Justin said. "You'll have to be the one to take her statement."

"Understood. You did good there, Detective." She turned and headed to the EMS truck.

He stumbled around the side of the garage and heaved up his guts in the weeds.

****

THE NEXT DAY, Justin, Bess Peters, a couple of troopers, and a team of evidence techs swarmed Reed Keniston's house from attic to cellar. After a shooting, Justin should've been put on administrative leave, but he'd persuaded the lieutenant to give him two days to wrap up the rest of the case.

He couldn't just sit at home, stewing. He needed to *do* something. He'd royally screwed up by not listening to Sheri's first message. He could've stopped Keniston two days ago. Could've prevented the kidnapping, the terror she'd endured. He swore at himself—again—and dragged in a breath past the ache in his chest. He focused on the evidence in front of him.

The array of bagged and tagged items was spread out on the dining room table. When Sgt. Dow finished recording the latest one, Justin picked up the bag. This one was a small bottle bearing a scrawled label identifying it as chloroform. Bastard had likely used it to keep Sheri knocked out while he transported her here and tied her to a chair.

Sheri.

Justin rubbed his tired eyes, clenched his jaw against a shudder. Comet had set up a racket, but the neighbors who heard Sheri's alarm the other time had gone to visit their daughter. So nobody heard, nobody came to her aid.

Based on her statement, he guessed Keniston had used a chokehold on her, cutting off the blood flow to her brain. Justin bet she'd fought him like last night, but Keniston learned from his failed effort with the rope that he needed an edge with a woman who had some defensive skills. Impressed the hell out of Justin that before she lost consciousness, she pulled the ring on her high-tech alarm to send an SOS to his cell. If only he'd seen that alert sooner.

He'd fucked up on that as well.

Beside the chloroform were tablets folded inside a white paper labeled Rohypnol, used to render her compliant. But she'd regained alertness too early and fought him. If Justin and Bess hadn't already been on the road— No, no more wallowing in his fuckups. Not now anyway. Later over a glass of fine bourbon. Or three. He'd raise his glass to the heroine.

The victory belonged to Sheri for her courage and strong runner's legs. In the end, she was the one who beat the bastard.

Except for last night's witnessed attempted murder, other evidence of Keniston's crimes was minimal. His death made no difference to closing the case. The cellar contained barbells and other exercise equipment, the way he kept himself in shape. No crime in pretending *not* to be in prime shape. But there the techs had found a coil of rope like he'd used to tie the noose and some old lobster-trap line. From a closet they collected a black raincoat similar to the one Spear's attacker wore and a pair of brass knuckles stuffed inside a boot. If that device had traces of Spear's DNA, it would close that case. *If.* Otherwise, Keniston's confession to Sheri he'd killed Spear and Rankin, and Noah Tardiff seventeen years ago, was based only on her statement.

Bess walked in holding her tablet and a phone. She jerked her head for him to follow her. They took seats in the living room, her on the couch and him on the facing chair. "Good to sit on something soft for a change. Check this out. She held up Keniston's cell phone. "I brought it with me because I didn't have time to go through it last night."

"Fucker planned to photograph his handiwork with the noose."

"Exactly. But you'll see." She scrolled backward and then handed him the phone.

The first image showed Adam Spear's arms and legs splayed out on that sloping boulder at Echo Cliff. The second showed his legs bent to complete the swastika symbol.

A little rush of adrenaline jacked his pulse. *Got him.* "Why do you think he did that?"

"Maybe he thought Spear's bullying was Nazi-like, or maybe he saw the limbs almost formed the symbol and thought it would be funny. The ropes, the brass knuckles, chloroform, all stuff he should've gotten rid of and didn't. Like Sheri told me, he thought he was smarter than everybody else."

"Arrogant fucker." He returned to the phone images. One of Miriam crumpled at the foot of her stairs, her blouse smoothed in position. The next of Keniston's own gas range, the back of it with a light focused on the compression nut he would later disassemble. The last brought bile into Justin's throat. Sheri tied to the chair, unconscious, her head lolling to one side.

He swallowed and handed back the phone. "Good work, Bess, but I thought you were digging into his laptop."

"I was, but Stan's faster than me, and I wanted to show you what I found." She handed him the tablet. "I copied his browser history. Some interesting websites and videos."

Justin ran a finger down the list, a how-to of his crimes. A site selling brass knuckle weapons. What driving problems loose lug nuts could cause. An article on hypothermia. A video on coupling and *un*coupling a range's gas lines. How to perform a chokehold.

"About the gas," she said, "he was lucky Genie didn't turn on the kitchen light, but she told me she smelled the gas as soon as she stepped inside. She knew better. You don't suppose the dipwad actually neglected one factor in his master plan?"

"More than one." He gestured toward the bookshelf to his left. Front and center on the middle shelf was a red leather book, spine out. "Hid it in plain sight. The techs took pictures of this earlier, but until now, I haven't had a chance to see what Miriam Littlefield wrote about her appointment with Keniston."

"The fateful appointment." She shook her head.

Justin donned his latex gloves before sliding out the

journal. He paged to the April 10 entry and read, *"I'm positive that was Reed in the gazebo early this morning. I didn't see his cane, but I know the way he tilts his head, and that nose! And then he left as Adam Spear ran past. I am devastated!!! Must think what to do."*

Justin pumped a fist. "More evidence."

"Backs up the photos he took. What about the next week?" Bess said.

He flipped pages. "Daily stuff first. She invited Reed for tea and dessert when she saw him in the village. She expected him to arrive around eight."

She heaved a sigh and slumped deeper into the couch. She was as exhausted as him after being up almost all night. "Then that's it. She didn't have a chance afterward to write about that meeting. And Keniston took the journal with him."

"Right. Nada after this." He riffled a few blank pages but then— "Wait. There's something else. It's not in her old-style looped handwriting. This is a cramped script, almost print but connected in some places."

She sat up straight, peering at the pages he'd turned toward her.

A charge of excitement crackled through him, and his heart hit a higher gear. "It's a dated list. Starts with how he planned and killed Adam Spear. The reason for the swastika? It made a better photo. He goes on to describe each attack, each murder. Ends with kidnapping Sheri. And he rants about how each person wronged him or insulted him or snubbed him."

"He let ancient slights become an obsession and hid it all from everyone until he could have his revenge."

"But we'll need confirmation. A handwriting expert."

"Looks the same to me," Bess said, "as on papers in Keniston's desk."

"Bingo."

Chapter Thirty-Three

FROM THE HALF-OPEN doorway, Sheri watched Deb brush polish on her grandmother's fingernails. Deb's mom stood nearby. Miriam was well enough to be moved into a regular hospital room and off IVs, and Deb had said she wanted Sheri to come.

Driven back to Miriam's house Wednesday night, she'd given her statement to Detective Peters, describing how Reed kidnapped and drugged her and relating the crimes he'd admitted. Including the biggest shock of all— he'd murdered Noah. Her emotions swung back and forth in such an erratic manner she still couldn't process that revelation.

Then Deb arrived and insisted she spend the night at her house. She bundled her into the van for a reunion with an ecstatic little dog.

Sheri finally took Comet with her to Weymouth the next day, but even so, the house and her heart seemed empty. She hadn't seen Justin since he rescued her. Probably for the better, although she kept reliving the feeling of his arms around her, the thump of his heart against hers.

And now, four days later, she must face another turning point. What if Miriam wanted to abandon the memoir? She shouldn't, not just because Sheri needed the work, but because she had a unique voice and such wonderful stories to tell. And then there was Comet.

"Sheri, I see you there. *Do* come in, my *very* dear ghost."

She hurried into Miriam's open arms. After three weeks in a drugged state, her hug was weak but fervent, and her arms and chest not slender but bony.

"Oh, Miriam, I'm so thrilled to be able to hug you." Sheri eased from the embrace and sniffed back tears.

The older woman's lips curved in a smile as warm and beautiful as the one that had welcomed Sheri a little over a month ago. Unlike the still, pale form she'd last seen, this was the Miriam she knew. She wore a quilted-silk bed jacket in a violet that matched her eyes and perfect makeup including mascara and eye shadow. And instead of the room smelling antiseptic and medicinal, the scent was Chanel.

"My dear, I'm *thrilled* to *be* hugged." Miriam smiled at Deb and Vera on the other side of the hospital bed. "And to see my *family*, although that *tyrant* of a surgeon won't let me go home anytime *soon*. Apparently I need a *hip* replacement and then therapy."

Clearly Miriam's brain had recovered its acuity, if her high dudgeon was any indication. It seemed wise not to mention that. Sheri murmured her sympathy.

A wash of pink colored Miriam's cheeks. "I do feel such a *fool* for thinking I could *persuade* Reed to turn himself in."

It had been beyond risky to let a man who'd committed premeditated murder know she'd seen him in the gazebo, but there was no point in making her feel worse about it. Deb and her mom had probably reassured her ten times over, but Sheri would give it a go.

"He was your nephew, your brother's grandson. Totally understandable you wanted to try."

"Thank you for that," she said. "At some point I may *believe* it myself."

Vera cleared her throat. "The shock of Reed's crimes has hit Sydney and Gil unbelievably hard. Syd told me that because he became the son they'd never had, they blinded themselves for years to his apparent lack of empathy and other quirks. Well they were more than quirks, but…"

Deb curved an arm around her mom's shoulders. "None of us realized the resentments and violence inside him."

At a speaking look from Miriam, Vera said, "That's our cue to depart. Time for you two to talk business."

After hugs and kisses all around, mother and daughter left.

Miriam patted the bed. "Have a seat, Sheri."

She eased down. Miriam was probably still in pain. She braced herself.

The other woman took her hand. "Before we do talk business, I must not let a *moment* go by without *thanking* you. My dear, you saved my life. *Twice*, according to my family. Thanks are hardly enough, but it's all I can *offer.*" Her eyes twinkled. "Although I might have *something* in mind."

"Seeing you alive and alert and on the mend is all the thanks I need. Luck played a part both times, that I was in the right place when you needed help."

"Then we'll not *speak* of it again, but just *enjoy* working together on our project."

The heaviness in Sheri's chest lifted. "I'm ready whenever you're able to continue."

"*I* am ready to get back to work *now*, but I'll have to see what that *tyrant* will allow."

"The doctor. Tell him I promise not to tire you too much."

Miriam started to lean forward, but winced and settled back again. "Damn. I suppose I'll have to *accustom* myself to limits. For now." Her expression morphed into the sour one she'd affected earlier when talking about her surgeon. "Apparently my family have been conspiring to *insert* themselves into my memoir. Even invited some of my *friends* to share stories with you."

Sheri focused on a wrinkle in the bed covering. She couldn't say the anecdotes were suggested in case Miriam didn't recover. *Think.* After a long moment, she looked up. "No one in your family knows about the journals. They thought I needed to be kept busy, you see. The decision of whether to include any of the anecdotes is of course yours. I did enjoy most of the memories people shared."

"Most." Miriam uttered an unladylike grunt. "Bring what you have tomorrow. I'd like to *read* them. Then we'll see. This is *my* memoir, after all."

"I have a question. That night, when Reed, well, that night, why were you phoning me?"

"Ah, to explain what was in the boxes." She shook her head. "I don't remember the rest. That's it."

Taking that as a dismissal, Sheri picked up her bag.

"One more thing," Miriam said. "Comet."

Sheri's throat tightened. She'd known the time would come. Without Comet she'd be totally alone.

"Again I'm in your *debt*. Deb tells me you've taken *such* good care of her. It pains me, but I see no way I can have a dog. It will be a long time before I'm able to do more than hobble around like an old *woman*! If you agree, I'd love for you to *keep* Comet."

"Oh, yes, I adore Comet." A laugh bubbled up. "That's your thank you, isn't it?"

"I *suspected* you'd agree." Miriam beamed and opened her arms. Sheri went happily into her fragrant embrace. "But it's on the *condition* that you bring her *with* you once I'm home. Or maybe at the rehab clinic. Do you think they allow *dogs*?"

****

AFTER THEY FINISHED with Reed Keniston's house, Justin's reprieve had expired, but Bess tied up related loose ends. He mulled those over Tuesday as he drove south on I-95.

With assistance from the Feds and a judge, Bess uncovered why Quentin Frost was hard to find. He'd emptied his bank account, signed his house over to a sister, and left the country for George Town on Grand Cayman Island. So much for his main squeeze, Angela Spear.

The new information persuaded a judge to grant a search warrant for the law office. Frost had apparently found the financial account passwords in Spear's office computer and used them to transfer the offshore investments to a new account in his own name. The United States had no extradition treaty with the Caymans, so the theft stranded Angela with only the house and savings and whatever life insurance Adam had. Now that Steve had moved home, Justin figured he'd have even less incentive to grow up.

Two days later the other puzzle was solved. After Bess had learned a bartender named Libby Stein came on too strong to Owen in the Old Port, she was suspicious, picturing dollar signs in the woman's eyes at the sight of the good-looking local attorney. Bess asked Owen to return to the bar, and sure enough, Libby hit on him again. He slipped his empty glass into his pocket. Her fingerprints ID'd her as Elizabeth Rockburn, wanted in Massachusetts for embezzlement. Portland PD picked her up, along with several burner phones and fake IDs.

Bess interviewed her at the Portland Police Department on Middle Street. Elizabeth aka Ellie aka Liz admitted she'd had a relationship with both men. She said Adam claimed she went through his briefcase and dumped her for no reason. And Steve was a sweet guy but a loser. She took the first exit as soon as the cops started looking at him for his dad's murder. Pressed about Adam's financial papers, she shrugged and said Steve asked her to look at them. That was all they could get out of her.

After Bess had shared that with Justin early Tuesday morning, she said, "That winds everything up."

"Not quite," he replied. "I have some groveling to do."

"About time." As he'd hurried to his truck, she called, "Good luck."

Chapter Thirty-Four

SHERI TUCKED TWO more reference books beside the rest in her file box. Her folders of printouts would go in her big tote. She had a couple of interviews tomorrow morning, but should be out of Miriam's house by late afternoon at the latest. The bathroom renovations were scheduled to begin the next day, Thursday. Carpenters first, Deb said. When Sheri returned, she'd spend no more nights, only days working with Miriam at the hospital or the rehab facility.

Detective Peters had tried to talk her into protective custody, but she'd refused. She'd be safe in Weymouth, where she had an alarm system and a tenant in the other half of the duplex.

Remaining in this house longer would only keep fresh memories she was strong-arming out of her consciousness. Justin's impossibly blue eyes, soft as he was about to kiss her ghosted in front of her. His voice, rumbling as he held her tight, echoed inside her.

Darkness swamping her heart, she sank onto the desk chair and pressed a hand to her stomach. If only she could pack up her emotions as easily as she packed her belongings. The pain that had tightened Justin's features meant that his mother's terrible betrayal, reinforced by girlfriends' lies, still evoked strong emotions and resentments. Telling her had made no difference. His reaction changed nothing. She'd been right to have kept her secret from everyone. What she'd done, what she'd caused could not be forgiven.

****

SOMETIME LATER THEY lay in each other's arms. He didn't care how long, for moments or hours. Holding her felt right, as if they'd always had each other.

Propped up on one arm, she tilted her head and eyed him. She was beautiful, her gaze happy and sated, her hair a bright cloud around her shoulders. "You told me why you searched for my daughter. What about the *how*?"

He sent her a half grin and wrapped his fingers around a lock of her hair. "I confess I told my sister about looking for your daughter. Since it wasn't an official investigation, I needed a reporter's help."

"I should've known." She flung an arm up toward the ceiling. "Rosemary. Rosemary. Rosemary. She wants to meet me. Oh, Justin." She pressed a quick kiss to his lips and burst out laughing.

"Ah. Now that's what I've been missing."

Epilogue
Sixteen Months Later

SHERI STOPPED IN the arch leading from the kitchen and adjusted the basket in her arms. Warmth glowed in her chest at the scene in the living room.

Justin and his brother-in-law sat with Sam's year-old twins on the carpet. From an armchair, Annie was snapping photos of the men with the babies. Little Ted— never Teddy, not for a boy named Ted Williams Kincaid—resembled the Wylde side of the family, with hair the same dark brown as Annie and Justin, but still only fluffy down. Ted ripped the gift wrap from a tiny baseball mitt and squealed his delight. Two tot-size baseball bats lay beside the picture books he and his sister Lisa had already opened.

Annie grinned. "Perfect. They both got baseball equipment. Sam will definitely show these off to his team." Signs were good he'd be moved up soon from Triple-A to Boston.

"No sh— Um, no kidding," said Sam, tempering his language in front of the babies. "The guys will get a bang out of seeing our little prospects."

Sheri carried her basket in and took a seat beside where Justin leaned against the sofa. She set out four crystal flutes. They had missed the family birthday party thrown by the senior Wyldes a week earlier because Justin had been deep in a manhunt, and Sheri had arranged a visit with her daughter.

The twins weren't worn out yet, but they'd exhausted Comet, who snoozed on one end of the sofa. They'd kept the little dog running after balls and after them while the burgers cooked in the small backyard.

319

After mini cupcakes for the babies, everyone had come inside to relax.

Justin popped the cork on the champagne. "You might want to practice with the kiddos a little first." He jerked a nod toward Ted, who was chewing on his mitt, soaking it with baby drool.

"Softening the leather. That's my boy." Sam waggled his mustache and turned to his daughter. "Lisa, baby, show your uncle your swing."

The little girl grinned at her dad from beneath curls a shade lighter than Sam's caramel color. She swung her bat for all she was worth, knocking herself onto her diaper-padded bottom and sending Justin scooting out of the way.

Annie hooted with laughter along with Sheri, who said, "Justin, you'd think it was a real Louisville Slugger and not soft foam."

"Old instincts kick in, honey." His cheekbones colored, but he laughed as he levered himself up onto the cushion beside her. He curved an arm around her shoulders.

Sheri leaned into his muscled heat. During the first months after their reconciliation they'd clashed over a few issues. Longing to keep Justin's trust, she learned to overcome holding her thoughts and motivations locked inside, and Justin learned she needed time before opening up. As they had moved toward emotional intimacy, their relationship flourished.

Shunting aside her musings, she poured bubbly for the adults while the twins accepted milk. Ted took his sippy cup and joined his mom in her chair.

Lisa climbed up on Sheri's lap with hers and snuggled in, a warm little body. Sheri sighed with pleasure. She'd missed this enjoyment of a child growing and learning, but she couldn't regret her choice now. Rosemary was a well-adjusted, bright, and happy teenager. And bless her parents for bringing the two of them together. So far she'd accepted what Sheri told her about Noah, which was only that he'd died before she was born.

Annie set her flute on the end table and gestured in a wide arc. "The house looks great, all updated. I love the muted tan and gold on the walls, restful and colorful at the same time." She winked at her brother. "And not even a mess with my brother living here. Yes, I know the signs."

"Signs?" Sam's gaze scanned the room, his brows beetled.

"Sports magazines in the powder room basket, his fishing gear in the garage."

Justin shook his head. "You should be a detective, sis. I moved in a few months ago. We thought we should see how it was to live together since we're getting married."

"Aha," Sam exclaimed, "the reason for bubbly and not beer."

Joyous whoops, hugs, and congratulations all around. The twins, who had been drifting into sleep, jumped up and shrieked in excitement. Comet raced circles around the humans. Annie hugged Sheri, saying how great it would be to have a sister, and Sam joked about never thinking he'd see the day, but Sheri was the woman to keep Justin in line. Annie elbowed him in the ribs, but Justin laughed.

"Have you told your parents?" Annie sank onto the floor and brought out toys from her big tote in an effort to calm down her revved-up children.

"Not yet," Justin said. "We want a small family wedding, only a few friends, nothing big and formal. We want it to be more about the marriage than the wedding. Maybe in the spring, when Sheri's dad can get away from the charter boat."

"Be sure to keep Mom out of it," his sister said. "She'll make it the event of the year."

"My mom too," Sheri added. Justin had charmed her mom enough that Barbara decided her daughter marrying a cop wasn't 'unseemly.' "So far we've managed to keep the two women apart. We want a plan first."

"Good luck. And from what you've said about Miriam Littlefield, she'll want a hand in it."

"You might as well stop a tornado," Justin said. "The reason we haven't told her yet."

Sheri grinned. Deb was sworn to secrecy, but they couldn't keep the news from Miriam much longer. She considered herself their matchmaker. Her memoir had gone to a proofreader, so the printing and Big Reveal would be soon. They'd tell her then. Sheri had worried about Comet's reaction when taken to Miriam's, but after a joyous visit there, the little dog readily came home with Sheri.

Annie shook her head. "Does Rosemary know?"

"I told her last week when we went to a concert at the university. She's thrilled. I asked her to be in the wedding, and her mom agreed." Sheri leaned forward and placed a hand on Annie's shoulder. "I'd like you to be in it too along with my bestie Deb Delano."

"Absolutely!" Annie hugged her. When she sat back down, she wiped away a tear.

"Crap." Justin slapped his forehead. "Then I probably have to ask Sam here to be best man."

Sam lifted his daughter, who was drowsy again, onto his lap. "An obvious choice. I've always been the best man anyway."

Justin nodded toward a drooping Ted, again sucking on his baseball mitt. "Someday we'd like a rug rat or two like these little guys." He turned to Sheri, his lips curved in that slow, crooked grin that made her whole body smile. "I love you, Sheri."

"And you are my heart, my everything." She snuggled in the warm curve of his strong arm and let the banter and teasing of the others wash over her.

Time and Justin's support had diminished the pain and trauma of Reed's horrific crimes. Both Bess Peters and Justin had received commendations for their work on the case. Hearing Justin share their thoughts on children expanded the sweet joy inside that still amazed her.

When she'd returned to Dragon Harbor, she never expected to find her heart. And she'd never, ever expected to be this happy, this loved and secure. Soon she'd be part of Justin's big, loving family. Maybe someday she wouldn't feel the need to pinch herself every day to make sure it was all real.

Thank you for purchasing
this publication of The Wild Rose Press, Inc.

For questions or more information
contact us at
info@thewildrosepress.com.

The Wild Rose Press, Inc.
www.thewildrosepress.com

www.ingramcontent.com/pod-product-compliance
Lightning Source LLC
Chambersburg PA
CBHW051137030726
47504CB00004B/909